Delirium Tremens

Daniel Ryan Lundquist

Published by Barbed Hook Books

Hardcover ISBN: 979-8-9943981-0-4

Paperback ISBN: 979-8-9943981-1-1

Second Edition

Contents

ACT I

Chapter One: The Inventory

John Glisner came awake the way a man surfaces from dark water: gasping, disoriented, and already tired.

His mouth tasted like pennies and old whiskey. His tongue felt too big for his teeth. The headache behind his eyes was not a pain so much as a pressure, a steady thumb pushing inward. When he swallowed, his throat rasped like sandpaper.

Sunlight knifed through the crooked blinds and painted hard stripes across his bedroom wall. The brightness made his stomach roll. He squinted and tried to remember when he had come upstairs, when he had pulled the covers over himself, when he had stopped being a person and started being a body.

There was only the familiar, unreliable blur of the night before: a bar light smeared into a comet; Hunter's laugh; a bottle passed back and forth like a microphone; his own voice promising someone, again, that he'd be good.

He sat up slowly. Denim pulled against his skin. His shirt was still buttoned wrong, the collar crooked. Yellow stains bloomed across the front of his jeans, dried into darker islands. He stared at them for a beat, waiting for the shame to land in the place where it usually landed.

Nothing landed. Not yet.

The apartment was silent in that unnatural way it got when Alice wasn't moving around downstairs. Alice always moved. Not loudly, not with the stomping impatience of someone trying to be heard. She moved with purpose - a cup rinsed, a dish set to dry, a light turned off in a room she wasn't in. The small domestic sounds that told him somebody was holding the world together.

His throat tightened. He swung his legs off the bed and stood, bare feet searching for the cool familiarity of carpet.

His calves screamed. Dark bruises climbed both legs like spilled ink. He looked down, tried to fit an explanation around them, and came up empty.

A memory tried to surface - concrete, a curb, laughter, his own hand slamming into something hard - then slid away, slick as oil.

He rubbed his face, a hand dragging over stubble and clammy skin.

"Alice?" His voice came out cracked. "Hey. Babe?"

No answer.

His phone lay face-down on the nightstand, screen smeared with a thumbprint. When he tapped it awake, the brightness stabbed his eyes and a cascade of notifications slid down—missed calls, unread texts, the digital proof of a night he couldn't remember surviving.

ALICE (13).

The timestamps ran down the screen in a neat, horrifying ladder: 12:48 a.m. 1:02. 1:17. 2:05. 2:11.

The last message was short enough to feel like a fist: "Please come home. Please."

Under it sat a reply from him, sent at 2:11 a.m.—a single line, all lowercase, like it had been typed with a sloppy thumb in the dark: "i'm on my way. love you."

John stared at it until the letters stopped looking like language. He didn't remember sending it. He didn't remember leaving. He didn't remember being the kind of man who actually came home when he said he would.

A voicemail icon pulsed beside her name. He pressed it. A second of hiss filled his ear, then the beginning of her voice—

He stopped it, thumb slamming the screen hard enough to sting. Hearing Alice right now felt like letting the morning decide what it meant.

He tried calling anyway. It rang twice and rolled into her recorded greeting, bright and casual, a version of her still alive inside a machine. John hung up before the beep, throat closing.

The phone trembled in his hand. Or maybe it was him. Probably him.

He padded to the bathroom and splashed cold water on his face. The mirror gave him back a version of himself he didn't want to claim: puffy eyes, a split at the corner of his lip, a faint bruise blooming along his cheekbone. He stared at that bruise too, waiting for the shame, the anger, any emotion that would anchor him.

Still nothing.

Downstairs, the living room and kitchen were too clean for the night he couldn't remember. The white carpet looked like it had survived. The coffee table held two empty cups, set neatly side by side, as if someone had tried to make normal out of something that refused to be normal.

The couch sat with its back to him. Over the armrest spilled a curtain of red hair.

Relief arrived first. Small, stupid relief. She had fallen asleep down here. She was mad, sure, but she was here.

He moved closer and tried to shape his voice into gentle.

"Hey," he said, soft as he could manage. "Wakey-wakey. Rise and shine, sweetheart."

He stepped around the couch and the room changed.

Vomit stained the carpet in a wide orange smear. Bits of chicken sat in it like broken teeth. Dark blood threaded through the mess, too much blood, the kind of blood that didn't belong outside a body.

His stomach dropped. The air itself felt wrong, thick with a sweet-metal smell.

"Alice." He didn't mean to say her name like that. It came out as a question he already knew the answer to.

She lay twisted on the floor, half against the couch. One arm was pinned beneath her as if she had tried to push herself up and couldn't. Her hands were smeared with blood, and her left ring finger was bare except for a pale band of skin. Her face was turned toward him, eyes open and unfocused, mouth parted as if she had been trying to speak and the words had gotten stuck behind her teeth.

John took one step, then another, like his legs were negotiating with reality.

He knelt. His fingers found her shoulder. The fabric of her shirt was damp and cold.

Something in him finally broke loose.

His scream filled the apartment, bounced off the immaculate white walls, and came back to him doubled.

John's fingers found her neck, searching for a pulse as if he could bargain with reality by refusing to believe it. There was nothing—no flutter, no give. Her skin was cold in the wrong way.

He rolled her gently and the weight of her head told him everything. The smear on the carpet had already started to tack up at the edges; it made a faint tearing sound when her shoulder shifted.

His phone was in his hand before he remembered reaching for it. His thumb missed the screen twice. When the 911 operator answered, John heard himself making sounds that were supposed to be sentences.

"Okay," the operator said. Her voice was calm in the way calm voices always were during catastrophe. "I need you to check for breathing. Put your hand on her chest. Do you see it rise?"

John pressed his palm to Alice's sternum. The fabric of her shirt was cold and damp; underneath it, her body had the wrong stillness, like furniture. "No," he whispered. The word scraped out of him.

"All right. I'm going to tell you what to do next."

He tried to roll Alice onto her back the way the operator instructed. She was heavier than he remembered. Her hair dragged across the carpet with a soft, terrible sound. His fingers slipped on blood and vomit and he gagged, but he kept moving because stopping felt like giving the universe permission to make this true.

"Start chest compressions," the operator said. "Put the heel of your hand in the center of her chest and push hard. Count out loud for me."

John did it. He pushed down. Her ribs did not crack the way movies promised, but something inside her gave with a small, wet resistance that made his stomach flip. "One," he said, and his voice broke. "Two. Three." His hands shook so badly his palms slid. "Four."

The apartment tilted. The clean white walls swam. He counted anyway, because counting was something a person could do when nothing else made sense.

Sirens rose somewhere in the distance—thin at first, then louder, then closer until they seemed to be inside his skull. Between compressions he saw small, ridiculous details: the two coffee cups on the table like a domestic joke; the cabinet under the sink slightly ajar; a chemical tang riding the air beneath the metallic sweetness of blood.

A hard knock rattled the front door. Then another. "Police!" a voice shouted. "Sir, open up!"

John stumbled to the door, legs rubbery, palms smeared red. He fumbled the lock and yanked it open.

Paramedics pushed past him with a gurney, their movements efficient, practiced. One of them—a woman with tired eyes—knelt beside Alice and checked her neck, her wrist, her pupils. John watched her face change by degrees from focus to something gentler and worse.

"I'm sorry," she said, not looking at John, as if speaking to the air made it easier. "I'm so sorry."

A uniformed officer stepped in front of John as more people filled the room. "Sir, I need you to step outside," he said. His gaze flicked down to John's bruised calves and back up again. "Now."

John's mouth worked. He wanted to say She was fine, she was fine, she was alive when I— but he didn't know when she had been alive. He didn't know what he had done. He only knew the way the paramedic pulled a sheet over Alice's body, covering her face first, and how that single gesture hit him harder than any blow.

Out on the porch, cold air and rain-wet wind slapped him awake. Neighbors stood at cracked doors in the building across the way, eyes wide, hands over mouths. John stared back at them like they might explain what he had missed.

Behind him, inside the apartment, someone started laying down tape. The word CRIME SCENE flashed through his mind like a neon sign he couldn't turn off.

* * *

Hours later - it could have been hours, it could have been years - John sat in the back of a police cruiser with a foil emergency blanket draped over his shoulders like a cheap cape.

He watched the city slide by through the glass. It didn't look different. That was the worst part. Traffic moved. People walked dogs. A man carried a grocery bag with a loaf of bread sticking out like the world had the audacity to keep eating.

Bread.

The sight pulled at John in that cruel way ordinary things did now—like hooks in soft tissue—because it belonged to a life where mornings had shape and smell and purpose.

He saw Alice at the little kitchen counter in their first apartment, hair twisted up with a pencil because she couldn't find a clip. She had flour on her cheek and she didn't know it. The radio played something soft and stupid, and she was humming off-key while she pressed a piece of dough flat with the heel of her palm.

John had been behind her with a mug of coffee—real coffee, not the stale, burnt stuff from gas stations—and his arms around her waist. He had kissed the back of her neck and she had laughed like it surprised her. Not the brittle laugh she used later when he tried to talk his way out of a lie. A clean laugh. A laugh that sounded like permission.

"You're going to make a mess," she had said, but she didn't move away.

"I'm already a mess," John said into her hair.

"That's not true," she replied automatically, the way she always corrected him when he tried to turn self-pity into a joke. She had turned her head enough to catch his jaw with a flour-smudged kiss. "You're just dramatic."

He remembered thinking then—God, he remembered it so sharply—that he had lucked into something he didn't deserve. That if he held on tight enough, he could keep it. That love was a kind of insurance policy.

He watched her pull two plates from the cabinet and set them on the table like she was setting a stage. Two forks. Two napkins. Two cups—mismatched because they hadn't owned anything long enough for it to match.

The cups were what did it, later. The cups sitting on the coffee table this morning like a domestic joke.

He hadn't let himself think about how they'd ended up there.

In the memory, Alice slid into the chair and tucked one leg beneath her. She leaned forward, chin in her palm, studying him in that soft, assessing way she had when she was trying to choose her words carefully.

"We should get a rug," she said.

John blinked. "A rug."

"A rug," she repeated, smiling because she knew it sounded ridiculous. "For the living room. You said you liked those clean, bright spaces. Like in those stupid magazines."

"I like you," he said, and meant it. It was so easy then to mean things.

Alice reached across the table and took his hand. Her fingers were warm, flour-dusted, real. "I want it to feel like home," she said. "Not like... a crash pad. Not like we're waiting for something to go wrong."

The word wrong sat between them like a small shadow. John had laughed, because laughing was his oldest trick.

"Nothing's going to go wrong," he said. "We're fine."

Alice squeezed his hand a little harder, and in her eyes there was the briefest flare of something that would become familiar later: doubt, buried under hope.

"Okay," she said. "Then prove it. Help me pick one."

They went that afternoon, because back then he still did things when she asked. They drove to a warehouse store that smelled like cardboard and plastic wrap and ambition. They walked rows of couches and lamps, hands brushing, shoulders bumping like teenagers.

Alice stopped at a display of rugs and crouched down, running her fingers over the fibers.

John stared at the tag. "That one's white."

She looked up at him, grinning. "Yes."

"You're out of your mind."

"Maybe," she said. "But I'm not living my life like I'm afraid of my own furniture."

John's mouth twisted into a smile that felt easy. "You know I spill things."

"I know," Alice said. Her grin softened. "So don't."

The way she said it—simple, confident—made it feel like a choice he could actually make. Like the future wasn't already wired.

They bought the stupid white rug.

They hauled it up the stairs to the apartment sweating and laughing, and when they unrolled it across the living room floor, the room changed. It looked like a place where people planned to stay.

Alice stood on it barefoot, arms crossed, surveying their tiny kingdom. "See?" she said. "It's bright. It's clean. It's—"

"White," John supplied.

"White," she agreed, and she laughed again. "A blank slate."

Blank slate. Like the past could be wiped away by decor.

That night she ordered Thai food and they ate cross-legged on the rug because they didn't have a coffee table yet. Alice poured wine into plastic cups because the glasses were still in a box somewhere. John watched the red liquid tremble in the cup and felt his body do that subtle, hungry lean toward it.

He told himself it was nothing. He told himself he was allowed.

Alice raised her cup. "To us," she said.

"To us," he echoed.

The first spill happened the same night.

John knocked his cup over reaching for the remote, and red wine bled into the white fibers like a bruise blooming under skin. For a second he just stared, horrified, because it felt like an omen—because it felt like proof that his hands were not built for clean things.

Alice didn't yell. She didn't gasp. She just laughed—one sharp bark of it—and sprang up to grab paper towels.

"It's fine," she said, kneeling, dabbing at the stain with brisk purpose. "It's a rug, John. It's not sacred."

He watched her hands move, quick and capable, and something in his chest loosened.

"You're mad," he said.

"I'm practical," she corrected. She glanced up at him with a look that was half warning, half affection. "But if you spill whiskey on it, I'll kill you."

John laughed because it was funny then. Because the idea of whiskey in their bright living room felt like a joke.

Later—weeks later, months later—he would stand in that same living room with a glass that wasn't wine, telling himself he deserved it, telling himself he needed it, telling himself she was overreacting. He would watch her stop laughing. Watch her stop correcting him. Watch her get quiet in a way that was worse than anger.

But in the memory, she was still laughing, still wiping the stain like it was the kind of problem you could solve with enough paper towels and patience.

Alice leaned back on her heels and looked at the rug, pleased with herself. "See?" she said. "Not permanent."

John stared at the faint pink shadow in the fibers and felt something tighten under his ribs, a premonition he didn't have words for yet.

"Yeah," he said, forcing his mouth into a smile. "Not permanent."

Alice reached for his hand again, and he let her.

His fingers were steady then. His skin was warm. His heart beat at a normal human pace.

He sat in the cruiser now, wrapped in foil like a cheap leftover, and wondered when exactly the stain had stopped being a stain and become the whole rug.

His hands shook so hard his teeth clicked. The officer in the front asked him if he needed water. John nodded. When the bottle touched his lips, he couldn't remember how to make his hands hold it steady.

At the station, they put him in a small interview room that smelled like old coffee and disinfectant. Detective Hargrove—tired eyes, loosened tie—asked him the same questions three different ways while a young patrolman, Officer Lane, sat in the corner with a notebook and tried not to watch John shake.

"Where were you last night?"

"When did you last see your wife alive?"

"Did she ever talk about hurting herself?"

John tried to answer. He tried to be helpful. The words kept slipping out of his grip.

"I was out with friends," he said. "With Hunter Wallace. We were drinking. I—" He swallowed and tasted bile. "I don't remember leaving. I don't remember getting home. I remember the stairs. I remember thinking I'd be quiet so I wouldn't wake her." He tried to picture the hallway, the door, the dark, and found only static. "Then I woke up. And she was..." His voice failed on the last word.

"What did you drink?"

He had to think. That fact alone made him want to vomit.

Hargrove's pen paused for the first time. "You don't remember leaving the bar?"

John shook his head. The motion made his skull throb. "It happens," he said automatically, and hated himself for how practiced the lie sounded. Blackouts. Like they were a quirky side effect instead of a warning label.

"How much did you drink?" Hargrove asked.

John tried to count—beer, whiskey, something in a plastic cup that tasted like syrup. He couldn't find the numbers. "A lot," he said. "More than I should have."

Officer Lane's eyes lifted from his notebook. The kid looked too young to have seen this much misery up close, but he was seeing it anyway.

Hargrove nodded toward John's legs. "You got those bruises last night?"

John looked down as if the bruises might tell him their own story. "I... I don't know," he admitted. "I don't remember falling. I don't remember anything hard enough to do that."

Silence settled in the room for a beat. The hum of the fluorescent light sounded suddenly loud.

"Did you and Alice argue?" Hargrove asked, gentler now, as if softness would make the truth easier to swallow.

John's throat tightened. A flicker of memory—Alice in the doorway, eyes shiny with anger; Alice's voice saying his name like a warning; a ring glinting in her hand—rose and dissolved before he could grab it. "We... we argued sometimes," he said. "It wasn't—" He swallowed. "It wasn't like that."

Hargrove didn't challenge him. He didn't reassure him, either. He just looked down and started writing again.

Hargrove wrote anyway, pen scratching, patient as a man taking notes on the weather.

* * *

They didn't let him leave after the interview.

Not right away.

John sat in a plastic chair in a hallway that smelled like lemon disinfectant and old coffee, and the station moved around him like he was a piece of furniture. Officers walked past with paper cups and radios crackling at their shoulders. Someone laughed at a joke down the hall, and the sound landed wrong in John's ears—too normal, too alive.

His hands wouldn't stop shaking.

He tried to pin them under his thighs. His legs bounced anyway.

A uniformed officer came out first. He avoided looking directly at John, eyes fixed on the clipboard in his hands like it was safer than a grieving man. "Sir," he said, "Detective wants you to come with us."

John blinked. "Am I being arrested?"

The officer swallowed. "No," he said quickly. "No. It's just... procedure."

John's mouth felt full of cotton. "Procedure for what?"

The officer hesitated. "For identification," he said.

The words did not register at first, because John's brain had already spent the morning registering too many impossible things. Then they landed, and his stomach rolled.

"I already told you it's her," John said. His voice sounded far away, like it belonged to someone on a phone line full of static. "I already—"

"I know," the officer said, softer. "I'm sorry. They still have to do it."

Detective Hargrove appeared behind him, coat on now, tie loosened as if that made any of this less formal. He held a small manila envelope in one hand. "John," he said, and his voice was as close to gentle as it got in a building like this. "We're going to the medical examiner's office. It won't take long."

John stared at him. "Why?"

Hargrove didn't lie. He also didn't give the full truth, because the full truth was sharp enough to cut. "Because we have to confirm it," he said. "Because it protects everyone involved."

Everyone involved.

John heard: you, too.

He stood on legs that didn't feel like legs and followed them out to a car.

The ride was short, gray streets sliding by under gray sky, and John watched the world through glass like it was a broadcast he didn't trust. His hands shook in his lap. His heart kept speeding up and slowing down as if it couldn't decide what rhythm grief required.

At the county building, the hallways were colder. The lights harsher. The air tasted like bleach and something faintly sweet underneath it that made his throat close.

A woman in scrubs met them at a double door. She was middle-aged, hair tucked under a cap, eyes tired in the way people's eyes got when they lived near death for a living.

"Hargrove," she said, nodding. Then her gaze slid to John. "Mr. Glisner?"

John nodded once. He couldn't trust his voice.

"Okay," she said, brisk but not cruel. "This is going to be quick. You can say no at any time. You can stop at any time."

John stared at her. "Stop what?"

She held his gaze for a beat, then softened her voice by half a degree. "Seeing her," she said.

The words made his throat tighten so hard he tasted bile.

The woman opened the double doors and led them down a corridor. The colder it got, the more John's skin prickled, sweat rising along his spine despite the chill. He tried to tell himself it was the building. He tried not to think about Hunter's warning—withdrawals can kill you—because dying here felt like adding another layer of absurdity to a day already drowning in it.

They stopped at a metal door. The woman swiped a badge and pushed it open.

Inside was quiet.

Not peaceful. Quiet like a held breath.

A gurney sat in the center of the room, a sheet draped over it with a practiced neatness that felt obscene. The outline beneath the sheet was unmistakable—shoulders, hips, feet. A human shape made small.

John stopped in the doorway, because something in him refused to cross the threshold. Like if he didn't step closer, maybe the world couldn't finalize itself.

The woman waited without rushing him. Hargrove stood a few feet back, hands clasped in front of him, eyes down.

John took one step. Then another.

His knees felt loose. His vision tunneled.

"This is Alice Glisner," the woman said quietly, as if naming it made it more manageable. "I'm going to uncover her face. Just her face."

John nodded, though he hadn't agreed to anything.

The woman folded the sheet back with careful hands.

Alice's face was pale, lips slightly parted. Her hair had been brushed away from her forehead, smoothed like someone had tried to undo the violence of the morning with a comb.

For one brutal second, John's brain supplied the wrong image—Alice in bed on a Saturday, half asleep, squinting at sunlight and asking him if he wanted pancakes.

Then the smell cut through him, sharp and chemical beneath the clean bleach of the room, and the fantasy snapped.

His stomach lurched. "Alice," he whispered.

Her eyes were closed now. That was a mercy. That was also worse, because closed eyes meant she had been turned from the world.

John stepped closer, fingers twitching as if his body wanted to touch her and his mind knew better. He stared at her mouth, at the faint bruise at the corner of her lip, at the small darkening under one eye that might have been an impact or might have been nothing.

He forced his gaze down, because there was one detail his brain had latched onto like a burr.

Her left hand lay atop the sheet.

Her ring finger was bare.

The pale band of skin where her ring should have been looked like a ghost.

John's throat closed. "Where's her ring?" he rasped.

The woman's eyes flicked to Hargrove, then back. "We didn't receive it with her personal effects," she said. "If it was on her, the paramedics would have removed it and logged it."

"It was on her," John said. His voice cracked. "It was—"

He stopped, because he didn't actually know. He didn't know what had been on Alice's hands at two in the morning. He didn't know what had happened in the hours his memory refused to carry.

Hargrove stepped forward, careful. "We'll look for it," he said. Not a promise, not comfort—procedure. "Could be at the apartment. Could've been taken off earlier."

John stared at Alice's hand and felt something open in his chest that wasn't grief exactly. It was fear. The ring missing felt like a message he couldn't read.

The woman covered Alice's face again.

John flinched as if struck.

"Mr. Glisner," she said, voice steady. "Is this your wife?"

John's mouth moved. The air didn't come.

He nodded once.

The woman exhaled softly. "Okay," she said. "That's all we need."

John stood there, staring at the sheet as if it might lift itself, as if Alice might sit up and tell him this was a joke and he was being punished and now he could go home and do it right.

Nothing happened.

Hargrove touched John's elbow lightly. "We're done," he said.

John jerked away as if the touch burned. His hands were shaking harder now. He could feel sweat on his upper lip. His heart skittered in his chest like it was trying to escape.

"Detective," John heard himself say, and the voice didn't sound like his. It sounded like a man begging without knowing he was begging. "Is she... is it—"

Hargrove's eyes held his for a beat. "The tox report will tell us more," he said. "Right now, it looks consistent with self-harm."

The phrase landed like an insult.

John shook his head, sharp. "No," he said. "No, she—she wasn't—"

Hargrove didn't argue. He didn't reassure. He just watched John the way you watch a man on the edge of a ledge.

"I'm going to say this once," Hargrove said quietly. "You don't leave the state. You answer your phone. You don't disappear. If you need to detox, you do it with a doctor. You hear me?"

John laughed—one dry, broken sound—because the idea of a doctor right now felt like a luxury reserved for people who hadn't already ruined everything.

"I hear you," he said.

He didn't know if he meant it.

Hargrove held out the manila envelope. "These are her personal effects," he said.

John took it with numb hands.

It was light. Too light.

He didn't open it. He couldn't.

They walked him back into the hallway, back into the world of fluorescent lights and footsteps and radios, and John realized with a jolt that some part of him had been waiting for Alice to be alive until this moment.

Now there was only the envelope in his hands and the pale ring-band on her finger in his mind like a missing tooth.

* * *

Back at the apartment, Detective Hargrove stood in the living room and stared at the couch while crime scene techs moved around him in shoe covers. Officer Lane hovered near the doorway, hands clasped, eyes flicking away whenever they landed on Alice.

The white carpet - so bright in the morning light - was stained now. A photographer crouched low, snapping pictures of the vomit, the blood, the trail it had made as if Alice had tried to crawl and couldn't.

A tech in blue gloves opened the kitchen cabinet under the sink and leaned back out.

"Detective?"

Hargrove walked over. He watched the tech lift a cardboard box from beneath the kitchen sink and slide it into a clear evidence bag. The label on the front was loud and ordinary: RAT POISON.

The box was open.

Beside it sat a half-empty bottle of wine, still uncorked, as if the night had been interrupted mid-thought.

"You think she mixed it herself?" the younger officer asked, trying to keep his voice low and failing.

Hargrove looked at the living room again, at the stairs leading up, at the bedroom door slightly ajar, as if he were trying to find the version of the morning John kept dropping.

He had seen this shape of tragedy before. Depression. Spite. A fight that no one else witnessed. A quiet decision made loud by a body on a carpet.

He could already feel the paperwork stacking up. He could already hear the phrases they would use to close it: no sign of forced entry; no evidence of struggle; consistent with self-harm.

"It looks clean," he said. "Cut and dried."

He didn't like how fast the words came.

"Husband?" the officer asked.

"John Glisner." Hargrove glanced at his notes. "Your friend says he's taking you to a family place up north while we finish the investigation."

"Adams?"

"Yeah." Hargrove adjusted his belt, eyes on the evidence bag like it might speak. "Van Drake Road."

The name sparked something unpleasant in the back of his mind - an old local story, a pharmacist, poison - but he shoved it aside. Legends were for later. Right now he had a dead woman and a husband who couldn't stop shaking.

"Tell the friend he can't leave the state," he said. "And put a car on that address in a day or two. Just to be sure."

* * *

When they released John that afternoon, the sky was the bleached white of an overcast day that couldn't decide if it wanted to rain.

Hunter Wallace was waiting in the lobby, hands in his pockets, jaw clenched like he was holding something back.

When he saw John, his face changed - not into pity, not exactly - but into something like grief shared by proximity.

"Hey," Hunter said. His voice came out careful. "Come on. Let's get you out of here."

John followed him toward the door. Halfway there, his gaze snagged on the evidence bag in Hargrove's hand as the detective walked past.

RAT POISON, the box read.

For a moment John smelled something sharp and chemical, like burnt plastic. For a moment he saw his own hand reaching under a sink in the dark.

In the flash of it, he wasn't in the lobby anymore. He was in his kitchen at two in the morning, the overhead light buzzing like a trapped insect. The cabinet under the sink yawned open. Something pale dusted his knuckles.

Alice was saying his name—tired, not angry, which was worse. He saw his own mouth move in reply, saw the shape of a smile that didn't belong on his face.

Then the moment snapped shut like a camera shutter, and he was back in the courthouse air with Hunter's hand on his elbow.

John stepped outside, and the air hit him like a slap.

Chapter Two: Van Drake Road

Hunter's Mercedes smelled like leather and pine air freshener, the kind you hang from a mirror when you want to pretend a vehicle is a fresh start.

John sat in the passenger seat and watched the city thin out. Buildings became warehouses. Warehouses became fields. Fields became the kind of open country that made him feel like the sky was closer and there was nowhere to hide.

Hunter didn't ask questions. He didn't say he was sorry in that automatic way people said it when they didn't know where to put their hands. He drove.

After ten minutes, John spoke anyway.

"They said it's suicide," he said. The word felt foreign in his mouth, like a piece of glass. "They said she was depressed."

Hunter's knuckles tightened on the steering wheel. "That's what they think."

"She wasn't depressed," John said. He heard the anger in his own voice and hated it. Anger was easy. Anger was familiar. Anger kept him from falling through the floor. "She was tired. She was tired of me."

Hunter glanced at him, then back to the road. "You don't know that."

John laughed once, bitter and small. "I do."

A mile marker flashed past. The road rolled ahead in long, empty stretches, flanked by cornfields stripped down to dead-yellow stubble. The land looked bruised. The trees at the edges were bare-limbed and dark.

John's hands still shook. He pressed them between his knees, trying to make them stop.

"I can't go back to the apartment," he said.

"I know." Hunter's voice softened. "That's why we're doing this."

They drove in silence until the city was gone behind them and the world had narrowed to road, field, and the occasional mailbox leaning like it had given up.

John swallowed. "I'm done drinking."

Hunter didn't respond right away. When he did, he kept his eyes on the road. "For real?"

"For real." John said it like an oath, like a prayer. "If I don't stop, I'm going to die. Or worse."

Hunter let out a slow breath. "Okay."

"Cold turkey," John added. "No taper. No bullshit."

That got Hunter's attention. He glanced over again, frown cutting deep. "John."

"Don't," John said. "Don't talk me out of it."

"I'm not talking you out of quitting," Hunter replied. "I'm talking you out of doing it alone in the middle of nowhere."

John stared out at the fields. The horizon was a hard line. Everything beyond it looked unreal. "I deserve alone."

"That's not how it works." Hunter's voice sharpened, then softened again. "Withdrawals can kill you. Seizures. Delirium tremens. Hallucinations. Your heart going sideways. People don't like to talk about that part because it ruins the whole neat redemption story, but it's true."

John flexed his fingers until his joints popped. "I drank, sure. But I'm not that guy. I'm not the shaking-in-the-street guy."

Hunter made a sound that wasn't quite a laugh. "You are literally shaking in my passenger seat."

John turned his face away. The shame arrived then, late as everything else in his life.

"If it gets bad," Hunter said, gentler now, "you call me. No pride. No penance. You call."

"Yeah," John said. "I will."

He didn't know if he meant it. He wanted to mean it.

They pulled off the highway a few miles later, not because John asked but because the Mercedes's fuel gauge had dipped below a quarter and Hunter had the habit of acting before a problem became a crisis.

The town was barely a town—two stoplights, a feed store, a shuttered diner with a sun-faded sign. The gas station sat at the edge of it with a row of pumps under a buzzing canopy light and a convenience store that smelled like burnt coffee and rubber mats.

Hunter swiped his card at the pump. "Bathroom's inside," he said. "Grab whatever you need. Water, snacks. Anything but booze."

John gave him a look that should have been offended and came out hollow. "Right," he said. "Because I was about to treat quitting like a buffet."

Inside, the air was warm and stale. A small television mounted above the counter played a daytime talk show at low volume. John walked toward the restroom and stopped without meaning to.

A display of tiny bottles sat by the register—miniatures arranged like candy, their glass shining under fluorescent light. The labels were bright and friendly. They looked harmless. They looked like relief.

His mouth watered again. His hands twitched, already reaching.

He forced himself to keep walking, one step at a time, like he was moving through deep water. In the restroom he leaned over the sink and ran cold water. His face in the mirror looked gray. His pupils were too wide, as if his body had already decided to panic.

When he came out, he grabbed two bottles of water and a pack of gum, something to give his jaw to do besides clench. At the end of the aisle, a stack of bait buckets and mouse traps made a little hardware shrine. RAT POISON sat there too, the same loud letters as the box in Hargrove's hand. John's stomach lurched.

"Rats are bad this year," the cashier said when he saw John staring. He was a thick-necked man with a mustache and a name tag that read BRETT. "They'll eat the wiring right out your truck if you let 'em."

John made a sound that might have been agreement. He couldn't trust his voice.

An old man at the coffee station turned and looked them over, eyes narrowed as if he could smell trouble. His gaze landed on Hunter. "You Wallace's boy?"

Hunter stiffened. "Yeah," he said. "Just passing through."

The old man's mouth tightened. "You headed up Van Drake?"

John felt Hunter's glance slice toward him, quick and warning.

"Just for a night," Hunter said, too casual. "Checking on the place."

The old man shook his head slowly, not quite pity, not quite disgust. "Storm's coming," he said. "That road gets mean in weather. And that house..." He let the sentence trail off like it didn't deserve a full ending.

The old man's eyes flicked to John, then back to Hunter. "Your daddy used to come in here when storms knocked the lines down," he said. His voice dropped until it was almost swallowed by the hiss of the coffee machine. "He'd buy ice and batteries like that made him safe."

Hunter's posture went rigid. "We're not staying long," he said.

"Ain't about how long," the old man replied. "It's about what you bring with you." His gaze lingered on John's shaking hands. "That road don't care if you're passing through."

He leaned in a fraction closer, as if the next part was something you didn't say at full volume. "If you hear that house phone ring after dark," he murmured, "you let it ring."

Hunter tossed cash on the counter without waiting for change. "Come on," he said to John, and there was something in his voice that wasn't impatience. It was fear wearing a normal mask.

Outside, the sky had darkened by a shade, clouds gathering low and heavy over the fields. John climbed back into the Mercedes with cold water in his hands and an old man's unfinished sentence crawling through his thoughts.

A green sign appeared ahead: ADAMS - 12 MILES.

Hunter slowed as the road narrowed and the fields gave way to a line of old oaks that formed a blunt, dark border around a property. The trees stood close together, their branches woven so tight they looked like a wall.

"That's it," Hunter said. "It's right up here."

A gravel drive branched off and climbed a small rise.

The farmhouse sat at the top like something waiting.

Red brick. Two stories. A porch with a sagging awning. The windows were dark, reflecting the cloudy sky. Behind it, a barn leaned half into itself, vines climbing the brickwork in green veins. Two massive oaks stood in the yard like sentries, their trunks thick enough that John couldn't have wrapped his arms around them.

Hunter pulled into the drive and killed the engine.

For a moment, neither of them moved.

"You sure about this?" Hunter asked.

Hunter stared at the house through the windshield as if expecting it to blink.

The key ring in his hand held only two keys. They looked too small for a place this big. He rolled them over his knuckles once, twice, an anxious habit.

John listened to the quiet. No traffic. No distant sirens. Only wind in branches and the faint creak of the barn settling into itself. It was the kind of quiet that made a man hear his own blood.

Somewhere in the trees a crow made a single, harsh sound and went silent again.

Hunter cleared his throat. "I haven't been here in a while," he said, like an apology he didn't want to say out loud.

John looked at the house. It wasn't pretty. It wasn't welcoming. It wasn't his apartment with white carpet and clean walls and all the evidence of Alice's life stuffed into drawers like a secret.

But it was far away.

"Yeah," John said. "I'm sure."

* * *

Inside, the house smelled like old tobacco and wood polish, like someone had tried to clean memories out of the walls and failed.

Hunter carried John's bags up the stairs to the room he had grown up in - the larger of the two bedrooms upstairs -

without being asked. He moved through the spaces like he was walking through a museum of his own childhood.

"Dad never stopped smoking in here," Hunter said, making a face. "Even after Mom died. Even after the doctors told him it was a bad idea."

"He seems like he had opinions," John said, trying to make it a joke.

Hunter's mouth twitched. "He did."

They did the tour fast. Kitchen with peeling linoleum. Cabinets empty. Yellowed fridge unplugged. Living room with heavy leather couches and an old television that looked like it belonged in an antique store. A red corded phone sat on a side table like a relic from a simpler apocalypse.

"Landline still works," Hunter said. "At least it did the last time I checked. Reception out here is garbage."

On the wall above the side table hung an old black-and-white photograph in a cracked frame. A group of men and women stood on this same porch, stiff and formal, as if the camera itself had asked them to hold their breath.

At first John couldn't tell what felt wrong about it. Then his eyes adjusted and his stomach dropped.

Masks. Half-masks and full ones, feathered and blank, pale shapes where faces should have been. The gloss of the photo had spiderwebbed with age, but someone had scratched at it anyway—two of the figures had their eyes gouged out by deep, angry lines.

John didn't remember seeing the picture during the quick tour. He was sure he would have.

Hunter noticed where John was looking. Without a word, he reached up and turned the frame facedown on the table, as if that was enough to keep it from staring back.

John nodded. The phone comforted him more than it should have.

Upstairs, across from Hunter's old room, was a smaller bedroom painted a dull red. The door was shut.

Hunter hesitated a beat before moving on. "That room's always been... weird."

John glanced at the door. "Weird how?"

Hunter shrugged. "Just weird. Dad kept it closed. Said it was storage. If you need extra blankets or whatever, check the closets in my room. There's a trunk under the bed too."

As Hunter turned away, John lingered a half step behind.

The red room door wasn't special. It was just a door—painted, closed, ordinary. And yet the air around it felt wrong, cooler, as if the hallway had a draft that only existed in that one spot.

There were faint scratches near the knob, thin lines in the paint that looked like someone had dragged fingernails down the wood and then tried to pretend they hadn't.

John leaned closer without meaning to. For a heartbeat he thought he smelled bourbon again, impossibly faint, like the memory of a drink.

Hunter's voice called from downstairs, breaking the moment. John stepped back and followed, telling himself he was imagining patterns because his brain didn't know how to sit still.

They went back downstairs and out the rear door onto the porch that faced the barn.

"Don't go in the barn," Hunter said quickly. "Floor's rotted. Basement's basically a pit. It'll swallow you."

John followed Hunter's gesture. The barn looked worse up close. Sections of the roof had caved in. Bricks at the base had melted in spots, fused with green glass like someone had poured a bottle into lightning.

"Lightning strike?" John asked.

"That's what Dad always said." Hunter's eyes stayed on the barn. "He never fixed it. Never wanted anyone messing around in there."

Hunter led him around the side of the house to two heavy wooden doors set into the ground under a slanted awning.

"Storm cellar," Hunter said. "Basement access is outside only. Annoying in winter. But you won't be here in winter."

John heard the certainty in that and wondered if Hunter believed it.

* * *

They sat in the living room as daylight thinned and the house filled with long shadows.

Hunter sat on the edge of the leather couch like he didn't trust it to hold him. The room smelled like old smoke and wood polish and something faint beneath that—stale sweetness, like liquor spilled years ago and never fully scrubbed out.

John sat opposite him, hands clasped so tight his knuckles ached. The shaking in his fingers had become a constant, low-grade vibration. Not violent yet. Just insistent. A reminder that his body was keeping score.

For a while they didn't talk.

The house made small noises around them—wood settling, a soft tick somewhere in the walls—quiet enough to ignore if you weren't listening for meaning.

Hunter cleared his throat. "So," he said, forcing casual. "You ate anything today?"

John stared at him. "My wife's dead," he said flatly.

Hunter flinched. "I know," he said. "I'm not—" He rubbed a hand over his face. "I'm not trying to make small talk. I'm trying to keep you from passing out. You're pale as hell."

John swallowed. The thought of food made his stomach fold in on itself. The thought of the poison box under the sink—bright letters, ordinary cardboard—made it worse.

"I'm fine," he lied.

Hunter's mouth tightened. "You're not," he said. Then, softer: "I need you alive, John."

The sentence landed wrong. Too heavy for a friend. Too close to something like a vow.

John looked at him. "Why'd you bring me here?" he asked, and he hated how accusatory it sounded, like he was trying to make Hunter responsible for the fact that John's life had split open.

Hunter held his gaze for a beat, then looked away toward the dark window. "Because it's empty," he said. "Because no one bothers it. Because it's far enough that you can... stop."

"Stop," John repeated, bitter.

Hunter nodded once. "Stop drinking," he said. "Stop running your mouth. Stop getting calls from people who want answers you can't give them yet." He hesitated. "And because if you're going to do something stupid, I wanted it to be somewhere I can find you."

John's throat tightened. "Like what?" he asked. "Like I'm going to—"

Hunter's voice sharpened. "Like you're going to have a seizure in a bathtub," he said. "Like you're going to hallucinate and walk into the road. Like you're going to decide you don't deserve to live and do something irreversible."

John stared at him, anger rising because it was easier than fear. "You think I'm suicidal."

Hunter's jaw flexed. "I think you're in shock," he said. "I think you're withdrawing. I think you're guilty enough to do something stupid just to feel like you paid." He swallowed. "And I think you've never been good at sitting with pain without turning it into... action."

John's hands tightened. "Don't psychoanalyze me."

"I'm not," Hunter said. "I'm telling you what I've seen."

The words were sharp, but Hunter's eyes weren't. His eyes looked tired.

John leaned back, the leather creaking under him. "You're acting like this place is... dangerous," he said.

Hunter didn't answer immediately.

He stared at the side table where the red corded phone sat, heavy and old-fashioned, like a piece of history pretending it still mattered.

Then he spoke quietly. "This house makes people weird," he said.

John snorted once. "It's a house."

Hunter's gaze snapped back to him. "Yeah," he said. "And alcohol is just a drink. And grief is just sadness. And you're just a guy who's been 'fine' for years."

John's mouth opened. Nothing came out.

Hunter exhaled hard, like he'd said more than he meant to. "Look," he said, forcing his voice down. "I'm not saying it's haunted. I'm saying... my dad wasn't the same after he stayed here alone. Not after Mom died."

John's stomach tightened. "You told me she died when you were a kid," he said.

Hunter nodded. "Car accident," he said. "That's what everyone says." He swallowed. "She died on Van Drake Road. In a storm. Dad was driving. He walked away. She didn't."

John watched Hunter's throat work around the sentence. The house ticked softly in the background like a clock nobody had wound.

Hunter continued, voice lower. "After that, he moved us here," he said. "He said the city had too many reminders. He said the land was quiet. He said it would be... clean."

Clean. John felt the word scrape something raw in him.

"It wasn't," Hunter said. "It was just quiet enough that his head got loud."

John stared at him. "You never told me that."

Hunter's mouth twisted. "It's not a fun story to bring up over beers," he said, and there was the sting of it—an accidental indictment of their friendship's shape.

John looked away first.

Hunter rubbed his palms on his jeans. "Dad started making rules," he said. "Little ones at first. Lock the doors by sundown. Don't go into the barn. Do not go under the house. Don't leave food out." His gaze flicked to the phone again. "And don't answer the landline after dark."

John felt his skin tighten. "Why?"

Hunter gave a small, humorless laugh. "Because he said it was an offer," he replied.

John went still.

Hunter watched his face, measuring whether he'd gone too far. "He drank too," Hunter added quickly, as if that explained everything. "He was grieving. He was paranoid. He was—"

"Or he was right," John said, and the words came out before he could stop them.

Hunter didn't deny it. That was what scared John.

Hunter leaned forward, elbows on his knees. "This is what I'm saying," he told John, voice firm. "You're going to be in a bad place physically tonight. Your brain is going to try to make meaning out of noise. You are going to see things that might not be there."

John's hands trembled against each other. "DTs," he said, and tried to make it sound like a diagnosis instead of a curse.

"DTs," Hunter agreed. "And grief. And guilt. And this creepy old place." He held John's gaze. "So you listen to me. You do not go exploring. You do not go into the barn. You do not go into the storm cellar. If the power goes out, you stay in one room and ride it out."

John stared at him. "You can't tell me what to do."

Hunter's jaw tightened. "I can," he said. "Because you asked me to bring you somewhere you couldn't drink yourself to death, and I did. And because if you die out here, I'm the one who has to carry you back."

The word carry landed like a threat and a plea at the same time.

John swallowed. His mouth tasted like pennies again.

Hunter's voice softened, but it didn't lose firmness. "And if that phone rings," he said, nodding at the landline, "you let it ring."

John's pulse kicked. "You don't believe in that," he said.

Hunter's eyes held his. "I believe in you making bad decisions when you're cornered," he replied. "I believe in you reaching for whatever stops the shaking." He paused. "If the house offers you something—anything—you call me first."

John stared at him, and the anger in his chest thinned into something else. Fear, maybe. Or shame that came too late to be useful.

Hunter hesitated, then offered, quietly, "I can stay tonight. If you want."

John's throat tightened. The thought of another person in the room with him—watching him shake, watching him sweat, watching him unravel—made something panicky in his chest start clawing. "No," he said too fast. "No. I just... I need quiet."

Hunter's jaw worked. He didn't argue. "Okay," he said, but he didn't sound convinced.

He stood, keys in hand. "I'll go get you food," Hunter said instead. "Real food. Not whatever Dad left in the pantry."

John swallowed. The thought of eating made his stomach twist. The thought of being alone made his chest tighten.

"Thanks," he said. He meant it.

Hunter stood by the door with his keys in hand. "You call if you need me. Day or night," he said. "And if it gets weird—if you start shaking so hard you can't hold a glass, or you start seeing things—you call. Don't try to tough it out."

"I will."

Hunter studied him for a moment, then stepped forward and hugged him, quick and awkward. "I'm not good at this part," he admitted. "But I'm here."

John closed his eyes, breathed in leather and cold air and the faint scent of Hunter's cologne. For a fraction of a second, he let himself believe he could be held together by someone else's arms.

"Go," John said, and hated himself for how fast he said it.

Hunter nodded once, then left.

John watched the red taillights disappear down the gravel drive until the trees swallowed them.

Silence settled over the property.

John stayed on the porch until the cold pushed him inside.

When he shut the door, the latch clicked too loud, as if the house was marking the moment.

Chapter Three: The Mask

John unpacked like he was staging for a temporary disaster: essentials on the dresser, spare clothes in a neat pile, a toothbrush lined up beside the sink.

In the mirror above the bathroom vanity, his face looked less like a man and more like a bruise. His hands would not stop trembling. Sweat slicked his back, even though the house was cold.

He told himself it was grief. He told himself it was exhaustion. He told himself anything but the truth he had been avoiding for years: his body had gotten used to poison, and now it wanted more.

He lay down in Hunter's old bed and stared at the ceiling until the faint outlines in the plaster started to look like faces. He sat up again, heart hammering, and went downstairs for water.

The hall outside the bedroom was colder than the room itself, a draft rolling along the floorboards like something patient and low.

John padded down the stairs in his socks, one hand on the railing because his balance kept slipping. The house was old enough that every step had an opinion. The wood complained under his weight, then settled again into a silence so complete he could hear the blood in his ears.

At the bottom, he paused.

The living room was dark except for the faint gray seep of stormlight through the front window. The fireplace sat dead and yawning. The red corded phone on the side table seemed brighter than it should have in the dim—its receiver like a tongue, its coil like a vein.

Hunter's rules surfaced, uninvited: Do not answer after dark. Do not go under the house. Do not bargain.

John swallowed. His throat rasped. He tried to tell himself he was being ridiculous. It was a phone. It was a house. It was an empty property in bad weather. The only thing haunting him was his own nervous system, rewiring itself now that the alcohol was gone.

Still, he stepped wide around the side table as he moved toward the kitchen, like the phone might reach for him.

The kitchen was colder than the living room.

Not colder in a normal way, not a draft from a poorly sealed window. Colder like the air had been stored somewhere dark and then released. The fluorescent fixture above the sink buzzed when he flipped the switch, then came on in a weak, sickly wash. The light made the counters look as if they had been scrubbed too hard and too often, worn down to the grain.

He turned the faucet. Water sputtered, then ran.

The sound was too loud in the small room. The steady rush felt like it should have been comforting—proof of plumbing, proof of ordinary life—but his nerves read it as threat. His hands shook as he held a glass under the stream. The water splashed and jumped off the rim, tapping his wrists like cold fingers.

He took a sip.

Metallic. Not poison, not chemicals—just iron, just old pipes, just the same pennies taste that had been in his mouth since morning. His stomach clenched anyway, because his body had started treating every sensation like a warning.

He set the glass down and opened the refrigerator.

The interior light came on. The shelves were mostly bare. A jar of mustard. A carton of eggs with an expiration date that looked like a dare. A half-empty bottle of seltzer water with Hunter's handwriting on the cap in black marker: H. WALLACE, as if labeling a drink could keep the house from drinking it first.

John stared at the marker, at the casual certainty of it, and felt a small, mean wave of anger.

Hunter had a name that stayed.

Alice didn't.

He slammed the fridge door harder than he meant to. The sound thudded through the house and went on too long, echoing off unseen rooms. He waited for it to die, for the house to forget he was here.

The silence that returned did not feel like forgetting. It felt like listening.

John's phone buzzed in his pocket—a single sharp vibration.

His heart kicked hard enough to make his vision spot. He fumbled the device out with numb fingers, expecting Hunter's name, a text, a question, a check-in.

The screen lit up.

WEATHER ALERT: FLASH FLOOD WARNING.

The time in the corner read 1:17 a.m.

John blinked. That couldn't be right. He looked toward the window, toward the gray smear of sky. It was night, yes, but not that deep. He had driven out here in the late afternoon. He had sat with Hunter while the light thinned. He had watched taillights disappear down the drive.

His thumb tapped the time. The screen hesitated, as if thinking. Then the numbers jumped.

9:04 p.m.

John exhaled shakily and laughed once, a dry little sound with no humor. "Okay," he whispered. "Okay."

His phone had always been glitchy. The signal out here was garbage. Batteries did weird things in the cold. That was all.

He slid the phone back into his pocket and realized his hand was still shaking like it had never stopped.

He opened the pantry.

Cans lined the shelves, old labels faded to the color of bone. A bag of rice. Two boxes of saltines. A stack of paper plates. Hunter had tried, at least, to make this place habitable.

On the bottom shelf, half hidden behind a dusty crock pot, was a yellow legal pad.

John crouched and dragged it out.

The top page was filled with a list written in heavy, angry strokes.

LOCKS.

The word was underlined twice, the pen gouging through paper.

Beneath it were smaller, tighter notes:

— doors by sundown

— phone unplugged

— no cellar after dark

— line stays unbroken

— do not answer after dark

John stared at the list until the letters stopped looking like letters and started looking like scratches.

He could almost see Hunter's father writing it, hunched over this same counter, making rules the way a drowning man makes plans.

John stood and put the pad back where he'd found it, as if touching it longer might make him part of the rule-maker's life.

His stomach twisted. He tried to tell himself it was hunger. He hadn't eaten since... since he couldn't remember. The thought of food made bile rise, but he forced himself to act anyway because action felt like control.

He found a saucepan, filled it with water, set it on the stove. The knobs were old and stiff. He turned one.

Nothing happened.

No click. No hiss. No pilot light. Just silence.

He tried another. Then another, more forceful. The knob protested and then turned, but the burner remained dead.

John stared down at the black metal grates and felt something prickle along his arms.

Power outage, he told himself. Or the propane's off. Hunter said the place was old. Old houses had broken things.

He looked up at the microwave and saw the clock blinking 12:00.

So, yes. Power.

He walked to the back door and peered out through the small window.

The rain had eased into a steady fall. The yard beyond was a dark, moving shape. Somewhere out there, the gravel drive disappeared into trees. Somewhere farther, the road waited.

If the power was out, the porch light would be out too.

But the porch light was on.

A dull yellow bulb burning over wet steps.

John's mouth went dry.

He turned back to the kitchen and felt the air change again, subtle as a mood shift. He realized the fluorescent light above the sink was no longer buzzing.

It was silent.

Still on, still casting that weak wash over the counter—but silent, as if the house had decided it didn't like noise in this room.

His pulse sped.

He reached for the light switch and flipped it off, then on again.

The buzz returned. A thin electric hum.

He flipped it off.

The buzz died.

He flipped it on again and held his breath.

No buzz.

The light came on clean and quiet, like a candle in a church.

John stood there with his hand on the switch, trying to decide whether he was frightened by the light making noise or frightened by it not making noise.

His mind did what it always did when it couldn't solve a thing: it went looking for the quickest exit.

A drink would smooth this. A drink would stop the shaking. A drink would make the buzzing and the silence feel like the same thing again.

He clenched his jaw until it hurt.

"No," he said out loud, because out loud was harder to ignore.

The word seemed to hang in the air.

Then the landline clicked once in the next room.

John froze.

It wasn't a ring. It wasn't even a dial tone. Just a small mechanical sound, like a throat clearing politely before speaking.

He waited for Hunter's voice in his head to tell him what to do.

Don't answer.

John backed out of the kitchen slowly, glass of water in one hand, because holding something made him feel less like a ghost.

In the living room, the phone sat as it had. Receiver cradled. Cord coiled.

Nothing moved.

John stared at it until his eyes watered. He could feel his heart in his ribs, could feel sweat cooling on his back, could feel his hands vibrating around the glass.

"Get it together," he whispered.

He took a sip of water. The metallic taste bloomed again.

The front window drew his attention the way a magnet draws a nail.

Outside, the rain turned the yard into a shifting mirror. The oak branches moved in slow, heavy arcs. The porch light painted a wet oval on the steps. Beyond that was only darkness and the suggestion of trees.

John's brain made shapes out there because that was what brains did. Fence posts became shoulders. A hanging branch became a crooked arm. The world offered patterns and his mind grabbed them because it wanted to name the threat.

He looked away from the window and toward the staircase.

Upstairs, the hallway was a black throat.

He remembered Hunter's rules again, and something else Hunter had said, quieter, almost like he hadn't meant it to be heard: This house makes people weird.

John took a breath, then another.

He walked to the front door and checked the lock.

It was a simple deadbolt. Solid. Ordinary. It turned with a satisfying click.

He tried the doorknob. It didn't give.

He checked the chain—there was no chain. Old house.

He checked the latch on the screen door behind it—still, no chain.

John's mouth tightened. In his head, he saw the masked figure from the yard earlier, the polite wave, the stillness, the way those eyeholes had looked like coins.

But that had been at the apartment, he reminded himself. That had been later. That had been—

No.

His thoughts were slipping again, time folding in on itself like wet paper.

He set the glass down on the mantle and rubbed his face with both hands.

He needed to sleep. He needed to ride out the night. He needed to stop trying to solve a world that had already decided it didn't care what he needed.

He picked up the glass again and turned from the door, heading back toward the stairs with the dull stubbornness of a man returning to a sinking ship because it was the only ship left.

Halfway back to the living room, he saw movement through the front window.

A man stood in the yard under the closest oak.

The figure was too far away to make out details at first. Then lightning flared in the distance - not a strike, just a bright pulse behind thick clouds - and the man's silhouette sharpened.

He wore a dark tracksuit. His head was covered by a ski mask that made his face a blank oval except for the eye holes. Those eye holes looked like two black coins.

John froze, glass of water halfway to his mouth.

The man raised one hand in a slow, almost friendly gesture, like a neighbor acknowledging a neighbor.

John didn't know why he lifted his own hand in return. It was reflex. It was politeness. It was the terrible human urge to normalize the unthinkable.

"Hey!" John shouted through the glass. His voice sounded small in the big room. "Who the hell are you?"

The man did not move.

John's pulse thudded in his ears. The house around him felt suddenly too large, too empty. The front door was only ten feet away, and yet it felt like a mile.

He set the glass down hard enough that water sloshed over the rim, then grabbed the fireplace poker from beside the hearth. His hands shook so badly it rattled against the metal stand.

He yanked the front door open and stepped onto the porch.

"Hey!" he called again. The cold air burned his lungs. "This is private property."

The yard was wet from earlier drizzle, the grass dark and flattened. The oak tree's branches spread overhead like a black umbrella.

The man was gone.

John stood there, poker raised, feeling ridiculous and terrified at the same time.

He walked down the porch steps, scanning the yard, the tree line, the barn. There was nowhere to hide. The fields beyond the oaks were empty.

John moved toward the oak, boots sinking slightly in the wet ground. He kept the poker raised, ridiculous as it was. The closer he got, the more certain he became that he would find evidence—footprints, snapped branches, anything to prove his eyes weren't lying to him.

Under the tree, the grass was flattened in a rough oval, as if someone had stood there a long time. But the ground was too wet to hold a clean print. Rain had smeared everything into formless dark.

He reached out and touched the oak's trunk. The bark was cold and slick. A notch had been cut into it—fresh wood exposed beneath the dark outer skin—like a mark made with a knife.

John stared at that notch, his mouth suddenly dry. A tally. A claim. Or just damage from some bored trespasser with a blade.

A gust of wind rattled the branches overhead and something tapped against the porch roof—acorns, hard as knuckles. John jerked back, heart hammering, and forced himself to return to the steps.

No footsteps. No snapped branches. No rustle in the grass.

Only the sound of wind pushing through dead leaves.

John backed up the steps and shut the door. He locked it, then checked the lock again as if repetition could make it stronger.

When he set the poker down, his hands left damp prints on the metal.

* * *

An hour later, Hunter's car crunched up the gravel drive and broke the silence.

Relief hit John so hard it made him dizzy. He met Hunter on the porch before the engine had stopped.

"You look like hell," Hunter said, taking in John's sweaty face and shaking hands.

"Somebody was out there," John said. He forced the words through his throat. "A guy. In a ski mask."

Hunter's expression flickered - surprise, then skepticism, then something that looked too much like recognition.

"Out here?" Hunter asked.

"Under the oak," John said. "He waved at me."

Hunter set the grocery bags down and looked past John at the yard, as if the masked man might still be standing there, patient as a scarecrow.

"Could've been kids," Hunter said finally. "Or a hunter. People cut through fields sometimes."

"In a ski mask?"

Hunter shrugged, but it wasn't convincing. "Maybe he didn't want his face eaten by bugs. It's the South. People are weird."

John watched Hunter's face instead of the yard. "You recognized him," he said.

Hunter's jaw flexed. "I recognized a ski mask," he replied. "It's not exactly a fingerprint."

"That look on your face wasn't 'maybe bugs,'" John said. His voice came out sharper than he intended. "That was 'I've seen this before.'"

Hunter stared at the groceries as if the labels might tell him what to say. When he spoke, his voice was quieter. "Dad used to talk about someone out here," he admitted. "Years ago. A guy that would show up around the property line. Never close enough to catch. Always... watching."

John felt his skin tighten. "In a ski mask."

Hunter didn't answer right away. The silence was an answer anyway.

"He called him 'the Mask,'" Hunter said finally, and tried to laugh, but it died in his throat. "Like it was a story you tell kids so they stay inside."

Hunter kept his eyes on the groceries as if looking at John might make this real. "After my mom died, Dad got... jumpy," he said. "He'd wake up at two in the morning and stand at the window like he was waiting for somebody to step out of the trees."

He swallowed and forced a laugh that didn't land. "One night I came downstairs for water and he was in the living room with a shotgun on his lap. Just sitting there in the dark. He told me, 'If you see him, you don't wave. You don't talk. You come inside.'"

John felt his skin tighten. "Did you ever see him?"

Hunter's jaw worked once. "I don't know," he said. "I was a kid. Dad was drinking. And this house... does things to people."

His gaze drifted toward the living room, toward the landline on the side table—receiver seated in its cradle like a mouth that could open. "He used to make me unplug it at night," Hunter said quietly. "Swore it rang anyway. Said the first ring was an offer. Said the second ring was how it got its hooks in."

Hunter finally looked at John then, and his expression wasn't skepticism anymore. It was warning. "So if you hear it, you don't play brave. You call me."

"Is it a story?" John asked.

Hunter looked past him, out the front window, as if expecting to see that blank oval face again. "I don't know," he said. "But if you see him again, you don't wave. You come inside. You lock the door. You call me."

John let it go because Hunter's voice had lost its humor, and arguing suddenly felt like tempting fate. He didn't want to push hard enough to make Hunter say the thing that hovered beneath all the explanations: there were no neighbors close enough to make this casual. There were no kids for miles.

Hunter brought the bags inside and started unloading. Bottled water. Soup. Bread. Bananas. A huge bottle of orange sports drink. Ibuprofen. A cheap flashlight. A battery lantern.

"I grabbed vitamins too," Hunter said, pulling out a bottle. "And some of that powdered stuff - electrolytes. If you're serious about quitting, you're going to sweat like crazy."

"I'm serious," John said.

Hunter looked at him for a long moment. "Okay," he said again, but the word had changed. It wasn't agreement this time. It was resignation.

He nodded toward the stairs. "Just... don't go digging around in places you don't need to. Dad left a lot of junk. Some of it isn't safe."

"Like the barn," John said.

"Especially the barn." Hunter's voice tightened. "And that basement. Door sticks. If you go down there, don't close it behind you."

John stared at him. "Why?"

Hunter opened his mouth, then shut it.

"Because it sticks," he said finally. "Because Dad never fixed it. Because old houses do weird things. Pick one."

John wanted to press. He didn't. He was too busy trying not to imagine a heavy wooden cellar door closing like a jaw.

* * *

Hunter left just after dark.

He had offered to stay again, but John had refused again. He watched the car disappear down the drive, the headlights sweeping over the barn for a brief moment. In that flash of light, the barn's broken windows looked like empty eye sockets.

John went inside and locked the door, then stood in the entryway listening to the house settle around him.

His first instinct was to call Hunter. Not because Hunter had magic answers, but because a living voice on the line would prove the world outside this property still existed.

John fished his phone out of his pocket. The screen lit his damp palm an anemic blue-white. For a second he stared at the clock and couldn't make it match what his body felt.

8:17.

It might have been 8:17. It might have been 3:00 in the morning. Time had been unreliable since he'd found Alice on the floor. Grief made minutes elastic. Withdrawal made them jump.

At the top of the screen, the signal bars flickered like a bad joke—one bar, then none. The carrier name blinked in and out: SOS Only. No Service. SOS Only again.

"Come on," he whispered, as if the phone could be persuaded.

His thumb hovered over Hunter's contact photo. He hit CALL.

The phone vibrated once, then flashed: Call Failed.

John tried again. Same result. On the third attempt the screen didn't even bother pretending. Call Failed appeared immediately, impatient as a slap.

He swallowed, throat raw. He walked three steps toward the living room window, then two steps back toward the kitchen, holding the phone up like a divining rod. The bars jumped to two—two—and his pulse kicked stupidly with hope.

He hit CALL again.

It rang once. Not through the speaker—just the small internal vibration of the device deciding it was doing its job. Then the screen froze and dumped him back to the contact list. No explanation. No call log entry. Like it hadn't happened.

His hands shook harder with irritation, with fear, with the simple physical outrage of a body deprived of its usual poison. He wiped his thumb on his jeans and tried texting instead, because texting was smaller, quieter. Less like begging.

You back yet? he typed, then deleted, because it sounded pathetic.

I'm fine. he typed, then stared at the lie until it made him nauseous.

He tried again, choosing something practical. Phone's dead out here. Just letting you know.

Autocorrect fought him, turning out into our, then into owe. He corrected it, then watched the letters wobble on the screen as his hands tremored.

Phone's dead our here. Just letting you know.

He grimaced and backspaced.

Phone's dead out here. Just letting you know.

He hit send.

The bubble appeared in the thread. The word Sending pulsed beneath it, as if the phone were breathing.

Then the bubble vanished.

Not failed. Not unsent. Just gone—clean as if it had never existed.

John stared, blinking hard. His mind immediately offered the simplest explanation: sweaty thumb, bad reception, glitch. He could hear Hunter's voice in his head, steady and practical: reception out here is garbage.

But his pulse kept hammering as if it didn't believe in garbage.

He tried again. This time he watched his own thumb like it was an untrustworthy animal.

Still no service. You okay?

He hit send. The bubble appeared. Sending pulsed.

Then the screen jumped.

The thread header at the top changed.

ALICE.

John's stomach dropped so hard it felt like falling. He hadn't touched her name. He hadn't scrolled. But there it was—her contact photo, the one from years ago when she'd been squinting into sunlight, one hand held up in mock protest.

The last message in the thread sat like a bruise.

Where are you?

He didn't remember that message. Or maybe he did and his brain had stuffed it in a locked drawer. There were dozens of those now—messages, moments, whole hours.

His thumb hovered over the text field.

For a sick second he imagined that if he typed back, if he answered, the world would reset. Alice would answer too.

She'd send one of her annoyed emojis. She'd tell him to come home and stop being dramatic.

John's throat tightened until he could barely breathe.

He locked the phone and shoved it back into his pocket so hard the edge of it bit his palm.

The house remained quiet. No voice. No vibration. No proof that he hadn't just hallucinated the entire thing.

His hands shook, empty now, as if they were looking for something to hold.

John forced himself into the kitchen, peeled the banana with clumsy fingers, and ate half of it without tasting it. He drank water until his stomach sloshed and his throat still felt dry.

He ate half a banana and forced down a bottle of water. His stomach cramped. His skin prickled as if ants were crawling beneath it.

He needed something to do with his hands besides tremble. In a kitchen drawer, he found a yellow legal pad curled at the edges and a pen that bled too much ink.

The first page was already written on in thick, slanted handwriting: CIGARETTES. COFFEE. GAS. Beneath it, underlined twice, a single word: LOCKS.

John stared at the list until he realized he was holding his breath. He tore the page off and crumpled it, but the underlined word stayed lodged behind his eyes.

The word pulled him sideways in time.

Alice at the kitchen counter in their second apartment, hair still damp from a shower, wearing one of his shirts like it belonged to her. The place had been bigger than the first— still cheap, still cramped, but with a real deadbolt and windows that didn't rattle every time a truck went by.

They'd been trying to make it feel like an adult home. That had been the phrase Alice used, half mocking, half hopeful.

John had come in late the night before, drunk enough that the hallway light had felt hostile. He remembered fumbling with keys. He remembered dropping them once, cursing softly so he wouldn't wake the neighbors. He did not remember turning the lock.

In the morning, Alice had found the door cracked open to the hall.

Not wide. Just open enough to let the strip of dim building light spill across their carpet like a warning.

John remembered her standing in the doorway, one hand on the knob, staring at the gap as if she couldn't make herself close it. Her face had been pale in a way John didn't know how to fix.

"I could have woken up and you'd be gone," she'd said. Not accusing. Just stating the shape of a fear.

"I was right here," John had mumbled from the couch, head pounding, mouth sour. "Nobody's going to break in."

Alice turned slowly. Her eyes were clear. Too clear. "You don't know that," she'd said. "You don't know anything when you're like that."

John had tried to laugh it off, because laughing was easier than accepting that he'd scared her. "We live on the third floor," he said. "What are they going to do, climb the building like Spider-Man?"

Alice hadn't smiled.

She crossed the room and sat at the table, pulling the magnetized notepad off the fridge. The one she used for grocery lists and little reminders—milk, coffee, batteries, replace lightbulb.

She wrote two words in thick, angry strokes.

LOCK THE DOOR.

Then she underlined it so hard the pen bit the paper.

John watched her and felt the irritation rise, reflexive. He hated being managed. He hated being reminded that his body could betray him, that his mind could vanish.

"You're being dramatic," he'd said, voice hoarse.

Alice's head snapped up. "No," she said, and the single syllable cut through his hangover like cold water. "I'm being realistic. Because you're not."

John opened his mouth to argue, but the argument stalled. It stalled because he could see the tremor in her hand as she set the pen down. Not fear of the world. Fear of him.

"I'm sorry," he'd said, quieter.

Alice stared at him for a long moment. Then her shoulders sank. The anger drained out of her like water leaving a tub.

"I know you are," she said. "And I know you don't mean to. But I can't keep waking up and wondering what version of you walked through that door last night."

John had stood up, unsteady, and crossed to her. He'd reached for her, and she let him. She always let him, even when she shouldn't have.

He kissed her forehead and tasted soap and shampoo and something saltier beneath it. "I'll lock it," he promised. "I swear."

Alice's eyes closed briefly, like she was trying to decide whether to believe him.

Then she leaned into him, and her voice went small. "I don't need you to swear," she said. "I need you to remember. Even when you don't want to."

Later that day she'd gone to the hardware store and come back with a sturdier deadbolt, as if metal could compensate for a man.

John installed it while she watched, sober and sweating, the screws biting into wood. Alice tested it three times, each click loud and final.

"There," she said. "Now it's harder."

John had meant to make a joke, something like you're turning our apartment into Fort Knox. But he'd looked at her and seen how exhausted she was by fear, and the joke died.

"Harder isn't the same as safe," he'd said before he could stop himself.

Alice's gaze held his. "Then stop being the easiest way in," she replied.

Now, in Hunter's house, John stared at the underlined word and felt the old shame press on him like a thumb to a bruise.

Locks, he thought. As if a lock had ever been the problem.

He could lock every door in this place and still not keep out what was already inside him.

He flipped to a clean sheet and wrote INVENTORY across the top. The letters came out crooked, the pen skating with every tremor.

He told himself it was practical. Water. Food. Batteries. A way to make this place manageable.

But the first thing his hand wrote was her name.

ALICE.

The ink looked too dark against the paper. His throat cinched. He tried to write a second line—anything that would make the name less final—but the words wouldn't hold still long enough to form.

A drop landed on the page. Then another. He wiped his face with the back of his hand and tasted salt.

He tore that sheet free, balled it up, and threw it away. Then he tore another. And another. The trash can filled with wadded paper like early snow.

Eventually he left the pad on the table, open to a blank page, because blank was easier than true.

By nine, his hands were shaking worse. By ten, his heart felt like it couldn't decide whether to race or stall.

He tried to watch television, something mindless, but the flicker made his eyes ache. He tried to read one of Hunter's old paperbacks and couldn't focus on a single sentence.

He sat on the couch and stared at nothing, feeling his own thoughts circle like vultures.

Alice's face kept appearing in his mind - not the way she had looked on the carpet, but the way she had looked in the kitchen when she laughed, when she rolled her eyes at his jokes, when she said his name like she liked the taste of it.

He shut his eyes hard, as if that could erase her.

He kept his eyes closed, breathing through waves of heat and cold, trying to will his nervous system back into a human shape.

Somewhere in the house, wood creaked. Not the small settling sounds he had been hearing all evening—the normal noises of an old building. This was a slow, deliberate creak, like someone shifting their weight.

John opened his eyes a slit.

The living room was the same. Couch. Coffee table. Armchair by the window like a patient listener. Darkness outside the glass.

Then the landline in the entryway made a soft click, as if a receiver had been lifted and set down again.

John's heart kicked. He held still, waiting to hear a dial tone, a voice, anything.

Instead, there was only the hush of rain on the windows and the faint sound of his own breathing.

When he opened them again, the television was on.

He was sure it had been off. He had unplugged it, hadn't he? Or had he only thought about unplugging it?

The screen glowed blue-white. Channels changed by themselves, a rapid-fire rotation: a cartoon; a late-night infomercial; a preacher with sweat shining on his forehead; static.

John leaned forward and grabbed the remote from the coffee table. The buttons were dusty, as if no one had used it in years.

He pressed POWER. Nothing happened.

The channels kept flipping, faster now.

"Okay," John muttered. "Okay. Great."

He reached for the plug behind the TV.

A voice behind him said, "Don't do that."

John whipped around so fast his neck popped.

A man sat in the leather armchair by the window.

He looked like the photographs Hunter kept in his wallet: Jim Wallace, Hunter's father. Same broad shoulders, same heavy brow. But the version of him sitting there now had a gray pallor to his skin, like wax left out in the sun. His eyes were bright, unnervingly alive. A cigarette smoldered between his fingers, though there was no ashtray and no smoke visible until John noticed the thin ribbon of it curling toward the ceiling.

John couldn't speak. His mouth opened and nothing came out.

"Sit down," Jim said, like he was the one who owned the place. He nodded at the couch. "You're making yourself worse."

John's hands were shaking violently now, but he forced them into fists. "You... you're dead."

Jim shrugged. "I'm a lot of things."

"This isn't real," John said. He heard the thinness of the sentence even as he said it. "This is withdrawal. This is—"

"Call it what you want," Jim said. He tapped ash that didn't exist onto the carpet that didn't burn. "Labels are for paperwork."

The TV flashed to a security-camera angle of a room John knew too well: his apartment living room. The white couch. The coffee table with two cups. The carpet stained orange.

John's breath caught. The image vanished a second later, replaced by static, then by the preacher again.

"What the hell is this?" John demanded.

Jim watched him with the tired amusement of someone watching a man argue with weather. "It's a house," he said. "Old houses have personalities. Some of them are just quieter about it."

"Hunter said you died," John said. "He said you had a heart attack."

Jim's smile was small and sharp. "I did."

John's heartbeat pounded against his ribs. "So why are you here?"

"Because you're here." Jim leaned forward, elbows on knees. The smell of cigarettes hit John - stale, sweet, and wrong. "And because this place likes company when it starts chewing."

"Chewing."

"You brought a lot of meat with you," Jim said. His gaze flicked over John like a butcher's evaluation. "Grief. Guilt. A habit that thinks it's a friend."

"Don't talk about my wife," John snapped.

Jim lifted his hands, cigarette between fingers, a gesture that was almost surrender. "You asked why I'm here. I'm answering."

John realized he was still standing. His legs were starting to quiver. He sat on the edge of the couch because he didn't trust them.

"What is this place?" he asked, quieter now.

Jim's eyes drifted to the dark window. Beyond the glass, the yard was a smear of shadow. "It's hungry," he said. "It's been hungry a long time. It takes what's already inside you and dresses it up in teeth."

Jim's gaze slid back to John. "It doesn't just scare you," he said. "Not at first. First it offers."

John's fingers tightened on the edge of the couch. "Offers what?"

Jim tilted his head as if considering the menu. "What you want. What you miss. What you think will fix you." His eyes flicked to John's shaking hands. "A drink, for a man who's trying not to shake apart. A voice, for a man who can't stand the quiet. A little mercy. A little forgetting."

John's stomach turned. "And then what?"

Jim's smile showed no teeth. "Then it takes something back. It always does. Sometimes it asks polite. Sometimes it takes without asking."

"That's insane," John said, but his voice sounded thin.

Jim shrugged again, and for a moment he looked almost tired. "Call it insane. Call it hallucination. Call it ghosts.

Doesn't matter what you name it. What matters is whether you accept the offer."

John swallowed. "That's not an answer."

Jim's laugh was a soft cough. "It's the only one you're going to get for free."

The TV snapped to another image—fast as a blink. A rain-blurred figure. Black knit over a face. Two hollow eyeholes that looked straight out at John. Then it was gone, replaced by static.

John jolted back. "That's him. That's the guy."

When he looked at Jim again, the chair was empty.

John didn't move for a moment because moving would make it real—would force him to choose which reality he lived in.

The chair sat exactly where Jim had been, cushion slightly indented, the leather catching the weak lamplight in dull folds. John stared at the imprint as if it might rise on its own and form a body again.

His skin prickled. Sweat cooled on his ribs.

Slowly, he stood. The tremor in his hands had settled into a fine vibration now, less violent than earlier but more constant, like his bones had been rewired wrong. He stepped toward the chair, half expecting the air around it to change temperature, to resist him like a magnetic field.

Nothing.

He reached out and touched the armrest.

The leather was cool. Ordinary.

John swallowed, then glanced down at the carpet. He remembered Jim tapping ash into it—remembered the tiny gray flakes falling like dandruff, remembered the impossible fact that the fibers hadn't singed.

There was a smudge there now, faint but visible. A small crescent of gray, like someone had pressed a dirty thumb into the weave.

John crouched. He pinched at it carefully.

His fingers came away clean.

He tried again, rubbing the spot with the pad of his thumb. The smudge didn't move. It wasn't ash. It was deeper, embedded—as if the carpet had been stained from inside.

His mouth went dry.

He leaned closer and caught the ghost of cigarette smoke, not just lingering in the air but threaded through the fabric itself.

"Okay," he whispered, though he didn't know who he was talking to. "Okay."

His gaze flicked to the coffee table. There should have been a cigarette there. A butt. A burn mark. Something. There was nothing—only Hunter's old coasters, warped from humidity, and the legal pad John had left open like a wound.

John straightened too fast and the room tilted. A brief wash of dizziness blurred the edges of everything. He grabbed the back of the chair to steady himself and felt the leather creak under his grip.

For a second he thought he felt warmth beneath his palm—residual heat, as if a body had just left.

Then the sensation was gone. Or it never existed. Or his brain, starving for dopamine and order, had invented it because the alternative was that a dead man had sat with him and offered advice.

He backed away from the chair and stared at the television. The screen was a dark mirror now. His own face hovered in it—gaunt, eyes bloodshot, skin slick with sweat. He looked like someone who belonged in a cautionary video.

"Withdrawal," he said out loud, testing the word. It sounded clinical. It sounded like a handrail.

The house answered with nothing. Just the faint tick of cooling wood, the low groan of wind, the distant percussion of the storm beginning to gather itself.

John sat down again, slower this time, and kept his eyes on the chair as if looking away might invite it back.

The cigarette smell lingered for a moment, then thinned until it was only the house's old stale air.

The television clicked off.

John sat in the quiet, sweat cooling on his skin, and tried to decide whether he had just hallucinated a dead man giving him advice.

Hunter's warning came back with uncomfortable clarity: withdrawals could turn a mind into a carnival. John tried to hold on to that like a diagnosis. Like an explanation that could keep him from falling apart.

He stared at the silent screen and told himself there was a reasonable sequence of events in which he was alone in a rural house, exhausted, shaking, and imagining a dead man in a chair. He told himself he believed it.

Outside, thunder rumbled like something clearing its throat.

Chapter Four: The First Offer

The storm arrived the way bad news does: quietly at first, then all at once.

Rain started as a soft tapping on the windows. Wind followed, pushing at the house with insistent hands. By midnight, thunder rolled close enough to rattle the glass in its frames.

John lay in Hunter's bed with his eyes open, listening.

Sleep refused to come. Every time he drifted, his body jolted awake as if it had remembered something urgent: drink, drink, drink. His skin alternated between fever-hot and gooseflesh-cold. His heart flopped in his chest like a fish on a dock.

He got up and paced the room, then the hallway, then the stairs. The house seemed to watch him move, a presence in the walls. He told himself it was paranoia. He told himself he was inventing threats because he couldn't bear the real one.

He went downstairs for water and found the kitchen colder than before. The air had that refrigerator-cold bite to it, even though the fridge was unplugged and dead. His breath fogged faintly when he exhaled.

The landline sat on the side table by the living room window, dark and silent. For a moment John stared at it, wanting—desperately—to hear it ring, just once, because a ringing phone meant the world outside this house hadn't forgotten him.

He reached out and touched the receiver, just to be sure it was seated properly in its cradle.

The phone clicked under his fingers, a small mechanical sound that seemed to echo through the whole house.

The receiver was heavier than he expected, the kind of weight that belonged to old objects that had outlived their purpose. He lifted it slowly, bringing the plastic to his ear.

For two beats there was nothing—no dial tone, no hiss, not even the comforting electronic hum of a dead line pretending it was still part of the world.

Then a thin static rose, so faint he wasn't sure it wasn't his own blood moving. It reminded him of holding a seashell to his ear as a kid, convinced the ocean lived inside.

John listened harder.

The static thickened for a moment, then dropped away into pure silence.

He swallowed and realized he could hear himself breathing, loud and wet and wrong. He could hear the faint click of his teeth as his jaw trembled.

He whispered without thinking. "Hello?"

The word fell into the line and vanished. No echo. No answer.

John pulled the receiver away and stared at it, irrationally offended. It was just plastic and wire. It was a tool. It was not supposed to feel like a mouth that refused to speak.

He set it back into the cradle.

The phone made a decisive little click, like a lock closing.

John froze. He waited for a dial tone. He waited for a voice.

Nothing.

He told himself it was the storm making the old wiring twitch. He told himself that because the alternative— because the alternative had a dead man sitting in Hunter's chair and a ski mask in the yard.

In the kitchen, the faucet dripped once, though he was certain he had turned it off. The single drop sounded like a footstep.

Upstairs, somewhere near the landing, a floorboard creaked.

John looked up toward the dark stairwell. The hair on his arms rose.

At the top of the stairs, the door to the small red room stood cracked open.

John stopped.

He was sure Hunter had left it shut.

A thin line of darkness spilled out into the hall.

He stared at the gap until his eyes watered. He told himself to go back downstairs. He told himself not to be an idiot.

Then, because he was John Glisner and his life was a record of choosing the worst impulse, he pushed the door open.

The room smelled like dust and old cloth. The walls were painted a deep, tired red that swallowed the weak light from the hall. A single wardrobe stood against the far wall, tall and narrow, its wood dark and glossy as if it had been oiled recently.

John stepped inside. The floorboards creaked under his weight.

The wardrobe was locked with a brass latch. The latch looked new compared to the rest of the room, too clean, too bright.

He didn't remember why, but his mouth watered.

He crossed the room. The air felt colder near the wardrobe, as if the wood radiated chill instead of warmth.

The latch clicked on its own.

John jerked back. He stared at it, waiting for it to click again, waiting for the house to admit the trick.

Slowly, the wardrobe doors eased open.

Inside was darkness, deeper than the room's shadows, as if the space did not lead to a simple set of shelves. John leaned closer and smelled something that made his stomach turn and his throat tighten at the same time.

Bourbon.

Not just alcohol - bourbon specifically, sweet and smoky, the scent of oak barrels and burned sugar. His body reacted before his mind could object. His tongue tingled. His hands reached out.

His fingers closed around a small wooden box set on a shelf. The box was carved with geometric patterns and fitted with a tiny brass clasp.

He brought it into the light and opened it.

Inside, nestled in dark velvet, was a shot glass filled to the brim with amber liquid.

The surface of the bourbon trembled, though the house was still.

John stared at it, hypnotized by the shine.

A thought arrived, smooth as a whisper: Just one. To steady your hands. To quiet your heart. Just one to get you through the night.

He could almost taste it. He could almost feel the burn sliding down his throat, the brief warmth blooming in his chest like mercy.

His hand shook so hard the bourbon sloshed against the rim.

He closed his eyes and saw Alice on the kitchen floor.

He saw blood threaded through vomit like dark string.

He heard his own scream, raw and animal.

He opened his eyes again.

"No," he said out loud, and the word surprised him with its steadiness.

He carried the box to the center of the room. For a moment he just stood there, breathing bourbon and dust and fear.

Then he raised the box over his head and threw it down as hard as he could.

Wood cracked. Glass shattered. Bourbon sprayed the floor, a sharp sweet smell that filled the room like a taunt.

John stared at the wreckage and felt, briefly, a fierce satisfaction. He had won a battle he hadn't known he was fighting.

Behind him, the wardrobe doors swung shut with a soft, decisive click.

The smell hit him all at once—sweet and sharp and intimate. It clung to the back of his throat the way guilt did. For a second he thought he could feel the bourbon inside his mouth even though he hadn't tasted a drop.

He bent over, hands on his knees, fighting the urge to retch. The room spun in slow circles around the broken glass and the wet stain spreading across the floorboards like a bruise.

"Not tonight," he whispered, though he didn't know if he was talking to himself or to the house.

John backed out of the red room on unsteady legs, keeping his eyes on the wardrobe as if it might lunge. The doorframe felt narrower than it had when he'd entered, as if the house was trying to make him squeeze past.

He stepped into the hallway and dragged air into his lungs until the bourbon-sweetness faded to something he could bear.

Then he reached back and shut the red room door.

It didn't close all the way at first. The latch met resistance, a soft catch like cloth snagging. John pushed harder. The wood thudded into place, and the old knob turned slightly under his palm as if someone on the other side had leaned against it.

John snatched his hand away.

"Stop," he muttered, not caring if the house heard him. "Just—stop."

He grabbed the brass latch plate on the outside of the door, searching for a lock that didn't exist. There was none. Just old paint and age-softened wood and the faint outline of where a different latch might once have been.

His pulse skittered.

He looked around the landing, eyes adjusting to the dim. There was a small table against the wall beneath a framed landscape print—something Hunter's mother might have hung because she'd wanted beauty out here. The table wobbled when John grabbed it, but it was solid enough.

He dragged it across the floorboards with a scrape that sounded like teeth. He shoved it against the red room door, bracing it beneath the knob. Then he tested the door with his shoulder.

It held.

John exhaled in a harsh burst, relief so sudden it felt like weakness.

This was rational, he told himself. This was a man taking precautions in an unfamiliar house during a storm. This was not a man barricading a door against something that could open latches without hands.

He stepped back and stared at his makeshift barricade, daring the door to move.

It didn't.

Not while he watched.

* * *

Downstairs, the house went colder.

John tried the thermostat. The needle sat stubbornly below fifty. He turned the dial. Nothing changed.

He turned on a faucet. Water came out in a weak trickle, colder than it should have been.

The overhead lights flickered. Once. Twice.

Then the power died.

The sudden darkness felt thick, like velvet thrown over his head. The house made a low settling sound, a long exhale.

John stood in the kitchen with his hands braced on the counter, listening to the rain pound the roof.

"Of course," he muttered. "Of course."

He found the battery lantern Hunter had left and clicked it on. A weak cone of light spilled across the floor.

The cold was already in his bones. He needed heat. He needed a shower. He needed anything that didn't feel like punishment.

In the living room, an old brick fireplace crouched beneath a mantel stained by decades of smoke. A stack of split logs sat beside it, half-covered by a dusty tarp.

John knelt and tried to build a fire the way people did in movies—kindling, then small sticks, then the heavy pieces. His hands shook so badly he kept dropping the wood. The sound of each clack on brick felt too loud in the quiet house.

For one sharp second he saw Alice in a different cabin, months ago, laughing as she snapped kindling and told him he was doing it wrong. The memory had warmth in it. The present didn't.

The memory came with such clarity it stole his breath.

It had been late October, cold enough that the air tasted metallic, the kind of cold that made fire feel like a necessity instead of a luxury. Hunter had lent them the place for a weekend—"Get out of the city. Breathe," he'd said, smiling like he was doing John a favor.

Alice had loved it immediately. She'd walked through the house barefoot, palms brushing the walls, as if she could read the history in the grain. She'd opened windows despite the chill and let the woods smell pour in. Pine and damp leaves and distance.

John had pretended to love it too.

He remembered standing in front of a fireplace much like this one—brick, soot-stained, stubborn. His hands had been steadier then. Not sober, but steadier. He'd been drinking at a pace he could still call controlled, the way men like him built lies: careful and convincing.

Alice had come up behind him, wrapping her arms around his waist, chin resting between his shoulder blades. "You look like you're trying to negotiate with it," she'd said, amused.

"I'm trying to start it," John replied, scowling at the kindling like it was personally offending him.

Alice laughed, warm and easy. "You're doing it wrong."

He'd glanced back at her. "And you're an expert?"

"I'm an expert at watching you refuse to ask for help," she'd said, and her voice had carried that familiar blend of affection and warning.

He had rolled his eyes. "I can do it."

"Okay," she'd said, and that one word had been a dare.

He'd struck match after match until the heads were gone, fingertips numb from frustration and cold. The kindling had refused to catch. Smoke had curled up, thin and mocking, then died.

Alice had watched him for a while, smiling like she was watching a child insist on tying his own shoes. Then she'd stepped past him, gentle but unyielding, and taken the matches from his hand.

"Here," she'd said softly, and her fingers had brushed his —a small touch that used to mean trust.

She'd arranged the wood differently. Not a pile, but a structure. A little deliberate architecture: kindling crisscrossed, paper tucked where air could feed flame. She moved with the confidence of someone who believed problems had solutions.

John had watched her, and the admiration in his chest had been real. It had also been sharp with resentment, because admiration was a kind of debt he never felt able to repay.

Alice struck a match. The flame bloomed steady. She held it under the paper, patient, and the fire caught as if it had been waiting for her permission.

She looked over her shoulder at him with a grin. "See? It likes me."

John had laughed—actually laughed—because the room had been warm and Alice was beautiful and the world still felt like something they could fix.

They'd sat on the floor in front of the fire with two mugs of cocoa she'd insisted on making because "we're not twenty-two anymore, John, we're allowed to be cozy."

He'd added whiskey to his.

Alice had pretended not to notice at first. Then she'd reached over and taken his mug, sniffed it, and raised her eyebrows.

"What?" he'd asked, defensive without meaning to be.

Alice had put the mug back down carefully. "Nothing," she'd said. "I just wish you didn't need it for everything."

"It's a weekend," John had said, too quick. "I'm relaxing."

"You always have a reason," she'd replied, still calm. That was what made it dangerous. When Alice got quiet, it meant she was choosing her words like they mattered.

John had stared into the fire and felt the old familiar irritation rise—the one that told him he was being judged, being controlled, being cornered.

Alice had reached out and touched his wrist. "I'm not trying to take something from you," she'd said. "I'm trying to keep you."

The fire had crackled. Warmth had washed over his knees. For a moment he'd felt the shape of a different life— one where he didn't choose the bottle every time his chest tightened, one where he didn't turn love into a negotiation.

He'd looked at her and almost said it. Almost said I'm scared. Almost said I don't know how to stop.

Instead he'd smiled and lifted his mug in a toast, making a joke out of the moment like he always did.

"To cozy," he'd said.

Alice had watched him over the rim of her cocoa, eyes soft and sad at the same time. "To cozy," she'd echoed, and her voice had sounded like surrender wearing a smile.

In the bedroom later, she'd fallen asleep quickly, face turned toward him, one hand curled near his chest.

John hadn't slept.

He'd gotten up in the dark, moved quietly so he wouldn't wake her, and poured himself another drink in the kitchen where the firelight couldn't reach. He'd told himself he deserved it. He'd told himself it was better than being angry. He'd told himself a hundred things.

When he came back to bed, Alice's eyes were open. Not angry. Just awake, watching.

"John," she'd whispered.

He'd pretended not to hear.

Now, in Hunter's house, John stared at the damp match between his fingers and felt the memory curdle into something sour. The warmth in it was still there, but it had teeth.

He struck another match.

He struck a match. The flame flared, then hissed out, damp and useless. The second match died the same way. The third stayed alive long enough to bite his fingertips before it guttered into smoke.

From somewhere upstairs came a soft creak—then another, spaced like footsteps. John froze with a dead match between his fingers, listening hard enough to turn the wind into words.

He backed away from the fireplace and grabbed his coat instead. Heat could wait. His body couldn't.

Hunter's words came back: Basement access is outside only. Don't close it behind you.

John hesitated.

If he was being rational - if he was a man who had ever been rational - he would have stayed upstairs and waited for morning, waited for Hunter, waited for daylight to dilute his fear.

But the cold pressed in, and his body demanded action the way it demanded bourbon: urgently, mindlessly.

He grabbed the flashlight, shoved his feet into boots, and pulled on his coat.

At the back door, he paused with his hand on the knob.

The storm outside made the glass vibrate. Wind moaned through the trees.

John pictured the masked man standing under the oak, watching, patient.

He opened the door anyway.

* * *

Rain hit him in a sheet.

The yard had turned to mud. Lightning flashed somewhere beyond the tree line, bleaching the world white for an instant. Thunder followed hard enough that it made the ground tremble.

John kept his head down and hurried around the side of the house to the storm cellar doors under the awning.

Water ran off the slanted wood in streams.

He set the lantern on the ground, knelt, and yanked at the metal ring handles.

The doors resisted for a beat, then gave with a wet groan.

Cold air rolled up from the basement like breath from a mouth.

John aimed the flashlight down. Wooden steps disappeared into darkness. The smell that rose was damp and sour, like soil kept too long in a closed fist.

He descended carefully, boots slipping on the slick boards.

At the bottom, he found a light switch and flipped it out of habit.

To his surprise, the basement lights came on.

Two bare bulbs hung from the ceiling, throwing a weak yellow glow over a concrete floor. The water heater sat in one corner, a rusted cylinder with pipes running into the wall. A workbench leaned against the far side, cluttered with old tools and coffee cans.

John let out a breath he hadn't realized he was holding.

The light made the basement look almost normal, which somehow felt worse. Normal meant he could pretend. Normal meant he could drop his guard. Normal meant the house could choose when to stop playing fair.

John moved deeper into the room, boots leaving wet prints on concrete. The air was colder down here, but it wasn't clean cold. It was damp and mineral, the smell of iron and old wood rot. He tasted it at the back of his throat.

A workbench ran along one wall, cluttered with forgotten lives: rusted tools, jars of nails, coffee cans with lids warped from humidity. In one corner, a stack of plastic storage bins sat like a barricade. A child's baseball glove lay on top of them, stiff with age, fingers curled as if still trying to catch something.

Hunter had been a kid here, John realized. Hunter had grown up under this roof with these smells, these shadows. He'd made rules for a reason, even if he didn't want to explain them.

A drip sounded somewhere in the dark beyond the bulbs' reach. Slow. Regular. Like a clock that didn't keep time.

John's hands trembled around the flashlight, though he didn't need it yet. The tremor traveled up his forearms into his shoulders, making him feel hollowed out. He tried to steady himself by focusing on something concrete, something solvable.

Heat. Pilot light. Turn gas. Ignite.

He crouched beside the old heater, staring at the small glass window where flame should have been. It was black.

"Come on," he whispered again, as if the machine cared.

He patted his pockets harder than necessary, searching for a lighter he knew he didn't own. His fingers kept catching on the edge of his phone, and the reminder of its uselessness made him want to throw it.

No signal. No voice. No tether.

He forced himself to look away and scan the workbench. The matchbook sat there like it had been placed for him—cheap cardboard, edges softened, the striker strip worn gray.

He picked it up and flipped it open.

Most of the matches were missing. The ones left were swollen slightly, heads dulled by moisture. He shook one loose and it stuck, stubborn. His fingers were too clumsy for delicate work now. He pried at it, and the match snapped in half.

"Goddamn it," John hissed, voice sharp in the small space.

The bulbs overhead swung slightly, though there was no breeze.

John froze.

They settled. Slowly. The light steadied.

He forced a laugh that sounded wrong. "Withdrawal," he told the basement, like naming it made him safe.

He pulled another match free, careful this time. He held it between trembling fingers and brought it to the striker.

For a moment he just stared at the tiny thing—the absurdity of relying on a sliver of wood to keep darkness back.

He struck.

He crouched beside the heater and stared at the pilot-light window. Dark.

"Come on," he whispered.

He patted his pockets for a lighter, found none. He hadn't smoked in years.

On the workbench, he found a small cardboard matchbook. The kind you used to get at diners. The logo on the front was faded beyond recognition.

He snapped it open with clumsy fingers and struck a match.

The match flared to life, bright and sudden.

At that exact moment, the basement lights went out.

Darkness swallowed the room so completely it felt physical. The only light was the tiny flame in John's trembling hand.

"No," John breathed. "No, no, no."

He held the match close to the pilot light window, squinting. The flame made shadows jump on the walls, sharp and frantic.

He turned the gas knob, held the match to the opening, and waited.

The match's heat licked his fingers.

Something moved at the edge of the light.

John's head snapped up.

In the dim matchglow, the far corner of the basement seemed deeper than it should have been. A patch of darkness that did not belong to the room's geometry.

Then, as the match sputtered, a pale shape emerged from that darkness.

A skull.

Not a decoration. Not a toy. A human skull, slick with moisture, empty sockets turned toward him.

His breath snagged. His heart hammered once, twice, and then his body did what it always did when terrified: it tried to run.

He jerked back, and the match fell from his fingers.

The flame winked out on the concrete.

Darkness slammed down.

John fumbled for another match in the open book, hands refusing to cooperate. He struck one. Nothing. He struck again. A spark, then nothing. The match head crumbled.

His throat tightened until he could barely swallow.

He forced himself to strike again, slower.

The match caught.

Light flickered back into being.

Water covered the floor.

It hadn't been there seconds ago. Now it spread in a shallow, rippling sheet, reflecting the match flame in broken pieces.

The water was rising.

John stared, mind stalling. Then cold flooded his boots.

"Jesus Christ," he choked.

Something splashed behind him.

He spun, match held out like a weapon.

The skeleton was closer now - not just the skull but the whole thing, a wet, articulated body pulling itself forward through the water. Bones knocked against concrete with a sound like dry sticks clacking together.

Its jaw gaped, as if trying to bite without flesh.

John screamed. The sound was swallowed by the storm outside and the basement's damp throat.

He bolted toward the stairs.

The water dragged at his boots. His feet slipped. The match flame fluttered wildly, then went out as water splashed up.

Darkness again.

John reached the stairs by touch, fingers scraping wood, and climbed blind.

Behind him, something scraped over concrete. Something splashed and slapped wetly against the steps.

"No!" John shouted, though there was no one to hear him. "No!"

He hit the cellar doors, shoved upward. Wind tore at them. Rain poured down.

For a heartbeat he couldn't get them open, and panic tightened into something sharp enough to cut.

Then the doors gave and he burst into the storm, hauling himself out like a drowning man.

He slammed the doors shut, threw his weight onto them, and fumbled for the metal rings to pull them tight.

From below, something hit the underside of the wood.

Once.

Twice.

The doors bucked under the impact.

John shoved harder, teeth clenched, shoulders screaming.

A third blow landed, so hard it made the hinges shriek.

Then everything went still.

John stood panting in the rain, chest heaving, hands shaking, boots full of icy water. When he swallowed, he tasted the cellar—iron and dirt—as if it had gotten inside him.

Lightning flashed.

In that bright instant, a figure stood at the end of the drive near Hunter's car tracks.

The man in the ski mask.

He was closer than before. Close enough that John could see the dark holes where his eyes should have been. Close enough that John could see the gleam of rain on the knit fabric.

The masked man took a step toward him.

Then another.

John ran.

Mud tried to keep his boots. Wind shoved at his shoulders like hands. John ran anyway, lungs burning, throat still full of the cellar's iron taste.

He didn't look back. The urge to see was almost as strong as the urge to live, and he didn't trust himself with both.

The farmhouse loomed through the rain, every window black. The porch light was out. The place looked abandoned, the way a mouth looks closed right before it bites.

John cut around the corner toward the front steps. His foot skidded on wet grass and he nearly went down. He caught himself and kept moving.

The front porch rushed up at him. He hit the steps too hard, stumbled, and grabbed the railing with numb fingers.

Behind him, something moved in the yard—fast enough that the sound didn't match the distance.

John reached for the front doorknob. His hand slid on wet metal. He grabbed again, hard, and yanked.

The knob turned under his shaking grip.

The door didn't budge. Not at first.

John hit it again, shoulder-first. Pain shot down his arm, bright and immediate.

For a terrifying second nothing happened, and then the latch gave with a sound like a tooth breaking. The door swung inward.

He fell into the entryway, catching himself on the wall. Darkness swallowed him. The house smelled of cold wood and old smoke and something sour beneath it, like a cellar that had been opened too long.

John slammed the door shut and threw the deadbolt. His fingers fought him. His hands were numb and shaking and slick with rain.

Outside, something moved fast across the porch boards —too fast to be footsteps, too heavy to be wind.

The impact came an instant later.

The door bucked under it, the whole frame groaning. The chain lock whined like an animal.

John staggered back, palms up as if he could catch the next blow.

Another hit landed—harder. The knob rattled under it.

Then silence.

Not relief. Not safety. A listening silence. The kind that told him whatever stood outside had decided it didn't need to hurry.

In that silence, the red corded phone on the side table rang once—sharp and old-fashioned, a sound from a different decade. It echoed through the house like a dare.

John stared at it, breath caught in his throat, and waited for it to ring again.

ACT II

Chapter Five: The Call

The house was cold and black. No hum of the refrigerator. No television glow. No porch light bleeding in from outside. He could hear only the storm and, under that, the blood rushing in his ears.

John's eyes adjusted by degrees. Shapes emerged—the outline of the couch, the coffee table, the narrow hall leading toward the kitchen. The red corded phone on the side table looked like a bruise in the dark.

Hunter. Call Hunter. Call anyone.

He moved too fast and clipped his shoulder on the corner of the coffee table; the pain helped—sharp, real, anchoring.

John fumbled his own phone out of his coat pocket with hands that didn't feel like hands. The screen was slick with rain. His thumb skated across it, leaving a smear, and the device refused to recognize him the way it used to. Face ID blinked and gave up. The passcode pad swam.

He tried anyway. Once. Twice. A third time with his teeth bared, as if anger could steady muscle and nerve.

Locked.

Of course. Of course it was locked. The universe was nothing if not consistent in the stupid places.

He wiped the screen on his sleeve and finally got it open. The battery icon glared a low red number at him. Three percent.

No signal bars. Then, as if the phone were reconsidering, full bars flashed for half a second before collapsing back to nothing.

Hunter. Call Hunter.

John jabbed the call icon. The screen read CALLING for a heartbeat. Then it stuttered into NO SERVICE.

His throat tightened. He tried again. Same result.

He opened his messages with the care of a man disarming a bomb. His last thread with Hunter was a neat list of practicalities—directions, a grocery list, the kind of mundane text you send when you're pretending everything is salvageable.

John started typing: I need help.

The phone corrected it into: I need it.

He stared at the words until his eyes blurred. He deleted them and typed again, slower. I need help. The cursor blinked, patient as a judge.

His screen dimmed. Low Battery flashed at him like an accusation.

John hit 911 before he could talk himself out of it. The keypad appeared. He pressed the numbers with shaking precision and lifted the phone to his ear.

Silence.

Then—a faint tone, not quite a dial tone, not quite static. The sound you get when you're between stations on an old radio. It rose and fell like breathing.

John yanked the phone away and stared at it. NO SERVICE. The words sat there, smug.

"Work," he whispered. "Please. Just—work."

The only answer was the storm ticking at the windows and the slow, intentional quiet of the house.

His gaze drifted to the landline on the side table. The red receiver sat in its cradle like a held breath.

Hunter's voice echoed in his head from earlier—too calm, too practiced: If that phone rings, you let it ring. You hear me? You let it ring.

The phone wasn't ringing now. It was just waiting.

John swallowed. His body was already leaning toward the receiver the way it leaned toward a bottle. Toward anything that promised relief.

He shoved the cell phone into his pocket as if hiding it would make it useful again.

He crossed the living room and grabbed the receiver.

The line should have been dead. The power was out, the house a relic, and yet the receiver gave him a dial tone—steady and confident, like the place had been waiting for him to pick it up.

Hope rose anyway, sharp and stupid. In this house, hope didn't feel like mercy. It felt like leverage.

He punched Hunter's number from memory, teeth clenched hard enough to ache. The rotary wheel dragged beneath his finger; each click sounded too loud.

It rang.

Once.

Twice.

Then—click.

"Hello?"

A woman's voice. Soft, close. Not the operator. Not some country stranger.

Alice.

John's throat locked.

"Alice?" The name came out ragged, almost a cough.

A pause, and he could hear breathing on the other end— slow and careful, as if she were listening to him listen.

"John," she said. His name the way she used to say it when she was tired. Not angry. Not pleading. Just... worn. "What did you do?"

"I—" He swallowed and tasted iron. "I didn't—Alice, I didn't do anything. I'm at Hunter's dad's place. I'm—"

"You're always 'at' something," she said, and the softness in her voice tightened like a wire. "At the bar. At Hunter's. At the boys'. At a party. At a place where I'm not."

The living room seemed to draw closer around him. The air felt damp, as if the storm had gotten inside.

"Alice... you're—" He could not say dead. His mouth refused the word.

"I waited," she said. "I waited in that living room with the ring in my hand and your boots on the stairs and your laughter coming through the door. I waited, and the whole time I kept thinking: maybe he'll see me. Maybe he'll see what he's doing."

John's stomach turned. A memory tried to climb up his throat—Alice standing at the foot of the stairs, pale and furious, eyes wet, voice shaking. Him smiling like a fool because he couldn't feel anything but the drink.

"That's not—" he started.

"You promised." Her voice sharpened. "Every time, you promised. You made a religion out of promises you didn't keep."

"Alice, I'm sorry." He meant it. It wasn't even a choice. The apology came from somewhere deeper than pride. "I'm sorry, I'm—"

"Stop," she said. "Don't do that."

"Do what?"

"Make it about you." The breath on the line sounded closer now, like she was leaning into the receiver. "You want absolution. You want someone to tell you it isn't your fault. You want to drink the guilt away and wake up clean."

The room tilted. The darkness seemed to pulse in time with his heartbeat.

"I'm trying," he said, a little too loudly. "I'm here to get sober. I'm doing it, Alice. I haven't had a drink."

"You're sober," she said, and the word was almost a laugh. "And you're still you."

The line crackled.

John squeezed the receiver. "Where are you? Are you—are you in the hospital? Did they—"

"No." The single syllable was absolute. "You don't get to look for me now."

"Alice, please."

The storm outside thundered, but it sounded distant—like it belonged to another world. The world where things made sense.

"I loved you," she said. "And you treated that like a guarantee. Like a paycheck you'd already earned."

"Alice—"

"You did this," she whispered.

The words dropped into John like stones.

The words didn't just hurt. They unlocked something.

For a blink he wasn't in Hunter's father's entryway, clutching a receiver that shouldn't have worked. He was back in his own kitchen with the overhead light off, the only illumination coming from the refrigerator's blue glow and his phone flashlight shaking in his hand.

The cabinet beneath the sink hung open.

A cardboard box sat among the pipes like a guilty secret, its label turned toward him in thick, patient letters: RAT POISON.

He could feel the weight of it even now, the dry rattle inside. He remembered thinking it was ridiculous, buying something so final for something so small. He remembered laughing too loud because the alternative was to admit he was scared of what a quiet house could do to a man who'd been drinking for years.

In the memory, Alice stood in the doorway in her socks, not stepping closer, not stepping away. She watched him the way you watch a stranger try on your life and wear it wrong.

John tried to grab the moment and hold it still. To force it to tell him what he'd done with the box. Whether he'd put it back. Whether he'd spilled it. Whether he'd left it where she could find it.

The memory tore away like wet paper, leaving only nausea and the taste of metal at the back of his tongue.

The dial tone returned. A flat, indifferent buzz.

John stared at the receiver, waiting for the voice to come back, to call him a liar, to forgive him, to scream. Anything. The buzz continued.

He set the receiver back on its cradle with care he did not understand, as if roughness would anger the thing that had borrowed her voice.

Then he felt something on his wrist.

A faint tickle at first—like a loose thread brushing his skin. Then another. Then a quick skitter that made his muscles jump.

John looked down.

In the dark, he could see movement where his arm met the phone. A crawling, living ripple.

He'd heard about the bugs. Rehab pamphlets called it formication, as if dressing it up in a polite word could make it less terrifying: ants under the skin, spiders in the corners, the brain inventing a swarm because it didn't know what else to do with panic. Delirium tremens. DT. The name sounded like a joke until it crawled.

"—No." The word came out as a whimper.

Lightning flashed through the living room window, turning the room white for a split second.

The receiver was alive with spiders.

They poured from the speaker holes and along the cord. Not a handful—hundreds. Their bodies glossy and black, legs too thin, too fast. They streamed down his forearm like water, vanishing into his sleeve. A wet heat followed them, as if his skin had become porous.

John screamed and flung the phone. The receiver hit the far wall hard enough to crack the sound in half. The base skidded off the side table, yanked by its cord, and dropped with a dull thud.

John clawed at his arms, slapping, scraping, trying to find purchase on things that weren't there. He yanked at his collar, fingers fumbling at buttons. His breath came in harsh, panicked bursts.

"Get them off—get them off—"

He stumbled backward, heel catching the edge of the rug, and went down hard. His shoulder hit the floor first; pain bloomed hot and bright. It didn't stop him. He rolled, grinding his arms against the carpet, scraping skin raw.

Another lightning flash.

No spiders.

None on his arms. None on the floor. None crawling away toward the shadows.

Only his own red scratches, and the phone in pieces like a broken jaw.

John lay there for a second longer, panting, hands shaking in the empty air, waiting for the next rush of legs over skin.

Nothing came.

The silence should have been relief. It wasn't. It was the moment after a bad dream when you're still sure something is in the room with you.

He forced himself upright. His shoulder screamed. His ribs answered with a deeper, duller pain that made him taste copper.

His arms were raw. Thin red lines crisscrossed his wrists and forearms where he'd clawed himself. The scratches looked real. They felt real. The spiders hadn't.

John crawled toward the broken phone on hands and knees, the way you approach a wounded animal. The base lay on its side. The receiver cord had torn loose and curled like a dead vine.

He shone his flashlight at the speaker holes. No webs. No legs. No glossy bodies smashed into the plastic.

His skin still itched anyway.

His brain supplied the sensation with obscene generosity: a phantom skitter along his collarbone, a tickle behind his ear. He slapped at nothing and hated himself for it.

Delirium tremens, the pamphlets said. Like giving it a Latin name made it less humiliating.

John swallowed hard and tried to breathe through the itch. In. Out. Slow.

The couch creaked behind him.

From the dark corner by the bookshelf came a sound like someone clearing their throat.

"Delirium tremens," a voice said. "That's what they call it when the drink finally stops letting you pretend."

John's head snapped up.

A man sat in the chair that wasn't supposed to have a man in it.

Jim Wallace—Hunter's father—was half visible in the light bleeding in from the storm. He looked like he had been left out too long. Skin sunk tight over bone. One eye dull, the other too bright. His mouth moved wrong, as if the hinge had loosened.

"You're—" John tried. His tongue felt thick. "You're not real."

Jim's laugh was dry as dead leaves. "That makes two of us, boy."

John pushed himself up, back against the couch. His palms were slick with sweat. "I can feel it," he said. "I can feel everything. The water. The bugs. The cold. That masked —thing—outside. If it's all in my head, why does it feel real?"

Jim leaned forward, elbows on knees. "Because your body don't care what's real. Your body only cares what it thinks is about to kill it." He nodded toward John's hands. "Look at you. You're shaking like a dog in a thunderstorm. You've got sweat on your lip and your heart's running a race."

John glanced down. His hands trembled. Not violently, but enough that he couldn't hide it.

"Withdrawal," Jim said. "Grief. Fear. Guilt. You stirred that pot and now you're surprised it tastes like poison."

"Don't." John swallowed. "Don't talk about her."

Jim's expression softened—not kind, but less sharp. "I'm not talking about her," he said. "I'm talking about you."

John's jaw tightened. "I didn't kill her."

Jim's eye flicked toward the shattered phone, then back. "Didn't say you did."

Silence. The storm hissed against the windows. Somewhere, deep in the house, wood creaked—just the settling of an old frame, John told himself. Just that.

Jim spoke again, quieter. "This place likes people who lie to themselves. It's got a taste for it. Like blood in the water."

John stared at him. "So what is this? The house? You? The masked man? The—things?"

Jim's shoulders rose and fell. "Could be your brain on fire. Could be ghosts. Could be both." He met John's eyes. "But I'll tell you something true either way."

"What?"

Jim held up one finger. "Don't drink what it offers."

John's mouth twitched in something like a bitter smile. "I'm not."

"Good." A second finger. "Don't follow the mask."

John remembered the shape in the yard. The quiet wave. The way his own hand had lifted in answer like a reflex. A third finger. "And if it shows you the truth..."

Jim paused, and for a moment the room felt smaller.

"...pay the price," Jim finished.

John swallowed hard. "What price?"

Jim's smile was thin. "Same as always. Pride. Comfort. The story you tell yourself to sleep at night."

A crack of thunder shook the windows. The light flickered—not electricity, but lightning—showing Jim's face more clearly for an instant. The rot was worse than John wanted to admit. The old man's suit hung wrong on him, as if it belonged to someone who had once been alive.

John pushed himself to his feet. Anger, fear, and exhaustion braided together until he didn't know which feeling he was wearing.

"I'm not staying here," he said. "I'm not. I came to get sober, not—" He gestured wildly at the broken phone, the darkness, the storm. "Not this."

Jim's gaze drifted toward the front door. "Then leave."

John looked that way too. The door stood quiet, its chain lock intact. The last slam had stopped. Maybe the masked man was gone. Maybe—

A slow, deliberate scrape sounded on the porch, as if something heavy had dragged itself along the wood.

John froze.

Jim didn't look surprised. "He likes to wait," he said, almost conversationally. "Likes to make you come to him."

John's heart kicked. He backed away from the door toward the kitchen. "Hunter," he said, voice breaking. "I need to call Hunter."

"You already did," Jim said.

John glared. "No. I didn't. I called—" His throat closed around her name.

Jim's expression didn't soften this time. "You called, boy. You just didn't get who you wanted."

John's mind swung like a door in wind. "Then what am I supposed to do?"

Jim tilted his head, listening. The scrape on the porch stopped.

Then, from somewhere deeper in the house, came a sound John hadn't heard since before Alice died. Music— tinny, cheerful, wrong in this darkness. An accordion, playing a bouncing tune that did not belong in a house that cold.

John stared toward the living room where the television sat in shadow.

Jim's remaining eye gleamed. "That," he said, "is the house offering you something."

John's mouth went dry. "What?"

Jim's smile returned, and it looked like a cracked tombstone. "A distraction," he said. "And a door."

Chapter Six: The Pharmacy

The fluorescent lights in Satterfield's Pharmacy made Hunter feel like he was being examined.

Everything under them looked a shade worse than it did outside: the bruises under a clerk's eyes, the yellowed corners of the linoleum, the thin sheen of sweat on Hunter's palms as he pushed a basket down the aisle.

He had come in for water. That was what he'd told himself. Water, a couple bottles of sports drink, maybe crackers. Practical things. The kind of things you could stack on a counter and pretend you were still dealing in the normal.

But he'd walked past the cooler and ended up here instead, in the vitamins, staring at bottles with names that sounded like prayers.

The detox kits were locked behind plastic, like shame required a key.

Thiamine. Magnesium. B-complex.

Names like spells. The kind of thing you bought when you wanted to believe the body was a machine with replaceable parts.

Hunter had spent the last three days reading pamphlets and message boards, trying to learn the difference between discomfort and danger. Shakes were expected. Sweats. Nightmares. Confusion. But every article, every warning label, every sober-person forum thread landed in the same place: seizures. Heart failure. A brain that decided the world was full of insects and enemies.

He'd told John not to do this alone. John had laughed, promised he'd be fine, promised he just needed a quiet place and a few days. Hunter had heard the lie in the word quiet.

You don't let a man quit alone.

You don't let him do it in a house that wants company.

It wasn't a mantra. It was a rule—one of the few that mattered. And it tasted, in Hunter's mouth, like something close to guilt.

If John was going to survive the night, it would be because Hunter kept him tethered to the boring world: water, light, numbers on a thermometer, a car that started when you turned the key.

In the first-aid aisle he added electrolyte packets and an old-fashioned digital thermometer.

At the end of the row he stared at a small display of sleeping pills and felt something cold move behind his ribs—how quickly a desperate brain could turn any object into an answer.

Two aisles over a woman argued softly into her phone about pick-up times. A kid in a hoodie scanned energy drinks like he was counting bullets. The normal world, indifferent.

Hunter almost put the sleeping pills back. He didn't trust them. He didn't trust himself to know the difference between helping a friend sleep and helping a friend disappear.

Hunter shoved the bottle into the basket and kept moving.

Hunter pulled a bottle of thiamine off the shelf and turned it in his hands. He could hear his father in the back of his mind, voice tight and certain.

He remembered being sixteen, standing in the doorway of this same pharmacy while his father bought a bottle of whiskey he didn't pretend was anything else. The clerk had said Have a nice night. His father had smiled like he believed it.

His father had carried the bottle out in a brown paper bag like it was groceries. In the truck he'd said, Don't tell your mother, and Hunter had said okay, because okay was what you said when you learned a family's rules were really secrets.

At the register the clerk—Marta, according to her name tag—rang everything up with the bored efficiency of someone who had seen every kind of emergency and learned not to flinch at any of them. Her fingernails were bitten down and painted a color that had started to chip, like she didn't have time for the details anymore.

She wore a cardigan two sizes too big and a small silver cross that kept flipping upside down when she leaned over the scanner. She looked tired in the specific way of someone who had learned how many emergencies came through a sliding door and how few of them ended clean.

Marta hummed. "Detox?" she asked, like she was asking if he wanted paper or plastic.

"Yeah," Hunter said. He heard the strain in his own voice and hated it. "Friend."

"That's a lot," she said, scanning thiamine, magnesium, sports drink, crackers. Her eyes flicked up to him. "Someone sick?"

Hunter forced a nod. "I know."

Marta's expression didn't change, but her gaze sharpened the way people's eyes did when they were reading something they didn't want to read. "Those are good," she said, tapping the thiamine bottle. "But if he starts seeing things or his heart does something weird, you don't try to tough it out. You take him in."

She said it like she'd said it before. Like she was reading from a script the county wrote in blood and ambulance lights.

Hunter's jaw tightened. "Something like that."

Marta slid the bag toward him. "Good luck," she said, and for a moment it didn't feel like a throwaway line. It felt like a warning.

Hunter grabbed the bag and stepped back out into the storm.

He glanced at the pharmacy window. Inside, the bright aisles made everything look staged, like a set you could step back into if you wanted to pretend the night wasn't happening. But the rain was real, and the road waited.

The parking lot lights threw rain into bright slanted streaks. Wind pushed at the hood of his jacket, trying to peel it back. He headed for his truck, boots splashing through shallow puddles.

In the silence he could hear the bag crinkle on the passenger seat like a small animal shifting when he climbed in.

The cab smelled faintly of damp dog and the stale coffee he never remembered to throw out.

"...severe thunderstorm warning remains in effect for—"

The radio sputtered. Static. Then a voice, too loud, too bright.

Hunter shut it off.

He started the engine and rolled out of town.

By the time he turned onto Van Drake Road, the world had narrowed to black trees, slick gravel, and the relentless percussion of rain.

Cell service dropped to one bar and then to none. The GPS line stuttered, then gave up. He knew the way anyway.

Everyone in town knew the way, even if they pretended they didn't.

Van Drake Road swallowed him whole.

Hunter swallowed hard and kept driving.

When he looked down again, the phone screen was dark.

Then the lock screen lit up—no ringtone, no vibration—and showed DAD in bright letters.

Hunter's blood went cold.

His mother had been dead for years. His father was alive, stubborn as a nail, and Hunter had spent most of his life learning which calls you answered and which ones you let die in the dark.

A smear of rainwater slid across the cracked glass, and the touchscreen misread it like a swipe. The contact card opened and closed in the span of a heartbeat.

When he snatched the phone up, it went dark again. No missed-call banner. No voicemail. Nothing he could show another person without sounding insane.

He set it back down face-first in the cup holder and kept both hands on the wheel.

Told himself it was water and cheap capacitive glass. Told himself that was all it was.

Recognition hit him anyway.

He did not tell himself what his father would have called it.

He told himself it was adrenaline. The storm. The responsibility.

A flash of lightning lit the empty lot white. For that instant Hunter saw his reflection in his truck window—eyes wide, jaw clenched, looking like a man bracing for impact.

The figure didn't move.

He drove past without slowing, eyes flicking to the rearview mirror.

Hunter's stomach dropped.

A man in a raincoat, face shadowed, standing too still.

Half a mile down, his headlights caught a figure under the awning of the closed gas station.

He kept going.

Hunter hit call. The phone rang once, twice, then dropped into silence like the line had been cut.

Then nothing.

Three dots appeared. Disappeared. Appeared again.

His pulse kicked. He typed: I'm on my way. Stay inside. Don't go looking for anything. I'm coming.

John's reply came back in two blunt bursts: It. I need it.

It could have been whiskey. It could have been the house. In John's mouth, need never needed a noun.

Hunter stared at the screen until the words stopped being letters and started being what they were—need with no object, hunger with no name.

For half a second his body decided it was a plea for help. Then his stomach turned and he understood: it wasn't help John wanted. It was relief.

Rain hammered the windshield hard enough to sound like fingers.

Hunter pressed the accelerator.

Chapter Seven: The Screen

The television clicked on by itself.

Not the soft, friendly glow John associated with late nights and mindless comfort, but a harsh, bluish rectangle that carved the living room out of the dark.

The television had been their truce once.

John could still see the old apartment living room the way it used to be before the grief and the drinking turned everything into clutter: Alice curled at one end of the couch with her feet tucked under her, a blanket pulled up to her waist; John sprawled at the other end with a glass on the coffee table, pretending the show was funny enough to be worth ignoring her silence.

When she'd asked him to talk—really talk—he'd always found a way to make the screen louder. One more episode. One more game. One more distraction, because distraction was easier than saying the thing out loud: I don't know how to be here without a drink.

Now, in the farmhouse, the television's light felt less like distraction and more like accusation. Like the house had found the exact frequency of his cowardice and learned how to broadcast it.

He drank again, and the screen kept laughing.

John had no answer that didn't hurt him to hear.

Alice's gaze dropped to the glass in his hand. "Then what is it?" she asked.

"It's not competition," John snapped.

"I can't compete with that," she said, nodding toward the TV.

Alice stood in the kitchen, looking at him, and John watched something in her face set like concrete.

The sitcom roar filled the apartment. Fake laughter. Fake problems. People who always forgave each other in twenty minutes.

Instead, he lifted the remote off the counter and turned the volume back up from the kitchen doorway, as if sound could erase everything.

He could have put the glass down. He could have said I'm sorry and meant it. He could have followed her back to the couch and sat in the quiet and let the ugliness sit between them until it became talk.

John remembered staring at her then and feeling, for one honest second, the shape of what he was doing. The way his choices left marks. The way her hope had been thinning for months.

Alice's eyes had gone wet. She blinked hard, once, as if refusing to spill. "I don't think you're a monster," she whispered. "I think you're scared. And I think you keep choosing the thing that makes you feel brave for ten minutes."

"I want you to stop," he'd said, and his tongue had already started to feel thick with false confidence. "I want you to stop acting like I'm some kind of monster."

John had taken a swallow. The burn had been relief. Immediate, obedient relief. It made the room tilt into something he could handle.

"Is that what you want?" she asked, voice soft. "To win?"

Alice had watched him do it like she was watching a door close.

John had poured anyway, the sound of liquid into glass loud in the small space.

Alice had followed him into the kitchen. "Don't," she said.

He stood up, walked to the kitchen, and opened the cabinet over the fridge without thinking. The bottle had been there, half-full. He had left it there on purpose, like a test, and then forgotten he was taking it.

He had looked away then, because the quiet in her voice made his skin crawl. He needed noise. He needed to drown the truth in something safe and familiar.

"No," she said. "You're sitting next to me. That's not the same thing."

John's laugh had been brittle. "I'm sitting right here."

Alice's mouth twitched. Not a smile. Something like grief. "You know what's dramatic?" she said. "You disappearing behind a screen every time I ask you to be here."

"Stop making everything..." He searched for a word that didn't sound like what it was. "Stop making everything dramatic."

"Stop what?" she asked quietly.

"Stop," he said.

He leaned forward, trying to take the remote. Alice held it higher, just out of reach.

He could still remember the exact sensation of heat in his chest then, that flare of resentment that always came before he reached for a drink. Resentment because she was right. Resentment because she wouldn't let him pretend.

"You're not," Alice said. "You're worse when you say you're fine."

John had shrugged, a small motion that felt like armor. "I told you. I'm fine."

"I'm acting like I live here too," she said. "I'm acting like this matters."

Alice's eyes had fixed on his in a way that made him feel seen. Not the version he performed for work or friends. The real one. The one who kept secrets from himself.

"Jesus," he said, and he meant it as a joke, but it came out sharp. "You're acting like I'm doing something to you."

John had reached for the remote. Alice moved it behind her back.

Her voice wasn't angry. That had been the worst part. Anger would have given him a fight to pick, a reason to feel righteous. She sounded tired. Like she'd been carrying the weight of his habits around in her pockets and her arms were finally shaking.

"It's always been a day," she replied.

John had glanced at the black screen reflection and seen himself: older than he wanted to admit, eyes tired, a man already practicing his excuses. "Can it wait?" he asked. "It's been a day."

"We need to talk," Alice said.

She hadn't smiled. She'd muted the TV. In the sudden quiet, the canned laughter from the screen became pantomime. People with open mouths and no sound.

John had laughed, trying to make it playful. "Hey."

Alice had reached over and taken the remote out of his hand.

John had known. He had known in his bones what was coming. The talk. The careful voice. The reasonable words that made him feel cornered. He'd turned the volume up a notch anyway.

John remembered one night with a clarity that felt cruel now: the two of them on the couch in their first apartment, the white rug they'd bought like a joke spread under their feet. Alice had come in from the bedroom wearing one of his old T-shirts, hair still damp from a shower. She'd sat down beside him and waited through a whole commercial break without saying anything.

It was the way he used it when she was trying to reach him.

Not because she was above it - she watched her own shows, laughed at the same dumb commercials, quoted lines from sitcoms like they were scripture. It wasn't moral for her. It was personal.

Alice had hated the way the television stole him.

Now the same blue-white light didn't feel like comfort. It felt like a spotlight. Like the house had found the only thing that ever made him sit still and decided to use it as a leash.

The accordion music jumped in volume, tinny and bright. An old black-and-white broadcast. A man in suspenders grinned at the camera as he played, cheeks puffing, fingers flying.

John stood at the edge of the room and watched, waiting for the punch line.

The stormlight flashed again and again outside the windows, but the TV stayed steady—its own little world that didn't care about weather.

He edged closer. The remote sat on the coffee table where Hunter had left it earlier. John picked it up and thumbed the power button.

Nothing changed.

He tried channel up, volume, input—each press answered by the same cheerful music, the same bouncing tune. The remote worked; the little red light at its tip blinked obediently. The TV ignored him.

"Okay," John whispered. "Okay. Fine."

John stepped closer until the blue light washed his face. The screen made his eyes feel dry, like he'd been staring into a welding arc.

He crouched and ran the flashlight beam behind the television, hunting for a cord.

There was one—thick and black—snaking down toward the outlet. He followed it with his hand, fingers brushing dust and the brittle edge of a baseboard.

The plug was already out.

It lay on the carpet beside the wall, prongs exposed, as if someone had yanked it free and forgotten to put it back.

John stared at it, waiting for his mind to supply the missing explanation. Power outage. Old house. Loose connection. Anything.

The television kept playing.

The accordion music bounced on, bright and cheerful, as if mockery could be broadcast.

John picked up the plug. It was warm. Not warm from his hand—warm as if current had been running through it a second ago.

A faint vibration thrummed against his fingertips, so slight he might have imagined it.

His stomach tightened. He held the plug up to the flashlight beam. The prongs were clean. No scorch marks. No melted plastic. Nothing that said fire or fault or reason.

"No," he whispered, and the word came out like a plea.

He shoved the plug back into the outlet with a jerky motion.

It didn't change anything.

The TV didn't flicker. The music didn't hiccup. The screen stayed steady, confident, like the house had its own power source and didn't need permission from the grid.

John's hand fell away from the wall. His fingers were shaking so hard the flashlight beam jittered.

Fine, he thought. Fine. If the house wanted him to watch, he would watch.

Because the other option was to admit he was losing his grip on what was real, and he didn't have the strength for that yet.

The man on-screen played another minute and then took an exaggerated bow. He stepped out of frame.

The camera did not cut away.

It stayed on the empty room behind him.

John's scalp prickled. The set—bare floor, two windows, a wardrobe against the wall—looked familiar in the way a bad dream can feel familiar. Like you've been there, but only while asleep.

He leaned closer.

The paint color.

The angle of the windows.

The wardrobe—dark wood, brass keyhole, a scratch near the handle.

John's stomach dropped.

"That's upstairs," he whispered.

The TV wasn't showing a studio. It was showing the second bedroom at the top of the stairs—the one with the locked wardrobe and the empty closet. The one he had left with the door open and the lights on because something in him refused to let it go dark again.

Only the room on the screen was dark. Not dark like a room with no lights. Dark like the light had been swallowed.

A soft creak came from upstairs.

John froze, remote still in his hand.

Another creak—higher, closer to the ceiling. The sound of weight on old boards.

On the TV, one of the windows in the upstairs room began to rise. Slowly. Smoothly. No hands visible. No squeal of stuck paint. Just a steady lift, like an invisible arm doing the work.

Wind blew in. The curtains fluttered.

A gloved hand appeared on the sill.

Then another.

John's mouth went dry.

The masked man pulled himself into frame with the patient efficiency of someone who had done this before. Dark hoodie. Gray track pants. The ski mask, blank and human and wrong. He didn't look around. He didn't hesitate.

He stepped into the room as if he owned it.

At the exact moment his boots hit the floor on the screen, John heard the same dull thump upstairs.

Real sound. Real wood. Real vibration through the bones of the house.

John backed away from the TV.

He remembered Jim's warning, sharp as a nail: Don't follow the mask.

Another part of him—older than drinking, older than guilt—refused to be prey. Refused to cower while someone walked his hallways.

John turned and moved fast through the kitchen, hands searching drawers by memory and desperation. He found a flashlight first, cheap plastic, batteries probably half-dead. He clicked it on.

A weak cone of yellow light sputtered to life.

He grabbed the biggest kitchen knife he could find, the blade cold and honest in his hand. Then he paused, breath hitching as he realized something.

His car keys weren't here. His wallet wasn't here. His phone was in his pocket, blinking NO SERVICE like a verdict.

Everything he had in the world was in this house.

And something had just climbed in through the window.

John returned to the living room.

The TV still showed the upstairs bedroom. The masked man stood perfectly still, head tilted, as if he were listening.

John held the flashlight beam on the carpet in front of him, not daring to point it toward the stairs. He didn't want to announce himself. He didn't want to play by whatever rules the house wanted.

On the screen, the masked man moved toward the bedroom door.

Upstairs, the floor creaked in the same rhythm.

John's pulse hammered. It would be so easy to stay down here, to let whatever was happening happen. But if the man came downstairs—if he reached the living room—

John forced himself to move.

He stepped to the base of the stairs and listened. The masked man's footsteps paused on the landing upstairs, as if he had reached the top and turned.

The flashlight in John's hand trembled with his pulse.

He began to climb.

One step. Another. He kept his weight close to the wall, testing each tread before committing. The house felt like it was holding its breath.

At the top of the stairs, the second bedroom door stood open. The thin spill of flashlight beam showed the torn carpet and the red-painted walls.

John stopped and listened.

No footsteps.

No breathing.

Only the storm fading into a softer rain. Only his own blood singing in his ears.

"Hey," he called, voice low and rough. "You don't get to just walk in here."

The words sounded stupid the moment they left his mouth. But the sound of his own voice steadied him.

He stepped into the second bedroom, knife raised.

The flashlight beam swept the room.

Empty.

The wardrobe door sat slightly open, as it had earlier—its natural tilt. The closet door hung ajar. The window stood half open, rain misting the sill.

John moved closer to the wardrobe, the smell of whiskey still ghosting in his nose from earlier, memory trying to knit itself into temptation.

He refused to look inside.

A creak sounded behind him.

John spun.

The attic stairs—those narrow steps that rose above the living room—stood at the edge of the landing, a dark throat leading up. The sound had come from there.

A slow shift of weight. The soft complaint of old wood.

Someone had gone up.

John stared at the attic opening.

He hadn't noticed it before. Not really. It was part of the house's geography in the same way a scar can be part of a face—present, but ignored until it aches.

He could turn back now. Go downstairs. Lock himself in Hunter's childhood bedroom. Sit under a blanket and wait for morning.

He could also wake up to the masked man standing over him.

John tightened his grip on the knife and started up.

The attic stairwell narrowed, pressing his shoulders. The air grew colder with each step. Halfway up, the flashlight beam hit dust motes and made them look like ash floating in a crematorium.

At the top, the attic opened into a low-ceilinged room full of boxes and old furniture under sheets. The flashlight beam cut a cone through the clutter, and for a moment John saw nothing but a junkyard of family history.

Then the beam slid across something tall and still in the far corner.

A person-shaped silhouette.

John's breath caught.

The silhouette did not move.

"Who are you?" he asked, and his voice cracked. He swallowed, forced it steadier. "What do you want?"

No answer.

John took a step forward, flashlight and knife angled ahead like two bad ideas.

The silhouette shifted.

Not in a human way. Not a turn of shoulders or tilt of head. It stretched, as if the darkness itself had been pulled upward by invisible hands.

The outline grew taller. Longer.

Something like a neck rose toward the low attic beams, too long for a person. The head at the top sharpened into an angle that reminded John of a beak.

The flashlight beam wavered as John's hand betrayed him.

"Stop," he whispered.

The thing's face—if it had a face—turned toward him.

Where eyes should have been there were two dull points that caught the flashlight like wet stones.

It opened its mouth.

The scream that came out did not belong to any animal John knew. It wasn't a roar. It wasn't a howl. It was a tortured, human sound forced through something that was not built for language.

John stumbled backward.

The attic boards creaked under his heel, and the thing lurched forward with a suddenness that made his skin go tight.

He turned and ran.

The stairs down were a blur. He took them too fast, nearly pitching forward. Behind him the scream echoed again, closer, accompanied by the heavy slap of feet—or talons—on wood.

John hit the landing and skidded, knife scraping the wall, flashlight beam spinning wild. He caught the banister and swung himself down the main staircase.

Something hit the attic doorframe above with a crash, wood splintering.

John reached the bottom and lunged for the front door—

And froze.

In the small window of the heavy front door, framed by rain and night, was the masked face.

Close. Watching. Waiting.

The ski mask's eyeholes were two dark wounds. John couldn't see skin. Couldn't see expression. But he could feel attention on him like a hand on the back of his neck.

It raised one gloved hand and pressed the palm flat to the glass.

John backed away, heart hammering, flashlight beam caught on the mask and made it shine briefly like wet leather. He slashed the knife toward the glass in an instinctive threat.

The masked man didn't flinch.

Behind John, the attic thing screamed again. The sound carried down the staircase like smoke.

John's brain made a decision without his permission.

He ran for the back.

He vaulted the living room, snagged his coat off the rack without thinking, and burst through the kitchen into the back door. Cold air slapped him. The rain had slowed to a steady drizzle, but the yard was still slick with mud.

John sprinted off the porch, flashlight beam bouncing in front of him. He didn't aim for the driveway. He didn't aim for the road.

He aimed for the barn.

He ran with the house at his back—full of doors that weren't doors, full of rooms that watched him—and he didn't look behind him until he reached the broken, sagging outline of the barn.

Only then did he dare a glance.

The kitchen window glowed faintly blue in the dark—television light. The front door stood still. No masked face visible now.

But from the attic window upstairs, high above the porch, something moved. A long shadow passed across the glass as if something had leaned close to look out.

John shoved himself into the barn's doorway and dragged the door as far as it would go.

Inside, the air smelled of wet wood and old hay and rot. The flashlight beam picked out holes in the floorboards—black mouths waiting.

John swallowed and stood there, shaking.

For a moment, the quiet felt like mercy.

Then, somewhere in the dark behind him, a board creaked.

Not settling.

Not the wind.

A deliberate step.

John raised the knife and turned the flashlight beam deeper into the barn, praying for emptiness.

The beam caught only dust and darkness and the splintered ribs of old beams.

Still, he knew, the way you know you're being watched.

He was not alone.

Chapter Eight: The Barn

The barn door groaned when John leaned his weight against it. It slid an inch, then caught, warped by years of rain and heat. He shoved until the gap narrowed to the width of his shoulder and then jammed a broken shovel handle under the rail like a crude lock.

It was a gesture. He knew it. If something wanted in, it would come in.

Still, the small act of doing something—of making a choice—kept him from coming apart.

He stood with his back to the door and breathed through his nose, trying to slow the gallop of his heart. The flashlight beam shook in his hand and made the barn's shadows twitch.

The place was mostly empty. The remains of old stalls lined one wall, slats chewed by time. A hayloft overhead sagged. Ropes hung from rafters like dead snakes. The floorboards under his boots were gray and splintered, the gaps between them wide enough to swallow a foot.

John took three careful steps in and stopped when the boards complained under him.

He aimed the light down. Beneath the barn was darkness—space. He could smell it. Damp earth. Something sour. The floor wasn't just old; it was thin.

He turned the flashlight toward the far corner and found what he hadn't dared hope for: an old lantern, metal and glass, sitting on a crate as if someone had put it there recently. Next to it lay a box of matches wrapped in plastic.

Too convenient.

The house offering you something, Jim had said.

John stared at the lantern for a long moment, then moved toward it anyway. At this point, distrust was a luxury.

He lit a match. The small flame made the barn feel less like a mouth and more like a place. He set the match to the lantern's wick. It caught with a soft whoosh, and warm light spread across the boards.

The lantern wasn't oil. It smelled like kerosene—sharp, industrial. It felt out of place in a barn that old. Like a prop.

John set the lantern on the crate and kept the flashlight in his other hand. Two lights. Two thin promises against the dark.

He listened.

No footsteps from the house. No scream from the attic thing. No scrape on the porch.

Just the steady drip of rain through holes in the roof and the small pop of the lantern as it warmed.

John's legs trembled. He lowered himself onto an overturned bucket with care and then let his shoulders sag.

His mind tried to replay the phone call. Alice's voice—soft, accusing. The way it had said you did this like a verdict.

He shut his eyes hard.

"You're not here," he whispered. "You're not."

For a minute, the barn stayed quiet.

Then, faintly, came the sound of a horse.

Not a whinny. Not a stamp. The soft, wet sound of breath, followed by a gentle shuffle, like hooves shifting on straw.

John's eyes opened.

The lantern light trembled across the empty stalls.

The breath came again, closer. Warm and animal. John could almost feel it against his cheek.

He stood slowly, knife rising.

"Who's there?" he called.

No answer.

The horse breath sounded again—then a soft clink, like a harness chain.

John's stomach tightened. There were no horses here. He had seen the property. He had seen the empty fields.

He stepped toward the stalls, each movement careful to keep his weight on the strongest boards.

The lantern light reached into the nearest stall and showed nothing but broken boards and cobwebs.

But the smell—

It hit him as he moved: a heavy, sweet animal smell. Manure, sweat, old leather. The barn smelled suddenly alive.

John raised the flashlight and swept it across the stalls.

Something moved in the far one.

A shadow flickered behind slats. A bulk shifting.

John's breath hitched.

He took one more step toward it, and the floorboard under his boot snapped.

The sound was loud enough to feel.

John's foot plunged into darkness up to his shin. The rotten board gave way around it. He yanked himself back, but the plank beside it crumbled under his weight.

The barn floor collapsed.

The world dropped out from under him.

John pitched forward, arms flailing for purchase. His knife clattered away into the dark. The lantern tipped off the crate and spun, its flame flaring wildly.

He fell through the boards with a crack of wood and a burst of dust and hit something hard—dirt, packed and wet —so hard it knocked the breath out of him.

Pain shot through his ribs.

The lantern landed near him and rolled, glass intact, flame still burning. Its light revealed the underside of the barn: a low space of earth and stone, a pit dug beneath the structure. The air was colder down here, damp enough to slick his skin.

John pushed himself up on shaking arms and coughed, tasting dirt.

Above him, the barn floor was a jagged hole framed by broken boards. Through it he could see the rafters, the hanging ropes, the lantern light spilling upward.

And, for a moment, a shape blocking it.

Not a horse.

Not a man.

Something tall leaned over the hole as if peering down.

A long neck. A head that ended in an angle too sharp to be human.

John's body went cold.

The shape stayed still for one long second, silhouette crisp in lantern light.

Then it moved with sudden, sick speed.

A hand—no, not a hand. Something like a clawed forelimb—reached down into the hole, groping, scraping at the broken boards for purchase.

John scrambled backward on elbows, heels digging into wet dirt. His ribs screamed. His breathing turned shallow and frantic.

The thing's arm extended farther, joints bending wrong. It scraped along the broken beam and found a grip. It pulled. The boards creaked.

The creature leaned further over the hole, and John saw its face in the lantern light.

It wasn't a mask. Not cloth, not lacquer. In the lantern light it looked like bone—pale and cracked, too dry for something that breathed.

A beak shape, or the suggestion of one. The kind of shape a frightened mind reached for because it needed a word for wrongness. Where eyes should have been were dark hollows that caught the light like wet stones, and the throat was fringed with ragged clumps that might have been feathers... or hair.

The mouth—if it was a mouth—opened. The sound that poured out was human. Not a growl. Not an animal call. A raw, familiar anguish, forced through whatever shape this thing wore, and it made John's bones vibrate like a struck bell.

John clapped his hands over his ears and still felt the sound vibrating through him.

"Stop!" he shouted, and it was ridiculous. It didn't stop.

He forced himself to look away, to search for a way out.

The pit extended beneath the barn in a rough rectangle. One corner held stacked crates turned to mush. Another held a rusted set of tools half-buried in dirt. Along the far wall, a narrow passage yawned—an old access route maybe, or a collapsed root cellar door.

John crawled toward it, dragging his injured side, moving as fast as pain allowed. The damp earth sucked at his knees. The lantern's light followed, throwing his shadow long and distorted.

Behind him, boards snapped.

The creature was trying to widen the hole.

John reached the passage and shoved his shoulders into it.

It was tighter than he expected—barely wide enough for him to squeeze through. Dirt rained down from the ceiling as he moved. The smell of earth intensified, thick and metallic. He kept going anyway, because the scream behind him rose in pitch like something getting excited.

The passage angled up.

John saw a faint gap ahead—light. Not lantern light; something else. Moonlight, maybe. A way out.

He shoved forward, elbows and knees scraping, ribs burning. His mind offered a single clear thought: keep moving.

He burst through the end of the passage and tumbled out into rain and cold.

He landed on his hands in mud, gasping.

He was outside the barn, near its rear wall where the boards had rotted away enough to leave a gap. The storm had softened into a mist, but the cold cut him anyway.

John rolled onto his back and stared up at the barn.

In the jagged hole in the floor above, the lantern glow flickered. The scream had stopped.

For a moment, there was only the quiet hiss of rain.

Then something heavy hit the barn wall from the inside —once, twice—as if the creature had thrown itself at the boards in frustration.

A splintered plank punched outward, then fell. More boards bowed.

John didn't wait to see what happened next.

He forced himself upright, pain bright along his ribs, and ran—stumbling, limping—toward the tree line.

The woods waited, black and thick.

Behind him, the barn gave a long, tired groan, as if it were waking up.

John plunged into the trees without looking back.

Chapter Nine: The Line

The woods swallowed him.

Rain clung to the branches and shook loose in cold drops when he shoved past. The ground under the leaves was slick and uneven, roots waiting to trip him. John kept the flashlight low, just enough to see where to put his feet without advertising himself to everything else.

His side hurt with every breath. The fall in the barn had done something—bruised ribs, maybe cracked. Each inhale was a small betrayal.

He forced himself deeper anyway.

Out here, away from the house, the air smelled cleaner. Pine and wet bark. The kind of smell that belonged to places where people lived and died in ordinary ways.

If he could find the road, he could follow it to town. If he could find town, he could find a phone, a police station, anything.

He walked until his lungs burned and his legs threatened to quit. He kept expecting to hear something behind him—the scrape of the masked man's boots, the ragged scream of the thing with the beak.

Nothing followed.

The silence was almost worse.

John stopped beside a tree and leaned his shoulder into the trunk, breathing hard. He killed the flashlight for a moment to rest the batteries and let his eyes adjust.

Darkness pressed in from all sides. The leaves above dripped steadily. Somewhere far off, an owl called once and then fell silent.

John swallowed. He could feel his heart in his throat.

He clicked the flashlight back on.

The beam caught the pale curve of something low to the ground a few feet ahead.

John stiffened.

He aimed the light.

A length of rope, half buried under leaves, stretched between two trees. It looked old. Frayed. Like someone had once strung it as a boundary marker and then forgotten.

John stepped closer and saw that it wasn't rope at all.

It was a line of bones.

Small, pale vertebrae threaded on twine. Animal bones, cleaned and dried. A charm. A warning. Someone's idea of protection, or someone's idea of a trap.

Up close, the bones weren't all the same.

Most were small vertebrae, bleached and clean, but threaded among them were sharper pieces—splinters of rib, a tooth with its root still intact, a knuckle joint polished smooth by weather and time. Somebody had put care into it. Somebody had taken time to string a warning and make it pretty.

The charm swayed as if it were breathing.

John crouched beside the line and let the flashlight linger on the bones. Up close they looked too clean, too deliberate. Not a random animal carcass picked over by weather. These had been threaded by a patient hand.

The twine was wet and dark. It sagged slightly between the trees, and the vertebrae knocked gently against each other with every shift of wind—small, polite clicks like teeth.

His throat tightened. He told himself it was a hunting charm. Something locals did to keep coyotes away. Something dumb and rural and explainable.

Except the line was placed where a man would walk if he was trying to leave.

John reached out and touched one of the bones with the tip of his finger.

Cold. Smooth. It rolled slightly on the twine and bumped the next vertebra with a tiny, accusatory sound.

The itch crawled up his arm again, phantom legs remembered by skin.

"Okay," he whispered, and his voice sounded too loud in the wet woods. "Okay. I'm going to step over you. That's all."

He lifted the twine with two fingers, careful not to let the bones touch him. The line rose a few inches. The vertebrae slid and clattered softly, a little chain of bone wind chimes.

For a moment nothing happened.

John stepped forward and swung one leg over.

The instant his boot crossed the line, his stomach dropped as if he'd stepped off a ledge. The trees tilted. The flashlight beam swung wildly. His ears filled with a low roar —blood, rain, something else.

A smell hit him so hard it made his mouth flood with saliva: whiskey. Fresh and sweet and burning, like someone had uncorked a bottle under his nose.

His whole body leaned toward it. Toward relief. Toward the easy lie.

John jerked back, almost falling. The twine snapped against his sleeve. Bones clicked like laughter.

His heart hammered. His hands were shaking worse now, betrayal turning his muscles against him.

No, he told himself. It's withdrawal. It's panic. It's your body craving a memory.

Still, he stared at the line like it had just spoken.

He tried the knife next, because men like him always tried to solve fear with tools.

John steadied the flashlight against his knee, angled the blade at the twine, and sawed.

The wet fiber resisted. The blade slipped and bit into his thumb instead. A bright sting, immediate and real.

Blood welled and ran down the side of his hand, warm against the cold air.

John hissed and shook his hand once. The blood spattered onto the nearest bone, turning it briefly pink before the rain diluted it.

The charm swayed, and for a second the bones seemed to settle back into place as if satisfied.

John stared at his bleeding thumb. The cut was shallow. The lesson wasn't.

Don't cross, something in him understood. Not because the line was magical—because admitting that would be admitting everything—but because the woods were not his. The boundaries were not his. The rules were not his.

John let the twine fall back into place and stepped away.

John told himself it was animal. Deer. Fox. Anything except what his mind wanted to name when it was cornered: human.

John backed away, skin prickling. "No," he whispered. "No, no, no."

He turned and walked around it, deeper into the woods.

The flashlight beam jittered. Shadows moved where his mind expected them to move, and that was the problem—his mind expected them everywhere.

He tried to keep his thoughts on practical things. Road. Town. Help. Hunter.

Alice.

Her voice slipped back in anyway, soft and sharp: You did this.

John's jaw clenched. "I didn't," he whispered.

He walked another hundred yards and found the line again.

Not the same bones. Another one. Strung between two different trees, but the same construction—vertebrae and twine, swaying in the rain.

John stopped, confused. He had been walking in a straight line. Hadn't he?

He turned in a slow circle. Tree trunks. Wet leaves. Darkness. No landmarks he could trust.

The woods had a way of turning you around. He knew that. But this felt different. Like the forest itself had rotated while he wasn't looking.

A branch snapped behind him.

John spun, flashlight up.

The beam caught nothing but mist and ferns.

Then he heard breathing.

Low. Heavy. Controlled.

Not Jim's dry rasp. Not his own panicked gasps.

Animal.

John's hands went numb. He took a step backward and felt his heel slide in mud.

The breathing came again. Closer.

"Hey," John said, and his voice shook. "Hey! Get back. Get—"

A shape moved at the edge of the flashlight beam.

Large. Gray-brown. Low to the ground and thick through the shoulders.

A wolf.

John had never seen one in person. Only on television, in nature documentaries, where they looked lean and proud. This one looked like hunger made flesh. Its fur was wet and matted. Its head was oversized, jaw powerful enough to snap bone.

It stood perfectly still, watching him.

Another shape moved behind it.

Then another.

Three wolves, spaced out in the trees like sentries. They made no sound. No growl. No bark. No warning.

John backed away slowly. "Okay," he whispered. "Okay. I'm going."

The wolves moved with him, matching his pace, always keeping the same distance. Herding him. Not attacking, not yet, but making clear where he was allowed to go.

John's mind tried to argue. Wolves didn't do this. Wolves didn't plan. Wolves didn't—

But these weren't ordinary wolves. Nothing tonight had been ordinary.

He turned and walked the other way.

The wolves followed.

He tried another direction.

They adjusted, flowing through the trees with silent, terrible grace, guiding him like cattle.

John's pulse hammered. His breath came shallow to avoid pain in his ribs, which made him lightheaded. He stumbled once, caught himself on a sapling.

The nearest wolf stepped closer.

John froze.

Its eyes caught the flashlight beam and reflected—not the green shine of a dog, not the yellow glint of a deer. This was a flat, dull light like a coin at the bottom of a well.

The wolf held his gaze.

And then, impossibly, it blinked slow, as if bored.

John's mouth went dry.

A voice spoke from behind him.

"Don't run."

John whipped around.

Jim Wallace stood between two trees as if he'd been there all along, hands in his pockets, shoulders hunched against the rain. The flashlight beam made his skin look waxy and thin, stretched over his skull.

"You're kidding me," John whispered.

Jim glanced at the wolves with the tired irritation of a man looking at neighborhood dogs. "They're doing their job," he said.

"What job?"

"Keeping you in," Jim replied.

John's chest tightened. "In what? The property?"

Jim looked past John, toward where the house would be, if the woods hadn't swallowed everything. "In the story," he said.

John's frustration flared hot. "That doesn't mean anything."

"It means everything." Jim stepped closer, boots silent on wet leaves. "You can't outrun what you brought with you. You can't take a different road and hope it changes where you end up."

John swallowed. His throat felt raw. "I'm trying to leave."

Jim nodded as if John had said something obvious. "And the house is trying to make you stay long enough to understand why you don't get to."

John's grip tightened on the flashlight. "I'm not a murderer."

Jim's expression didn't change. "Never said you were."

"Then why—" John gestured at the wolves, the bone charms, the trees. "Why is any of this happening?"

Jim's remaining eye narrowed. "You ever see a man drown?" he asked.

John blinked. "What?"

"A drowning man doesn't look like the movies," Jim said. "He doesn't wave and holler. He panics. He clutches at anything he can reach. Sometimes he'll climb right up on a rescuer and push them under without even knowing he's doing it."

Jim's mouth tightened as if he'd tasted something bitter.

"I watched it happen," he said. "A man going under, not screaming, not waving—just disappearing in inches while everybody on the bank argued about whether it was real."

He looked at John, and for a second the deadness in his skin seemed like exhaustion instead of horror. "You think you're different because you didn't mean to hurt anybody," he said. "That's what drowning men always say. They don't mean to. They're just trying to breathe."

Thunder rolled far off, slow as a drumbeat. The wolves adjusted their stance without taking their eyes off John, as if even the weather was part of the pressure.

Jim leaned closer and lowered his voice. "And once you've pushed someone under, you don't get to call it an accident just because you were panicking."

John stared.

Jim's voice dropped. "You've been drowning for a long time, boy. In whiskey. In pride. In your own story." He nodded toward John's chest. "And you keep grabbing at people."

John's face went hot. "I loved her."

"I believe you," Jim said. "But love isn't a shield. Love doesn't make the harm disappear."

The wolves shifted, and John realized with a jolt that they were circling slowly, tightening the ring. Not in threat. In inevitability.

Jim lifted his chin toward the wolf closest to John. "That one's the line," he said. "Cross it and you'll learn something you won't like. Stay this side and you'll walk back to the house."

John let out a harsh breath. "So that's it? I'm trapped."

Jim shrugged. "You're tested."

John laughed, bitter. "Tested by who? The masked man? The bird thing? You?"

Jim's mouth twisted. "By you," he said.

A distant sound floated through the trees.

Music.

Not the tinny accordion now, but something warmer— fiddles and clapping, the rise and fall of voices. A party. Laughter.

John's head turned toward it before he could stop himself.

Jim watched him. "Hear that?" he asked.

John's pulse quickened. The music sounded impossible out here. The storm should have swallowed it. Distance should have swallowed it. Instead it felt close, like it was just beyond the next stand of trees.

"What is it?" John whispered.

Jim's expression went hard. "A door," he said again. "And a lie dressed up pretty."

John looked back at the wolves. They waited, patient and unblinking.

He looked at Jim. "If I go back," he said, "do I get out?"

Jim's gaze held his. "If you tell the truth," he said. "All of it."

John's stomach clenched.

He could feel the truth like a weight on his tongue—heavy and bitter. Not a single confession, not one clean, dramatic moment. A thousand small choices. A thousand times he'd chosen the drink, the joke, the boys, the easy version of himself.

Alice's face flashed in his mind: lips pressed tight, eyes shining, shoulders drawn in as if she were bracing for another impact.

John swallowed hard.

The music rose in the distance, bright and inviting.

Jim took a step back into the shadows as if he were giving John room to decide. "Do not bargain with the plantation man," he said quietly, and the phrase hit John strange—specific, oddly placed.

"The who?" John asked.

Jim's expression didn't change. "You'll know him when you see him," he said. "He'll offer you the easy exit."

John shook his head, too exhausted to argue. "I just want this to stop."

Jim's mouth softened in something like pity. "Then stop making it someone else's fault," he said.

John stared at him.

Jim dissolved into darkness—not vanishing, exactly, but stepping back until the trees and rain swallowed him. One moment he was there. The next he wasn't.

John stood alone with the wolves.

The nearest wolf turned its head toward the music, as if hearing a command.

Then it stepped aside.

A gap opened in the ring.

John's skin crawled. He didn't want to move. He wanted to sit down in the mud and scream until his throat tore.

But the music pulled at him, and the wolves' patience felt like a threat.

He started walking.

The wolves flowed behind him, not close enough to touch, but close enough that he could feel them.

The music grew louder with each step.

The trees thinned, and light appeared ahead—warm, golden light that did not belong to flashlights or porch bulbs. Lantern light. Firelight.

John pushed through the last line of branches and stopped dead.

The farmhouse yard had changed.

Lanterns hung from trees like glowing fruit. People moved in clusters, laughing, drinking, dancing. A fiddle sang. A woman clapped in time. The air smelled of roasted meat and sweat and pipe tobacco.

The house itself—Hunter's father's house—stood bright and whole, windows lit from within, paint unpeeled, porch sturdy. Not the damp, neglected place John had entered earlier.

It looked new.

It looked alive.

John stood at the edge of the yard, flashlight still in hand, and felt the world tilt.

Behind him, the wolves stopped at the tree line.

They sat.

And watched.

As if they had delivered him exactly where he belonged.

Chapter Ten: The File

Detective Hargrove didn't go home after his shift ended.

The storm had the city pinned down—rain sheeting off streetlights, wind worrying the gutters—yet the station kept humming with the same stale urgency it always did. Phones rang. Printers spat paper. Men and women in uniform moved like pieces on a board that never reset.

Hargrove sat at his desk with John Glisner's file open in front of him and felt, for the first time in a long while, the faint irritation of being unable to put something away.

The case should have been simple. A dead woman in a locked bathroom. A husband who had discovered her. A suicide note that could be read two ways if you were in the mood to be generous.

And a husband who shook like a man on the edge of a cliff.

Hargrove had seen grief a thousand times. He'd seen shock. He'd seen guilt. He'd seen the way people lied with sincerity because the lie was the only structure left to them.

John Glisner had all of it.

He also had the smell—the faint, sour sweetness that came out of pores when a body had lived on alcohol long enough that it started to mourn it.

Hargrove turned a page in the file and stared at the photograph of the apartment living room the techs had taken earlier. A white rug. Clean in the center, bruised at the edges with old stains that didn't quite lift. Two cups on the coffee table, one tipped on its side as if someone had started to pick it up and stopped.

Domestic detail. Ordinary evidence.

It made him uneasy anyway.

He slid the file aside and opened a smaller manila envelope: a property receipt. A few items logged from Alice's effects. Nothing that mattered to the case on paper. Nothing that mattered to a grieving husband except that it proved she had been real.

The ring wasn't listed.

Hargrove stared at the blank space where it should have been and felt the irritation sharpen. Missing property happened. Paramedics missed things. People took things. Spouses forgot what was on a hand in the worst moment of their lives.

Still.

He picked up his phone and dialed the medical examiner's office. He got voicemail. He left a short message that sounded less like a request and more like a reminder: confirm whether a wedding ring was recovered and logged.

Then he dialed John Glisner.

It rang until the voicemail picked up. A generic recorded voice. No name. No personal message.

Hargrove hung up and checked the timestamp on the file again. John had been released only hours ago. Not missing. Not yet. A free man with a dead wife and an addiction his body was about to cash in.

Exactly the kind of man who stopped answering his phone because he didn't want to hear what the world was going to ask of him next.

Hargrove leaned back and rubbed the bridge of his nose. The fluorescent lights made everything look a little sick.

Officer Lane paused at the edge of his cubicle. "Detective," he said, notebook in hand, careful as a man approaching a dog that might bite. "You still on Glisner?"

Hargrove looked up. "Something's off," he said.

Lane shifted. "Off how?"

Hargrove tapped the photo of the living room. "He's telling the truth the way drunks tell the truth," he said. "It's in there somewhere. But it's wrapped in excuses."

Lane nodded once, understanding without needing the specifics. "You want me to run the phone?"

Hargrove hesitated, then nodded. "Ping if we can. If he's in a hospital, fine. If he's in a ditch, I'd rather know before morning."

Lane left.

Hargrove stood and pulled his coat on. The smell of wet wool and stale coffee followed him out into the parking lot.

He drove back to the apartment building, wipers working hard against the rain. The city at night was a smear of reflected light. Everything looked like it had been rubbed with a thumb.

In the lobby, the same clerk sat behind the desk, watching a muted television. He barely looked up as Hargrove flashed his badge.

"Back again?" the clerk asked, trying to sound casual.

"I don't sleep well," Hargrove replied, and it was closer to truth than he liked.

The apartment door had been resealed after techs finished, but it opened easily enough with a key from evidence. Inside, the air was colder than it should have been. Not supernatural cold. Just the cold of a place where a life had stopped mid-motion.

The white rug waited in the living room like an accusation.

Hargrove walked the perimeter without stepping onto it at first, studying the stains. Old wine, maybe. Old whiskey, more likely. The kind of discoloration that told a story without anyone having to testify.

He moved to the kitchen and opened the cabinet beneath the sink.

A cardboard box sat there, pushed half behind a bottle of dish soap as if it had been hidden in embarrassment. Bright letters. Skull-and-crossbones warnings. Ordinary retail packaging for something that killed quietly.

Hargrove stared at it for a long moment.

People always chose the most ordinary containers for their final decisions, he thought. As if normal packaging made the act less violent.

He closed the cabinet and stood in the small kitchen, listening to the rain. The apartment building creaked around him. Pipes knocked once somewhere in the walls.

Hargrove thought of the husband's hands. The tremor. The way John's eyes had kept slipping toward the bathroom door as if it might open again and undo everything.

He pulled his phone out and scrolled to the number Hunter Wallace had provided earlier—friend, caretaker, concerned citizen.

He dialed.

It rang twice before someone answered with a breathy, distracted "Hello?" that sounded like it had been spoken into a steering wheel.

"Mr. Wallace," Hargrove said. "Detective Hargrove."

A pause. Wind noise. A turn signal clicking.

"Yeah," Hunter said, voice tightening. "Detective. I'm— can this wait? I'm driving."

"Where's John Glisner?" Hargrove asked.

The silence on the line lasted half a beat too long.

"With me," Hunter said finally. "He's safe."

Safe was a word people used when they weren't sure, Hargrove thought.

"Safe where?" he asked.

Hunter's breath came out in a short rush. "At my dad's place," he said. "Out on Van Drake. It's quiet. He needed... quiet."

Hargrove looked around the apartment at the debris of normal life and felt his jaw tighten. "Quiet doesn't detox a man," he said.

"I know," Hunter said quickly. "I know. I got him water, vitamins, food. I'm picking up more supplies now. I'm not doing this blind."

"Has he seen a doctor?" Hargrove asked.

Hunter didn't answer directly. "He wouldn't go," he said. "You saw him. He doesn't want a hospital. He doesn't want —"

The truth, Hargrove supplied silently.

"If he seizes, you call 911," Hargrove said. "Not after. Not when it's convenient. The moment it happens."

Hunter's voice hardened. "It's not going to happen," he said, and the certainty sounded like prayer.

Hargrove wrote the address down as Hunter recited it, rain drumming on the windshield in his imagination. Van Drake Road. The Wallace property. The kind of address you remembered because no one visited it unless they had to.

"What's your father's name?" Hargrove asked.

Another pause. "Jim Wallace," Hunter said, and his tone changed. Not quite fear. Not quite shame. A complicated, private thing.

Hargrove's pen hovered. He had seen the name before. Not in a homicide file. In something older. A domestic call. A welfare check. A rumor that never solidified into a report.

The name didn't attach to one clean incident. It attached to a fog of small paperwork and half-finished calls—the kind that lived in a county file room until the paper yellowed and the people involved either moved away or learned to stop asking for help.

A welfare check, three years ago, out on Van Drake Road. A neighbor's complaint about "lights in the trees" during a storm. A deputy's note written in tight block letters: SUBJECT REFUSED ENTRY. MET AT PROPERTY LINE. APPEARED SOBER. APPEARED ANGRY.

A domestic disturbance even older than that—noise, shouting, a woman crying. Responding unit listed as "cleared on arrival." No contact. No report of injury. A single line in the margin: HOUSE DARK. DOGS PRESENT. SUBJECT SAID NO ONE ELSE INSIDE.

A missing-person call that never became a case because the missing person turned up a week later in a motel in the next county, half-starved and too embarrassed to explain why he'd run. Hargrove remembered that one only because the clerk at the station had said, with casual superstition, Don't go out there alone.

Hargrove had laughed at the time. He'd been younger. He'd believed the county's fear was mostly boredom looking for a story.

Now, with Hunter's voice tight on the other end of the line and rain noise chewing at the signal, the file-fog felt less like boredom and more like a warning the county had learned to carry.

He opened his laptop with his free hand, balancing it awkwardly on his knee, and pulled up the incident database while Hunter continued talking—supplies, water, vitamins— practical words to keep panic from taking the wheel.

Hargrove typed WALLACE, JIM.

The screen populated with a short list.

Too short.

Not because nothing had happened, but because the incidents had never stacked into something that demanded a narrative. They were scattered. Small. The kind of events that never made headlines and never made prosecutors lean forward.

The kind of events that still taught a neighborhood which roads to avoid.

Hargrove clicked into the welfare check.

A deputy's bodycam note: REFUSED TO CROSS LINE. SUBJECT REQUESTED CONTACT AT FENCE POST. ADVISED "HOUSE IS BAD AT NIGHT."

Hargrove's jaw tightened.

He had heard that phrasing before—house is bad—spoken by people who wanted to sound sane while describing something that made them feel insane.

He clicked into the neighbor complaint about lights in the trees. The notes were thin. The deputy had written: CLAIMED "LANTERNS." NO EVIDENCE ON ARRIVAL. SUBJECT STATES "TRESPASSERS." SUBJECT ADVISED TO CALL IF SEEN AGAIN.

Trepassers. Lanterns. Storm. Van Drake Road.

Hargrove felt the pieces brush against each other without locking.

He wasn't a man who believed in ghosts.

He was a man who believed in patterns, in bad decisions repeating themselves, in places that became magnets for the same human failures—drinking, violence, secrecy.

And yet.

The name Jim Wallace sat in the file like a knot.

Hunter was still talking, voice fast now, as if speed could outrun the detective's questions. Hargrove heard, beneath the words, the edge of fear.

Not fear of the storm.

Fear of the address.

Hargrove closed the laptop and looked at the rain streaking his windshield. "Listen to me," he said, keeping his voice even. "If Glisner starts hallucinating, if he starts talking to someone who isn't there, if he gets combative—"

"I know," Hunter cut in, and the sharpness was defensive. "I've got him."

"Do you?" Hargrove asked, and surprised himself with the bluntness.

A pause.

Then Hunter exhaled, and for a second Hargrove heard something like shame come through the line.

"I'm trying," Hunter said. "Okay? I'm trying."

"You staying there with him?" Hargrove asked.

"I'm on my way back now," Hunter said. "Storm's bad. Roads are a mess. But yeah. I'll be there."

Hargrove listened to the wind on the line and pictured a two-lane road flooded in places, trees shedding branches like broken arms.

"Keep your phone on," Hargrove said. "If I call, you answer."

Hunter made a sound that was supposed to be agreement. It came out strained. "Okay," he said. "Okay. I will."

The line crackled. Hargrove heard a brief, high squeal—feedback, interference, nothing supernatural. Just weather and distance and cheap cell towers.

Still, it made the hair on his arms lift.

"Mr. Wallace," Hargrove said again. "If he starts hallucinating—if he talks about insects, voices, people in the room—don't argue with him. Get him medical help."

Hunter's breath caught. "He's already... shaky," he admitted. "But he's lucid. He's—he's okay."

Hargrove didn't say what he was thinking: men like that aren't okay until they're dead or sober, and sometimes not even then.

"I'll follow up," Hargrove said. "In the morning."

"Detective—" Hunter started, and then something thumped on Hunter's end of the call. A jolt. A curse. "Shit."

"What happened?" Hargrove asked, alert.

"Nothing," Hunter said too fast. "Pothole. I'm fine."

The call dropped immediately after.

Hargrove stared at the screen for a beat. No signal, it read. The same two words that had frustrated him a hundred times on rural calls.

He slid the phone back into his pocket and stood alone in the apartment kitchen, listening to the rain and the quiet that settled in places where the living had left.

In the living room, the white rug waited. The stains waited. The ordinary evidence of a life that had been eroded one spill at a time.

Hargrove walked back to the door and paused, hand on the knob.

He didn't believe in haunted houses. He didn't believe in curses. He believed in patterns. He believed in grief. He believed in what men did when grief didn't have anywhere to go.

Outside, thunder rolled, slow and distant, like something heavy shifting in its sleep.

Hargrove locked the door behind him and went back into the storm with Van Drake Road written in his pocket notebook like a warning.

And Hargrove didn't like cases that developed edges in the dark.

Whatever John Glisner was dealing with on Van Drake Road - sickness, grief, hallucination, something worse - it was now part of Hargrove's case.

Back at the station, Hargrove shook rain off his sleeves and set his coat over the back of his chair. The storm tapped the windows like impatient fingers.

He opened John Glisner's file again. The blank line where a wedding ring should have been listed stared back at him. The photo of the white rug looked like a bruise.

He picked up the phone and called dispatch.

"Dispatch," the voice said.

"Hargrove," he answered. "Run me a background on Hunter Wallace. Full."

A pause, then the dispatcher laughed once, the kind of laugh that meant yes, the county had delivered something strange again. "You got a feeling, Detective?"

"I've got a husband in withdrawal in a house with a flagged history on Van Drake Road," Hargrove said. "That's not a feeling. That's a problem. Pull every call tied to that address. And if Keene's working, ask him what he knows."

"Copy," dispatch said. Keys clicked. Paper rustled.

Hargrove hung up and sat still for a moment, listening to the storm and the old building settling.

While dispatch dug, he went down to evidence.

The evidence room was colder than the rest of the station. Fluorescents hummed above rows of shelves.

Hargrove flashed his badge and stepped between sealed lives.

He found the box for Alice Glisner.

There were details in there that didn't matter to a court. But they mattered to a person.

Inside were the things that had come from her apartment after she died: a cracked phone, keys in a plastic pouch, a grocery receipt, a cheap hair tie. A ceramic dish from the bathroom counter with a single earring in it.

No ring.

He closed the envelope and slid it back into the file as if putting it away made it less important. He put the box back, signed out, and returned to his desk.

Dispatch called twenty minutes later.

There was a pause, then the dispatcher lowered their voice. "Detective... about Van Drake."

Hargrove straightened. "Go on."

"I asked Sergeant Keene," the dispatcher said. "He told me to tell you: don't go out there alone after dark. If you have to go, bring someone. And if you hear music, don't follow it."

Hargrove stared at the phone. "Did he say why?"

"He said he went out there once," dispatch replied. "Came back and realized he'd been holding his breath the whole drive."

"Thanks," Hargrove said quietly. "Let Keene know I heard him."

He hung up.

He did not believe in notes that told officers not to go to an address alone after dark. He believed in the way a single night could ruin everything.

Hargrove opened a drawer, pulled out his rain jacket, and set his keys beside the file. He looked at them like a question he didn't want to answer yet.

Chapter Eleven: The Ledger

Hargrove clicked the Marianne Wallace entry. The report was sparse. Vehicle accident. Severe storm. Single survivor. Witness statements contradictory. No charges filed. Notes about grief and alcohol and a man who kept insisting the road had moved under his tires.

He felt the same small tightening he'd felt when he noticed Alice's ring was missing. The sensation that the case was developing edges. Not answers. Edges.

Wallace, Marianne - deceased.

One wasn't.

Hargrove scrolled slowly, reading the names. Most were strangers.

A 911 call with no voice on the line, location pinging to that address, dismissed as a misdial.

Two missing-person reports filed by out-of-county agencies with the last known location listed as Van Drake Road.

A fire call that ended with a note: NO FIRE FOUND. STRONG ODOR. RESIDENT REFUSED ENTRY.

Then the pattern shifted.

The list populated with the kind of dull repetition he expected at a rural address: noise complaints, trespass calls, a few welfare checks.

He opened the call history.

He checked the date. Eleven years ago.

Hargrove stared at it.

FLAGGED - DO NOT SEND SOLO UNITS AFTER DARK.

And then something that didn't belong among the clean municipal forms: a note field, typed in by someone who had either been bored or spooked enough to break protocol.

He clicked into attachments. Property history. Tax records. A scanned plat map with a thin rectangle of land like a coffin.

He opened one of the scans expecting dry deed language. What loaded instead was an inventory ledger from the mid-1800s, brown ink on ruled paper. Columns for value and rations. Under "labor" were first names written without last names, as if surnames were a luxury: Ruth. Eli. A handful of others. Hargrove stared at the entries longer than he meant to. It wasn't folklore. It wasn't atmosphere. It was paper. And, tucked behind it in a more recent incident report, someone had scrawled in pen: DON'T BARGAIN WITH THE PLANTATION MAN.

The name Blithe made his skin tighten.

Ownership: Wallace, Arthur (deceased)
Previous: Blithe, Everett (deceased)
Previous: Blithe Family Trust (dissolved)

The screen loaded slow, as if the computer itself was reluctant.

VAN DRAKE FARM - ESTATE PROPERTY

Hargrove opened the county database and typed the address Hunter Wallace had given him.

He sat alone at his desk with the storm tapping the station windows like impatient fingers. The building smelled of old coffee and toner and damp wool from officers coming in off the street. Somewhere down the hall a TV droned to an empty break room.

Not the geological kind. The human kind. The addresses that pulled trouble down into them and then pretended the surface was still solid. Where calls came in and paperwork went out and nothing ever quite got solved, only filed.

Sinkholes.

Chapter Twelve: The Masquerade

John stood at the edge of the yard like a man who had wandered into the wrong movie.

For a second he could still feel the farmhouse behind him—its sagging porch, its crooked railing, the thin wedge of light under the front door. The same ordinary geometry he'd been clinging to since Hunter left. He turned his head, expecting to see it, to use it as an anchor.

It was there.

And it wasn't.

The porch was lit, yes, but the light was wrong: too warm, too steady, as if the bulb had never flickered in the storm at all. The steps shone with wet gloss. The mud in the yard looked freshly churned, as if a hundred feet had already crossed it tonight.

John swallowed and tasted iron.

His hoodie clung to him, heavy with rain, and he realized the wet didn't feel cold anymore. It felt like sweat. His skin prickled beneath the fabric, that restless crawl that always came when his body couldn't decide whether it was freezing or on fire.

He reached for his phone by reflex.

The screen lit up, then dimmed, then lit again—struggling. In the corner the time jumped forward, then backward, then settled on something that didn't match anything: 4:44.

A weather alert banner sat frozen at the top, half-loaded, the words chopped:

FLASH FLOOD WA—

John stared at the broken sentence and felt his pulse climb. The device in his palm was solid. It was real. It was modern. It was the one object in his life that usually told him what the world was doing and when.

Now it couldn't even tell time.

He slid it back into his pocket as if hiding it could keep the yard from noticing. A stupid thought. But he was full of stupid thoughts tonight.

Somewhere near the barn, a low engine note throbbed— steady, mechanical.

A generator, John thought.

The idea was a relief. A rational hook. Of course a place like this would need a generator. Of course Hunter would have one. The sound explained the porch light. It explained the steadiness.

Then he blinked and realized the throb wasn't an engine at all.

It was music.

Not the clean pulse of a speaker. Not quite. Something older and rougher, a rhythm made from clapping hands and boots on dirt, from breath and laughter and a fiddle line that kept slipping into something like a hymn.

He looked down and saw an orange extension cord cutting through the mud near his feet, bright as a wound.

It ran toward the porch.

John's relief sharpened into unease.

The cord was there for one breath.

On the next, it was gone.

In its place, a strand of lanterns swung from branches, their flames steady, untouched by wind.

John's throat clamped. He told himself the cord had been in his mind. A hallucination. A brain trying to explain what it couldn't. Alcohol had taught him how quickly desire could turn into certainty.

But the mud on his shoe had the faint imprint of a ribbed rubber sheath, the kind extension cords wore. The detail was small enough to be ignored. It wasn't.

Nothing tonight was.

He forced himself to look back at the yard.

The people moved everywhere, faces flushed, voices bright. They were dressed as if for another century, yes—waistcoats, cravats, long skirts—but their movements weren't theatrical. No exaggerated gestures. No wink at the camera. They moved like this was normal. Like this was simply what happened here when the storm passed and the night decided to throw a party.

John's heart hammered hard enough to make his bruises ache.

The ache was another anchor: his ribs still hurt. His jaw still ached. His legs still carried bruises that didn't match his memory. Withdrawal didn't erase pain. Hallucinations didn't heal you.

He rubbed his sternum with the heel of his palm, trying to press his heartbeat down into something manageable.

"Okay," he whispered into the wet air. "Okay."

It sounded like a plea.

The yard answered with laughter.

The rain was gone. The air was heavy with summer warmth. Lanterns swung from branches, their flames steady, untouched by wind. Somewhere near the porch, a woman laughed—a bright, unguarded sound. The music was live: a fiddle, a hand drum, clapping palms, the rhythmic stomp of feet on packed dirt.

John swallowed and realized he wasn't shivering anymore.

His hoodie still clung to him, but the cold had let go as if someone had cut a rope. The rain in his hair felt like warm sweat now. He looked for his breath out of habit, expecting smoke, and found nothing. Summer air slid into his lungs, thick with heat and smoke and perfume.

The flashlight clicked once, twice, and died. The beam guttered out as if the party's lantern light had taken offense at his cheap, modern little sun. John stood there with a dead tool in his hand and a heartbeat that would not slow, and the fear shifted shape: not just fear of what might happen, but fear of where he'd been taken.

People moved everywhere.

Men in waistcoats and cravats. Women in long dresses with bare shoulders and pinned hair. White faces flushed with drink. They turned and glanced at John and then looked away as if his presence made sense, as if a man in jeans and a soaked hoodie belonged here.

His flashlight looked obscene in his hand.

He lowered it at his side. Even dead, he kept it, as if holding onto a piece of his own century could keep him from slipping all the way under.

Someone brushed past him and called, "Blithe, you old devil, you've outdone yourself!"

Another voice answered with a laugh—deep, easy, practiced.

John's skin prickled.

He moved forward because standing still felt like painting a target on his back. The yard's smells hit him in layers: meat roasting, spilled liquor, tobacco, sweat, crushed grass. Beneath it all, faint and sharp, the scent of something metallic—like blood on a hot day.

As he passed under the first lantern, its light warmed his face. The glow made the scene more real and more wrong.

A young man staggered into his path, holding a glass. He blinked at John. "You're late," he said with good-natured accusation, and then he smiled. "No matter. Drink."

John shook his head. "No, thanks."

The smell still found him—sweet rot and oak and the promise of quiet. His mouth watered, traitor that it was, and for a dizzy heartbeat he could almost feel the warmth of it sliding down his throat, turning everything soft around the edges. He swallowed hard and tasted only sweat and fear.

The man looked confused, as if John had spoken a foreign language. He shrugged and wandered off, glass sloshing.

John kept moving, eyes scanning for anything familiar— a car, a modern porch light, the outline of the gravel driveway.

He saw none.

What he did see, near the far side of the yard, was a line of figures standing apart from the party.

At the far edge of the lantern light stood a small knot of Black men and women in plain clothes—workers, not guests. They moved in controlled lines with trays and pitchers, eyes lowered, bodies careful in a way that read as practiced survival.

One woman had a pale scar across her wrist, like old rope burn. When John looked her way, she looked back. Not pleading. Not inviting. Her expression said, with brutal clarity, that she had learned what men wanted from a scene like this and she refused to give it.

John felt his guilt rush up, eager to turn their suffering into a stage for his own confession. He forced it down. This was not his to use. Not his to explain away. Not his to make poetic.

The sight landed like a slap because it wasn't a story. It was an economy. A violence that had rules and uniforms and people who laughed a few yards away as if the world were clean.

He took a step toward them anyway—instinct, a stupid reach for help. The woman's voice cut through the music, low and steady. "No," she said. "We are not your way out."

Before he could decide whether to listen, someone stepped into his path.

A man in a dark coat and a neatly tied cravat. Mid-thirties, perhaps. Hands clean. Eyes sharp. He carried himself with a quiet authority that didn't fit the party's loose, drunken energy.

"Sir," the man said, voice low enough to keep their conversation private. "You mustn't be seen like that."

John stared at him. "Like what?"

The man's gaze flicked over John's clothes, his wet hair, the flashlight. "Uncovered," he said.

John frowned. "Who are you?"

"My name is Phillip," the man replied. He hesitated, then added, "I can help you, but you must listen."

The cadence of Phillip's speech carried the era—more formal, more measured—but his eyes held something else. Not period charm. Not party politeness.

Concern.

John's throat worked. "Where am I?"

Phillip's jaw flexed. "You are where you are meant to be," he said. "And if you want to remain alive, you will do as the house requires."

"The house requires?" John repeated, incredulous. "This is—this is insane."

Phillip's gaze drifted toward the porch where a group of men laughed too loudly, slapping each other's shoulders. "Insane is a word for men who refuse to see what is before them," he said. He reached inside his coat and withdrew something.

A mask.

It was painted white and gold, shaped like a face with no expression, the eyeholes dark. The surface gleamed as if freshly lacquered.

John's blood cooled. He saw, all at once, the ski mask in the storm. The blank eyeholes. The fixed attention.

"Put it on," Phillip said.

"No." The refusal came quick and sharp.

Phillip's eyes narrowed. "You think the mask makes the monster," he said. "It does not. It only tells this place what role you will play."

John stared at the mask. "I'm not playing."

Phillip stepped closer, lowering his voice. "If you stand here barefaced, someone will notice you. Someone will ask questions you cannot answer. And when you cannot answer them, you will be taken inside." He paused. "That is not what you want."

John's stomach twisted. "Inside where?"

Phillip didn't answer. He held the mask out again, patient.

John glanced toward the line of workers again. Their eyes were down, hands moving, bodies in controlled motion. Not a single face looked toward him.

He realized with a chill that they were avoiding him. Not out of indifference.

Out of fear.

John took the mask.

For a second he just stood there holding it, turning it in his hands like an object that might reveal its purpose if he stared long enough.

It was lighter than he expected. The lacquered surface looked polished, but the inside was raw wood, unsealed, the grain rough beneath his fingers. Someone had worn it enough that the edges were darkened by skin oil, the way a tool darkened where it was handled most. John's thumb caught on a tiny nick near the cheekbone, a shallow gouge that looked like a fingernail mark.

His hands trembled around it anyway.

Not fear alone—withdrawal. His body still insisted on movement, on agitation, on doing something to earn the next breath. The tremor climbed into his forearms, made the mask quiver like a live thing.

He pressed the heel of his palm against his ribs and felt the bruise answer with a dull pulse. Pain meant time was still moving forward. Pain meant he hadn't simply slipped out of his life and into someone else's memory.

His phone buzzed in his pocket again.

John flinched hard enough that the mask almost slipped from his fingers. He fished the phone out.

No notification this time. No vibration icon. The screen was black.

He tapped it. Once. Twice.

Nothing.

A dead slab of glass in his palm.

He stared at his own faint reflection in the dark screen: a man in a soaked hoodie, face too pale, eyes too bright.

Behind him, lantern light drifted across moving bodies, turning them into ghosts.

John swallowed. The taste of iron was back.

He wanted, irrationally, to walk back to the farmhouse and slam the door and sit on the floor with his back against it and ride out the night like a fever. He wanted Hunter's truck lights. He wanted the station's fluorescent hum. He wanted any place where the rules were written down in a book instead of carved into the air.

Phillip was watching him, patient.

John hated that patience. It felt like the mask was already making a demand: choose.

John lifted the mask and held it an inch from his face.

The air behind it smelled faintly of sweat and smoke and something sweet that made his stomach roll, because sweetness had started meaning liquor to his nervous system. His breath warmed the inside of the mask and came back at him damp.

He thought, absurdly, of the white rug—of Alice kneeling with paper towels, laughing like nothing permanent could happen if you were quick enough.

He thought of his own voice on the apartment floor, screaming.

He thought of the moment he had called 911, thumb slipping, begging a stranger for instructions.

That was what the mask promised.

Instructions.

A role.

A way to behave that could make the world predictable again.

John's fingers curled along the cheek line. He could feel the tiny nick. The fingernail mark.

Someone had tried to take this off once.

Someone had failed.

His fingers hesitated on the smooth lacquer.

The mask wasn't cold the way he expected. It held a faint warmth, like it had been pressed to a face moments ago. That was the part that made his stomach roll—the idea of passing a skin from one man to the next, trading identities the way drunks traded stories at a bar.

From the corner of his eye, John saw one of the workers glance up. Just once. A young woman with her hair wrapped tight, hands red from scrubbing. Her eyes met his through the lantern light and the look in them was not fear. It was recognition, hard and steady, like she'd seen his kind before and already knew how this ended.

She dropped her gaze again before anyone else could notice.

John lifted the mask to his face and felt, with a sick little jolt, how easy it was to hide.

It fit too easily, as if the mask had been waiting for his face.

Behind the lacquer, the air tasted stale, like old breath trapped in varnish.

His hands trembled as he lifted it toward his face. "This is ridiculous," he muttered, but his voice sounded small.

Phillip's expression didn't change. "Do it," he said.

John slid the mask on.

The world changed immediately, not because the yard changed, but because his face did.

The mask cut his vision into narrow angles. The eyeholes were smaller than they looked from the outside, forcing him to turn his whole head to see. The lacquered edge pressed into his cheekbones, and the rough wood inside scraped at the skin near his temples. His own breath came back at him warm and damp, trapped, tasting of rain and panic and the metallic water he'd swallowed too fast.

For a second, the claustrophobia almost made him rip it back off.

He didn't.

He stood there with the mask on and listened.

Sound was different too. Muffled at the edges, as if the mask were a filter. The laughter in the yard became a low wash. The fiddle line sharpened, then softened. Individual voices blurred, and the whole crowd sounded like one organism, exhaling.

John's pulse thudded in his ears, too loud.

He reached up and touched the bottom edge of the mask, needing proof it was still just an object. The wood was warm already from his skin.

He tried to ground himself the way the therapist at detox had taught him when the room started to tilt:

Name five things you can see.

Lanterns. Mud. A woman's gloved hand. Phillip's coat buttons. The farmhouse porch light.

Name four things you can feel.

The mask on his face. Wet fabric at his shoulders. The ache in his ribs. The tremor in his fingers.

Name three things you can hear.

Music. Rain. His own breathing.

Name two things you can smell.

Smoke. Something sweet—perfume, liquor, rot. He couldn't tell which.

Name one thing you can taste.

Iron.

The exercise didn't calm him. It just made the yard sharper.

He took a step forward into the crowd.

No one stopped him. No one asked for his name. The mask was enough. It was admission.

As he moved, he caught sight of details that didn't fit the century the costumes were pretending to belong to.

A black cable ran under a table and vanished into shadow. It looked like an extension cord. John followed it with his eyes until his neck ached, and then the cable wasn't there—just a dark line of mud where someone had dragged a heel.

A woman in a high-collared dress lifted a glass to her lips. For an instant the cup looked disposable, thin plastic catching lantern light with a cheap shine. John blinked, and it was crystal again, heavy and cut, the kind of glass that belonged in a cabinet no one dared open.

A man leaned against a tree, smoking. The ember at the end of his cigarette glowed bright and modern, too precise. Then the ember flared and became the tip of a cigar, thicker, older, and the man's hand suddenly wore a ring too large to be comfortable.

John's stomach knotted.

Either his mind was scrambling to explain, inserting modern objects like subtitles, or the yard itself was slipping between versions of itself the way his phone had slipped between times.

He didn't know which answer was worse.

Phillip stayed near his shoulder as if escorting him. "Just breathe," Phillip said.

John's laugh came out thin. "That's what everyone says right before something awful happens."

Phillip's masked head tilted. "Sometimes it's also what you say right before you stop running."

John wanted to ask him what this was. He wanted to demand a rational label—re-enactment, fundraiser, hallucination, dream. He wanted the comfort of a noun.

Instead he let himself be moved through the crowd.

Hands brushed him—gloved, bare, cold. Someone pressed a drink into his palm and then, when he looked down, there was nothing there. The gesture remained, the ghost of weight.

John's ribs ached again, a dull flare that made him remember his body.

Not an observer.

Not a camera floating through a weird scene.

A man with bruises and sweat and a nervous system that had been trained to want poison.

He looked toward the farmhouse.

The porch light was still on.

He could see the front door now, open, spilling a wedge of warmer light into the wet night. People moved in and out, vanishing into the house and returning with their laughter slightly changed, as if the air inside carried a different pressure.

John's mouth went dry.

He knew, with the sick certainty of every addict facing a drink, that whatever was inside that house was an offer waiting to be accepted.

Phillip's voice came close to his ear, intimate even through masks. "You don't have to," he said.

John's heart hammered. "Don't have to what?"

Phillip didn't answer directly. He only said, "But you came."

John stared at the open door until his eyes watered.

Then he followed Phillip toward it anyway.

With it in place, he didn't have to manage his face. He didn't have to perform sobriety or contrition or bravery. He could be a blank shape in a crowd—one more lie among a hundred others. The relief was immediate, and that scared him more than the party did.

For a moment his world narrowed to the dark eyeholes and the muffled echo of his own breathing. The mask's edge pressed against his cheekbones. The lacquered surface felt too smooth.

Phillip exhaled softly, as if relieved. "Good," he said. "Now walk as if you belong."

"I don't," John said.

"You do tonight," Phillip replied. He nodded toward the house. "Come. Before Mr. Blithe's man sees you."

"Mr. Blithe," John repeated. The name tasted wrong.

Phillip didn't look at him. "You will meet him soon enough," he said.

They walked together along the edge of the yard. The party surged around them in waves: laughter, clapping, the scrape of shoes on dirt. John's body moved on instinct, matching Phillip's pace, trying not to draw attention.

With the mask on, people glanced at him and then looked away, satisfied by the lie. The mask made him invisible.

It also made him feel—hollow. Like he'd stepped out of his own skin.

John lifted a hand and touched the edge of the mask.

The lacquer was warm from his skin, slick with sweat along the rim. He could feel his own breath trapped inside it, cycling back into his face. Each inhale tasted a little more like him: stale fear, sour stomach, the coppery tang that came before he threw up.

He told himself it was just the heat. Just the crowd. Just the remnants of the storm sweat drying under his hoodie.

But the truth was simpler and uglier: the mask felt like the drink. Not the first drink, the one you pretended was social. The second, the third - the point where the world softened at the edges and you stopped having to be the man who had done what he'd done.

The mask made him invisible. It also made him safe from himself.

His fingers hooked under the chin line. For a second he hesitated, because Phillip's warning still rang in his head - uncovered - and because some instinct deeper than reason understood this wasn't about manners.

John pulled the mask away from his face by an inch.

Cold air slid in like water. Not cool night air. Cold like the inside of a freezer, sharp enough to sting his cheeks. The laughter nearby didn't stop, but it seemed to move farther away, muffled as if he'd dipped his head under bathwater.

Three people turned at once.

Not curiously. Not casually. Their masked faces snapped toward him with the same fixed attention, like animals hearing a branch crack.

John's pulse jumped. He looked past them and saw the line of workers again. One woman stood with a tray in her hands, her posture perfectly still. She didn't avert her gaze when their eyes met.

There was no pleading in her face. No fear. Only a hard, measured warning, the same kind you gave a child reaching for a stove.

John's hand froze on the mask.

A voice breathed near his ear. "Put it back."

Phillip hadn't been beside him a second ago. Now he was, close enough that John could smell smoke on his coat. Phillip's fingers closed over John's wrist - not gentle, not cruel. Certain.

John tried to speak. Nothing came out but a dry rasp.

Phillip's grip tightened. "Not here," he said, still low. "Not in front of him."

John swallowed and shoved the mask back against his face.

The cold retreated instantly. The muffled sound snapped back into fullness: fiddle and drum, clapping palms, the roar of voices. The three partygoers who had turned toward him looked away again as if someone had erased the moment from their minds.

Invisible again.

Hollow again.

John's hands dropped to his sides, trembling. He stared at the woman with the tray. Her gaze remained on him for one more heartbeat, then slid away - not because she was obedient, but because she'd delivered the message and didn't need to repeat it.

Phillip released John's wrist and leaned in, voice barely more than air. "This place rewards performance," he said. "It punishes truth. You understand?"

John nodded once, because he did. He understood too well.

They passed close to the line of workers. John caught quick looks now—eyes flicking up and away again. Not vacant. Not obedient.

Watching.

Judging.

Phillip's voice stayed low. "Do not speak to them," he said.

John's first impulse was outrage— at Phillip, at the party, at himself for standing there in a mask while people carried trays like furniture. Then he realized Phillip wasn't protecting John from them. He was protecting them from John: from questions that made a man feel righteous, from pity that demanded gratitude, from attention that could get someone hurt.

John gave a single, stiff nod. It wasn't agreement. It was understanding, and that felt worse.

John's throat tightened. "Why not?"

"Because they are not here for you," Phillip replied. His tone sharpened. "And because you are not the first lost man to arrive with questions and pity. Keep your pity. Keep walking."

John's face flushed beneath the mask. "I'm not—"

Phillip cut him off with a look. "Listen," he said. "The man who owned this house owned people, once. This place remembers. It doesn't forgive. It doesn't forget. And it will use anything you hand it."

John's pulse hammered. "And you?" he asked. "What are you? Are you—"

Phillip's jaw tightened. "I am one of those who keep the door shut," he said. "That is all you need to know."

A hand closed around John's wrist—warm, sweaty, certain—and tugged him toward the music.

A woman in a feathered mask laughed up at him, cheeks flushed from drink. "Don't brood in the shadows," she said, as if they were old friends. "Mr. Blithe didn't hang lanterns for you to stare at them."

John tried to pull free, but the crowd absorbed the movement and made it look like consent. Phillip's gaze flicked to him—warning, urgent—and then away, as if even that small attention might give him away.

They spun him into the dance line. Hands slapped his shoulders. Someone shouted a rhyme in a drawl too old to be real. Boots stamped. Skirts flared. The heat of bodies pressed in, and beneath it all ran the smell of whiskey—sweet and medicinal and impossible to ignore.

A glass brushed his knuckles. Dark liquid winked in lantern light. For one terrible heartbeat his hand almost closed around it on instinct, the way you reach for a railing on stairs. He yanked back as if the glass were hot.

For a second the craving wasn't a voice. It was a body memory: hand closing, throat opening, the sweet burn arriving like forgiveness.

His fingers twitched toward the glass. The mask pressed against his face and he thought, wildly, of the way a drink worked—how it let you stop being a person and become a shape. A blank. A lie. He forced his hand away and the relief he felt was sharp and ugly, because it came with the knowledge that some part of him had been willing.

Across the yard, a woman laughed with her head thrown back, hair pinned in a careless twist that made John's heart jerk. The tilt of her chin, the angle of her smile— it was Alice for half a second, alive and careless in the light.

For a heartbeat the yard tilted and he was fourteen again at some summer party, Alice's laugh lifting above the noise like a rope thrown to a drowning boy.

He saw her the first time he'd met her—not the exhausted woman at the end of their marriage, not the body under a sheet—but the girl with sunscreen on her nose and a cheap beer in her hand, grinning like the world didn't have consequences yet.

His throat tightened so hard it hurt. He took a step toward the laughter before he realized it belonged to someone else.

That was the house's real cruelty: it didn't just scare you. It showed you what you missed until missing became a kind of hunger.

And hunger, Jim had warned, made men stupid.

"Alice—" His voice made it to his tongue and died there. The woman turned. Not Alice. Just a stranger with bright eyes and a mouth stained with drink. She studied his mask and leaned in as if sharing a secret. "You look like you've seen a ghost," she said.

John's skin crawled under the lacquer. Behind the stranger's shoulder, the line of workers stood in the darker band beyond the lanterns—still, watching. For a blink the fiddles blurred into a thin, high ringing, like a hospital monitor that didn't want to stop beeping.

He stumbled out of the dance line, breath sawing, ribs protesting, and found Phillip again at the edge of the yard. Phillip didn't ask if he was all right. He only looked at John the way you look at a man about to step through a trapdoor.

A harsh voice barked from behind them. "Hey!"

John flinched and turned.

A man strode toward them, thick-bodied, shoulders broad, face red from drink or temper. He wore a coat, but it hung open. A pistol sat in a holster at his hip, the grip polished by use.

His eyes locked on John.

"You," he said, pointing. "I don't know you."

Phillip stepped in smoothly, placing himself half between the man and John. "Doug," he said, voice calm. "The gentleman is with Mr. Blithe."

Doug's stare didn't budge. "I asked him, Phillip."

Phillip kept his hands visible, palms open. "He is newly arrived," he said. "Mr. Blithe expects him."

Doug's mouth twisted. "Mr. Blithe expects a lot of things," he muttered. Then he looked John up and down again. "You're wearing the wrong clothes under that face."

John's mouth went dry. Through the mask, his voice sounded muffled. "I—"

Doug stepped closer, making John smell sweat and tobacco. "Take it off," Doug said. "Let me see."

Phillip's tone hardened. "No," he said.

Doug's eyes narrowed. "You telling me no?"

"I am telling you Mr. Blithe's guests wear masks," Phillip replied. "And you do not touch them."

Doug's hand drifted toward his pistol, lazy but ready.

John's body tensed, knife long gone, flashlight dead, ribs aching. He had nothing.

Then, from the porch, that deep, easy laugh sounded again.

"Douglas," a voice called. "Leave the poor man be."

Doug turned.

A man stood at the top of the porch steps, hands spread in a gesture of welcome. He wore a tailored coat, his hair neatly combed back. His face was handsome in the way that made you trust him before you'd earned it. His smile was broad and bright.

John knew him without being told.

Mr. Blithe.

Blithe descended the steps with unhurried confidence, as if the yard itself belonged to him in a way deeper than property lines. People made space automatically. Laughter softened into attentive murmurs.

Doug stepped back, deferential despite himself. "Sir," he said.

Blithe waved a hand. "We're celebrating," he said, still smiling. "No need for sour faces." He looked at John. "Welcome."

John held still. The mask made Blithe's gaze feel invasive. Like the man was looking through lacquer and skin into whatever lived behind.

"You look like a man who's seen a ghost," Blithe said pleasantly.

John's throat worked. "Where am I?"

Blithe's smile widened. "In my home," he said. "In my house, on my land, under my sky." His tone turned playful. "At least for the moment."

Phillip's shoulders were tense beside John. "Sir," he said carefully, "the gentleman is confused."

"Of course he is," Blithe replied, as if confusion were a charming trait. He stepped closer to John and lowered his voice. "Confusion is what happens when a man loses his story."

John's skin crawled. "My story?"

Blithe's eyes glittered in lantern light. "Come inside," he said. "The night is damp. Let us talk somewhere civilized."

John didn't move.

Blithe kept smiling, but his voice sharpened an edge. "Douglas," he said without looking away from John. "Escort our guest."

Doug's hand returned to John's shoulder, heavy as a clamp. "This way," he said.

John looked at Phillip, desperate. Phillip's eyes held a warning: Don't fight here.

John let Doug guide him.

They crossed the porch and entered the house.

The interior was not Hunter's father's dim, cluttered place. It was bright. Clean. Alive with movement. Candles in sconces threw warm light over polished floors. The air smelled of citrus peel and smoke and something sweet.

People milled through rooms with glasses in hand. Laughter rose and fell. A piano played somewhere, jaunty and careless.

Doug led John past the staircase and down a hall to a door John recognized by shape, if not by reality.

The office.

In the present, it had been dusty and unused. Now it looked occupied, lived in. Books lined shelves. A decanter gleamed on a sideboard. A fire cracked in the hearth.

Doug shoved John forward and shut the door behind them.

Blithe stepped around John and poured a drink into a glass without asking. The liquid was amber, catching firelight. It smelled of oak and sweetness.

John's stomach rolled.

Not because he wanted it—though some part of him did—but because the smell reached into him and pulled up a memory he had tried to bury.

Alice on the couch, eyes red-rimmed, holding her phone like it was a weapon. "You didn't come home," she'd said. "You didn't even call."

John on the stairs, too drunk to stand straight, laughing because his friends were laughing, because it was easier to be funny than to be sorry.

The smell of whiskey on his breath when he leaned over her, when he said something cruel and didn't even remember it later.

Blithe held out the glass.

John shook his head hard. "No."

Blithe's eyebrows lifted. "Ah," he said. "A man trying to become someone new."

John forced his voice steady. "I don't drink."

Blithe's smile turned thoughtful. "Not tonight," he corrected.

Doug stood by the door like a jailer, arms folded.

Phillip was not in the room. John felt his absence like cold.

Blithe set the glass down and moved closer, hands behind his back. "Tell me," he said softly, "what brings you to my house?"

John's mouth felt dry. "I'm—" He stopped. Any answer felt like admitting the lie. "I don't know."

Blithe nodded, delighted. "Honesty. Rare." He leaned in a fraction. "But you do know something, John."

John's blood chilled. "How do you know my name?"

Blithe's eyes gleamed. "This house knows," he said. "It keeps names the way it keeps stains."

John's rib pain flared as his breathing tightened. "What do you want from me?"

Blithe's smile returned, easy. "Want?" he echoed. "Want is a childish word. I prefer... appetite."

He turned and glanced at the decanter, then back at John. "You have appetite too," he said. "For relief. For blame. For someone to say you did everything you could."

Blithe watched John's face with an almost affectionate patience, as if he could see the shape of John's thoughts through the mask.

"Relief," Blithe continued, tasting the word like it belonged to him. "It's such a holy thing, isn't it? Men will kneel for it. Beg for it. Hurt the people they swear they love for it."

John's fingers curled. "I didn't come here for a sermon."

Blithe's smile widened. "No," he said. "You came here for permission."

John felt his stomach drop, the way it did when someone said out loud what he'd been trying to keep buried under excuses.

Blithe tilted his head. "Tell me," he said, softly now, "how many times did you rehearse your innocence today?"

John's throat tightened. "I'm not innocent," he said, and hated how the sentence sounded like a confession and a defense at the same time.

Blithe nodded as if pleased. "Good," he said. "Honesty, at least in theory. But that's not what you want."

He stepped closer. The room seemed to lean with him, as if the walls were listening.

"What you want," Blithe said, "is a story that lets you sleep."

John flinched. "Stop."

Blithe ignored it. "A story where her sadness was bigger than you," he said. "A story where the bottle did all the work, and you were just... nearby."

John's vision blurred at the edges. He saw Alice at the kitchen counter again, hands on the sink, shoulders tense as wire. Heard her voice: If you can't be here, just say so. Don't make me guess.

Blithe's voice slid under the memory like a knife. "You want the world to look at you and say, 'Of course it happened. She was sick. She was dramatic. She was fragile.'"

John's mouth went dry. He hated how easy it was to picture people saying it. How easy it would be to let them.

Blithe's smile turned almost tender. "Because then you don't have to admit the uglier truth," he said. "That you were there. That you were part of it. That you didn't put your hands on the poison, but you taught it where to land."

John lurched forward a step before he realized he'd moved. "You don't get to talk about her."

Blithe lifted his hands, placating. "I'm not talking about her," he corrected. "I'm talking about you."

He nodded toward the decanter again, not offering it yet. Not pushing. Just reminding John it existed.

"Two kinds of drink," Blithe murmured. "The one in the glass, and the one in the mind. You've taken both. You know the difference."

John's breath came sharp through the mask. "You don't know anything," he said, but the words felt weak even as he spoke them.

Blithe's eyes gleamed. "I know your appetite," he said. "And I know you came here because part of you is tired of being the villain in your own story."

For a heartbeat, John felt the temptation of it. Not the whiskey. The absolution. The warm, narcotic idea that he could walk out of this room lighter, cleaner, with someone else holding the weight.

And then he felt the hook under it. The cost he couldn't name yet.

His hands clenched until his nails bit his palms.

John's jaw locked beneath the mask. "You don't know anything about me."

Blithe's gaze sharpened. "Oh, but I do," he said, voice still gentle. "I know you lost a woman and the world expects you to feel something clean about it—grief, perhaps. But what you feel is dirtier. Anger. Shame. A little bit of fear."

John's throat knotted. "Shut up."

Blithe chuckled. "And there it is," he said. "The lovely, familiar sound of a man who hates the truth."

John took a step forward. "I'm leaving," he said.

Doug's hand moved toward his pistol.

Blithe lifted a finger, and Doug stopped.

Blithe smiled again. "Go," he said. "By all means."

John stared, thrown by the permission.

Blithe's voice softened. "But understand something before you do," he said. "There are men who come to this place looking for punishment. There are men who come looking for forgiveness. And there are men who come looking for a way to keep their hands clean."

John's pulse pounded.

Blithe leaned closer, smile fading into something colder. "Those men are the easiest to feed," he said.

John's mouth went dry. "Feed?"

Blithe spread his hands. "You feel it, don't you?" he asked. "This house pulling at you. Showing you things. Borrowing voices." His eyes flicked to the mask. "Making you wear a face so you don't have to wear your own."

John's hands clenched into fists. He could feel sweat under the mask, the damp interior pressing against his skin like a second face.

Blithe took another step closer. "Tell me, John," he murmured. "When she looked at you near the end... did she look like she still recognized you?"

John's vision blurred. "Stop," he whispered.

Blithe's smile returned, satisfied. "There it is," he said. "That's the bruise. That's the tender spot."

John surged forward on impulse, the urge to hit something, to break something, to silence the voice.

Doug caught him by the shoulder and shoved him back. Pain lanced through John's ribs. He gasped.

Blithe's face stayed pleasant, but his eyes were not. "Temper," he said. "Another appetite. Useful."

John's breathing came in sharp pulls. He looked at the door. "Let me out," he said.

Blithe nodded to Doug. "Escort him," he said. "But don't let him wander. He's a guest, after all."

Doug yanked the door open.

John moved past him, forcing his body to work through pain and fear. He stepped into the hall and headed for the front door, desperate for air, for space.

Behind him Blithe called softly, "Enjoy the party, John. It may be the last invitation you ever receive."

John didn't turn back.

He pushed out onto the porch and into the lantern-lit yard, the noise and laughter crashing over him again.

He tried to breathe.

The mask felt tighter now. The eyeholes narrower. The world framed by dark lacquered edges.

He moved toward the driveway—toward what should have been his car, his escape.

There, in the shadows beyond the lantern glow, a carriage sat ready. Black lacquer. Large wheels. A driver holding reins, face hidden by a hood.

Doug appeared at John's side like a bad thought. "Not that way," he said.

John kept walking. "I'm leaving," he said.

Doug grabbed his arm. John flinched, ribs screaming.

Doug leaned in, voice low and mean. "You don't leave Mr. Blithe's party without permission," he said. "You understand me?"

John met Doug's eyes through the mask. "I don't belong here," he said.

Doug's mouth twisted. "No," he agreed. "You don't."

John felt something cold in his gut.

He glanced back toward the tree line, toward where the wolves had sat.

The woods were dark again, no lanterns beyond the yard. The ring of trees looked like a wall.

And along that wall, scattered like stones, stood figures in plain clothes—workers, servants, whatever name this place used—watching the party with faces like masks of their own.

They didn't dance. They didn't drink. They didn't even pretend to smile.

They stood with their hands folded or hanging at their sides, bodies held still in the practiced way of people who knew motion could become an excuse for punishment. Lantern light brushed their faces and slid away without warming them, and John had the irrational thought that the light didn't want to touch them.

A few wore bruises the way other guests wore jewelry—dark marks at wrists, a split lip, a swelling along a cheekbone. Some stared at the ground. Some stared straight ahead.

One man met John's eyes and held them. Not begging. Not accusing. Just watching, as if weighing whether John was the kind of person who could be trusted with truth.

John looked away first, ashamed of how quickly his instincts reached for the mask to make him invisible.

Phillip was among them.

He caught John's eye and shook his head once. Slow. Clear.

Don't.

Doug tightened his grip. "Come on," he said. "Mr. Blithe wants to see you behave."

John stared at Phillip, desperate for instruction.

Phillip didn't move. He didn't rescue.

He only watched, eyes steady, as if waiting to see what John would choose.

The party music rose into a new tune—faster, brighter.

John swallowed hard.

He turned back toward Doug.

"Fine," he said.

But inside the mask, behind the lacquered lie, something else rose—small and ugly and familiar.

The certainty that if he didn't find a way out soon, he would never find one.

Chapter Thirteen: The Search

Hunter's phone had been silent too long.

He told himself that was the point. That quiet was what he'd driven John out here for - a place where the city couldn't press in, where the liquor stores weren't on every corner, where the noise of other people's lives didn't give John an excuse to drown his own.

But the longer the silence stretched, the more it felt like something else: a held breath.

Hunter sat at the kitchen table of his rental, staring at the cracked screen of his phone. Ten missed calls from him to John. Three texts that still showed delivered but never read.

He tried to picture John inside the house - sweating through the worst of it, pacing, cursing, begging the walls for mercy. That was normal. That was the sickness doing what it did.

And then his mind supplied a different picture, one he didn't like admitting even to himself: John alone in that old place, listening to the landline ring.

Hunter rubbed a hand over his face. He could still hear his father's voice from years ago, low and angry, the way it got when he'd been drinking and afraid at the same time.

"Don't answer it after dark."

Hunter had laughed then. He'd been sixteen and smart enough to think he was immune to superstition. His father had slapped him hard enough to make his ears ring.

"The house offers you things," he'd said. "It always asks for more back."

Hunter stood up so fast the chair scraped the floor.

He pictured John in that house, shaking, hearing things, making bargains without realizing that was what he was doing.

Hunter looked at his phone again. Three delivered texts. No reply.

But also responsibility. The kind his father had tried to pass to him like an inheritance.

Fear, yes.

Now, years later, sitting at his rental kitchen table with John's silence filling the room, Hunter felt the same shift.

He was afraid.

Instead, he had stood there in that kitchen and felt something shift. A recognition that his father wasn't just drunk and mean.

Hunter remembered wanting to throw the notebook across the room. He remembered wanting to run back to the city, back to friends and bright streets and the lie that grief stayed put if you didn't invite it in.

His father had looked at him with a terrible kind of clarity. "A receipt," he said. "For every time I thought I could pay my way out."

"What is this?" he'd demanded.

Hunter had stared at that last line until his eyes hurt.

If you see the party, you are already late.

If you hear her voice, do not follow it.

If you want relief, it will offer you a price that feels like justice.

And then, lower, half-smeared as if someone had tried to rub it away:

Do not answer after dark.

Do not cross the bone line.

Do not bargain.

Inside were lists. Doors. Windows. Times. Notes written in a hand that got shakier the farther down the page you went.

LOCKS was written on the front in thick marker, underlined hard enough to tear the paper.

His father had released him and gone to the desk by the window, the one with the warped drawers. He'd yanked it open and pulled out a notebook - cheap spiral, cover stained. He'd slapped it onto the table.

Hunter had frozen at the mention of his mother, the way her name always turned the air heavy.

"I'm trying to keep you alive," his father had whispered. "You think I like being this man? You think I like laying down rules like I'm some damn preacher? I'm doing it because I already watched your mother die on that road and I'm not watching you die in this house."

His father had stood over him, breathing fast, eyes wide with something Hunter didn't have a name for yet. Not rage. Panic.

The slap had come then, hard enough to make the room flash. He'd stumbled into the counter, heart hammering, mouth tasting blood.

"I understand you're drunk," Hunter had shot back.

"Listen," his father had said, voice low. "This place hears you. Not your words - your want. You understand?"

His father had grabbed his wrist and pulled him close enough that Hunter smelled the whiskey and the fear under it.

Hunter had tried to laugh it off. He'd wanted to be the kind of kid who didn't believe in anything he couldn't touch.

Hunter could still see the kitchen of that old house, his father standing barefoot on the cold boards, shirt unbuttoned, a bruise blooming under one eye that he swore he got from a cabinet door. His father's hands had been steady when he said it, too steady for a drunk. Steady like a man reciting rules he'd learned the hard way.

The memory didn't stop at the words.

Hunter stood up so fast the chair scraped the floor. He grabbed his keys, didn't bother with a jacket, and was out the door before his brain could talk him out of it.

The drive back to Van Drake Road took less than twenty minutes. The storm clouds had thinned, leaving the world washed and dark. The headlights cut through wet air, catching sheets of water on pine needles and the occasional flash of animal eyes in the brush.

As Hunter turned off the main road, his stomach tightened. Van Drake Road was a narrow ribbon of gravel that felt too old to be maintained by anyone living. The trees leaned toward it, branches knitting overhead, turning the road into a tunnel.

The house came into view at the end of the drive, and Hunter couldn't shake the feeling it had been waiting.

It should have looked the same as when he'd left. Same porch. Same sagging lines. Same dead windows.

But something in the yard looked wrong.

Hunter killed the engine and sat for a moment, listening. No music. No laughter. No hum of electricity. Just insects and the slow drip of water off eaves.

His phone had one bar of service. He texted John again: You OK? Answer me.

The message sat there for a second, then changed. Not failed. Not undelivered. It simply blinked and vanished as if he'd never typed it at all.

Hunter stared at the empty screen. His thumb hovered over the keyboard.

He typed again. Slower. You OK? Answer me.

The words remained this time. Delivered.

Hunter swallowed. He shoved the phone in his pocket as if it could burn him and got out of the truck.

The porch boards creaked under his boots. The front door was shut. The chain was latched.

"John," he called.

Nothing.

Hunter tried the knob. Locked.

He stepped back and looked at the windows. No light. No movement. The house looked abandoned, the way it always had from the road.

Then the television clicked on inside.

Hunter froze.

It was faint at first—a soft electronic whine, the particular static of an old set warming up. Hunter paused, waiting for it to resolve into something he could blame on weather or wiring. Instead it swelled into a low, bright sound, like a commercial jingle from another room. The noise didn't match the darkness in the windows.

Hunter swallowed and forced his hand toward his pocket. The instinct was habit more than belief, and now it felt childish.

He called again. "John!"

Still nothing.

Hunter moved around the house toward the side entrance. The grass was wet and high, soaking his jeans. He found the kitchen door and tried it.

It opened.

Inside, the air was colder than it should have been. Cold enough to raise gooseflesh along his arms.

The smell hit him next. Old wood. Damp. And underneath it, something sweet and rotten that made his stomach tighten.

"John?" he tried, softer now.

No answer. But the TV noise cut off abruptly, like someone had hit a mute button.

Hunter stood in the dark kitchen and listened to his own breathing. The silence in the house wasn't empty. It felt crowded, full of things holding still.

He took one step forward. Then another.

His eyes adjusted slowly. The outlines of counters. A table. A chair pushed slightly away, as if someone had stood up too quickly.

Hunter reached for the light switch and flipped it.

Nothing.

He pulled out his phone and turned on the flashlight. The beam carved a narrow tunnel through the dark. Dust motes glittered in it like ash.

He followed the hallway toward the living room.

Halfway there, he stopped.

The landline sat on the side table, exactly where it always sat. Red. Heavy. Ordinary.

And the receiver was off the hook.

Hunter stared at it. The dial tone was a thin, steady whine, too high in the quiet.

His skin prickled. He reached for the receiver, hesitated, and then lifted it back onto the cradle.

The dial tone stopped.

For a second the house felt like it had relaxed. Like it had been waiting for that correction.

Hunter exhaled shakily. He told himself this was simple. John had been here. John had used the phone. John had left it off the hook in a panic. That was all.

He turned toward the stairs.

Something moved at the top. Not a person—at least he couldn't prove that. Just a shift of shadow, the kind you could blame on wind and branches if you wanted to.

"John?" Hunter tried again.

Silence.

He climbed two steps and stopped. The air up there felt different - thicker, wrong, like heat trapped in a closed room.

A sound drifted down from the second floor, faint but distinct.

Something that sounded like a laugh.

Not John's. Not any voice Hunter recognized—if it was a voice at all.

It cut off. Then came the soft, deliberate sound of a door latch clicking—wood on metal, the kind of noise an old house made when it settled.

Hunter backed down the steps without meaning to. His heartbeat hammered in his throat.

He turned and moved toward the front door again, fast now, not caring how loud his boots were on the boards.

As he crossed the living room, the TV clicked on behind him again—maybe a power hiccup, maybe a stuck button, maybe nothing he could explain.

Hunter didn't look. He didn't give it the satisfaction.

He shoved the front door open and nearly fell onto the porch. The night air felt warmer, more real. He sucked it in like it was oxygen after near-drowning.

The yard was still empty. Dark. Quiet.

But beyond the edge of the lantern reach - beyond where the trees began - Hunter saw something pale on the ground.

A line.

Not paint. Not chalk. A thin border of pale fragments—bone, maybe, and salt—curving across the grass as if someone had tried to draw a boundary between the house and the woods.

Hunter stared at it and felt his father's handprint on his cheek again, hot and stinging.

"Don't cross it."

Hunter's mouth went dry. He took one step toward the line and stopped.

The darkness beyond it seemed to deepen, as if the tree line had moved closer—or as if the lantern light had simply shifted with the wind.

A sound rolled out of the woods, low enough that his body reacted before his brain could label it.

Not wind. Not insects—at least not the familiar kind.

Something low and distant, animal or engine, rolled through the trees.

Hunter backed up slowly until his heel hit the porch step. His hand went to his pocket and closed around his phone.

He called the number on Detective Hargrove's card, the one he'd shoved into his wallet after the apartment. It rang twice, then went to voicemail.

"Hargrove," the recorded voice said. "Leave your name."

Hunter swallowed. "This is Hunter," he said. "John Glisner's friend. He's not answering. I'm at the Van Drake place. Something's wrong."

He hesitated, because he didn't know how to say haunted without sounding insane.

"Call me back," he finished, voice tight. "Now."

He hung up and stood on the porch, staring at the bone-white line in the grass.

Behind him, inside the dark house, he thought he heard the phone ring once.

Just once.

Hunter didn't turn around.

Chapter Fourteen: The Road

John waited until Doug's attention drifted back to the porch.

Blithe had returned to the center of the party, laughing with his guests, playing the gracious host. Doug hovered at the edges like a watchdog, eyes hard, hand never far from his pistol.

John knew men like Doug. Not the coat and the pistol—those were costumes. The shape underneath was familiar: a man who liked being the one holding the keys, the one deciding who went where, the one who could say no and mean it.

He'd been Doug in smaller ways—standing in doorways, deciding when a conversation was over, using silence like a weapon. He saw Alice in it now, waiting on the couch with her keys in her hand, asking him if he was coming home or if she should stop pretending.

He took a slow breath through the mask, tasting sweat, and forced his voice to stay calm.

He turned back toward Doug and said, "Mr. Blithe needs you."

Doug's head snapped around. "What?"

John nodded toward the carriage at the edge of the yard. "He wants something fetched," John said. "Town."

Doug stared at him, suspicious. "Town's a long ride."

John leaned in slightly as if sharing a secret. "He said he wants it before morning," he lied. "And he said he doesn't want Phillip doing it."

Doug's mouth tightened at Phillip's name. Whatever rivalry lived between them, it was sharp enough to cut.

Doug spit onto the dirt. "What's he want?"

John's mind raced. "Supplies," he said. "Medicine. He said there's a... sick guest."

Doug narrowed his eyes. "Who?"

"Didn't say." John shrugged. "But he said you'd understand it's important."

Doug stared at John through the mask's eyeholes, trying to read what John wouldn't let him show. "You're new," Doug said. "You sure you heard right?"

John forced himself to hold Doug's gaze. "He said you," John replied. "He said you're the only one he trusts not to screw it up."

Doug's nostrils flared. Pride was an easy lever. Men like Doug were built with it.

Finally Doug grunted. "Fine," he said. "You're coming."

John's pulse stuttered. "Me?"

Doug's smile was thin. "If you're lying, I want you where I can see you," he said. He jerked his chin toward the carriage. "Move."

John followed, ribs aching, breath tight.

As they walked away from the lantern-lit yard, the music softened behind them. The warmth faded. The air grew cooler with each step into the shadows beyond the party.

The carriage waited at the edge of the driveway—black lacquered, wheels slick with dew. The driver sat hunched beneath a hood, face hidden. A pair of horses stood in harness, heads lowered, flanks shifting.

John's mouth went dry. The horses looked wrong.

Not sick. Not thin. But their eyes were too pale in the dark, their movements too slow, like puppets waiting for a hand.

Doug shoved John toward the carriage door. "Get in."

John hesitated.

Doug's voice sharpened. "Now."

John climbed in. The carriage interior smelled of leather and old perfume. He sat with his back straight, hands clenched, mask pressing against his cheekbones.

Doug climbed in across from him and shut the door hard. "Don't try anything," he warned.

John didn't answer.

The carriage lurched forward.

Outside, the yard lights receded, becoming a warm smear through the small carriage window. John watched them shrink, watched the house glowing behind them, and tried not to feel relief too early.

He had made one choice for himself tonight—something other than running blindly or obeying.

If he could reach town, he could reach a phone. If he could reach a phone, he could reach Hunter. Police. An ambulance. Reality.

The wheels thumped over ruts. The horses' hooves struck wet dirt with a steady rhythm.

Doug leaned back, arms folded, eyes half-lidded but alert.

John stared at the window.

The drive stretched ahead, framed by trees. Darkness pooled between trunks. The lantern light from the party did not reach far. Beyond it, the world looked like the present again.

John exhaled slowly.

"Where exactly you think you're going?" Doug asked suddenly.

John looked at him. "Town," he said.

Doug's smile twitched. "Town's a ways," he said. "Long enough for a man to do a lot of thinking."

John's ribs tightened around his breath. "I'm not here to hurt anybody," he said.

Doug snorted. "Aren't you?" His gaze flicked to John's hands. "Men who say that usually are."

John bit down on the response that rose automatically—the insult, the threat. Instead he said, "Why are you doing this?"

Doug's eyes narrowed. "Doing what?"

"Guarding him," John said. "Blithe."

Doug's smile turned sour. "He pays," he said. "He protects."

"From what?"

Doug's gaze flicked toward the window as if checking the dark outside. "From everything," he muttered.

The carriage wheels rolled over a patch of gravel and the sound changed. John felt it in his teeth. The driveway had ended. They were on the road.

His pulse quickened. "How much farther?" he asked.

Doug didn't answer.

The horses slowed.

The driver's hooded head lifted slightly, as if listening.

John's skin crawled. "What is it?" he asked.

Doug leaned toward the carriage window. He peered out and then cursed under his breath.

John shifted to look.

The trees on either side of the road seemed closer now, leaning in. The darkness between them looked thick, solid. The air had gone strangely still.

And then, ahead in the road, the lantern light stopped.

Not dimmed. Not faded.

Stopped.

As if the night itself had set down a wall.

John leaned toward the carriage window, squinting into the sudden divide.

It wasn't fog. It wasn't a shadow from the trees. The air itself looked different, as if the road ahead had been dipped in ink.

He pressed his palm against the glass. The pane was cold, colder than the night. His skin stuck to it for a moment before he jerked his hand away.

The lantern light didn't spill forward into that patch. It ended cleanly, an edge too sharp to be natural.

For a heartbeat John saw something beyond it - not trees, not road, but a suggestion of open space and a distant streetlamp, the pale sodium glow of the modern world. Then it was gone, swallowed back into darkness.

His mouth went dry. He grabbed the door latch, instinct screaming to get out and run, to cross whatever this was on his own feet.

Doug's hand slammed down on John's wrist. "Don't," Doug hissed.

John yanked back, ribs flaring. "What is that?" he demanded.

Doug's eyes darted toward the hooded driver. His voice went lower. "The line," he said, as if naming it made it less terrifying. "Now shut up."

John's heart hammered. The line. The bone-and-salt boundary from the yard, here again, wearing a different face.

The horses whickered low, uneasy.

Doug snapped, "Get on!" and banged a fist against the carriage wall.

The horses took one reluctant step forward.

The moment their hooves crossed into that darker patch, they reared.

The carriage jolted violently. John slammed into the seat, ribs flaring with pain. The horses screamed—not the shrill sound of fear alone, but something deeper, as if they had seen an open grave.

The driver yanked the reins, trying to steady them, but the horses fought, eyes rolling white.

The carriage tilted.

Doug threw himself forward, reaching for the door latch. "Stay in!" he barked at John as if that were helpful advice.

The carriage tipped further, wheel lifting off the ground.

John braced his hands against the seat, mask slipping slightly with the motion. He could smell horse sweat now—hot and sour.

Then he saw it.

Between the trees, just beyond the road's edge, shapes moved.

Low and silent.

Wolves.

Not three this time. More. A pack, gliding through the underbrush like shadows with teeth.

John's blood turned to ice.

Doug saw them too. His face went pale under its sunburn. "No," he whispered.

A wolf stepped into the road ahead of the horses.

It stood perfectly still, head lowered, eyes locked on the carriage.

The horses screamed again and bolted sideways.

The carriage toppled.

The world flipped. John felt weightlessness, then impact. Wood cracked. Glass shattered. His shoulder hit hard. His ribs exploded with pain.

He hit the ground and rolled, the mask scraping dirt. Mud filled his mouth.

He forced himself up, gasping.

The carriage lay on its side. The driver had been thrown; the hood lay crumpled in the mud, empty.

John stared at the empty hood and felt something inside him tip.

A driver without a face. A job without a man. Like the house had been borrowing the idea of a person and had decided it didn't need the rest. He thought of the masked figure in the storm and of the mask that had been on his own face and wondered, not for the first time tonight, if the house was running out of costumes.

Empty.

The empty hood lay there like shed skin.

John thought of funerals. Of suits on hangers. Of the way grief made clothing feel obscene because it pretended a body would return to fill it.

The house had dressed the carriage the way it dressed everything: with props and roles and the confidence that men would behave the way they always did when given a script. Driver. Guard. Guest. Victim.

John swallowed hard. In that moment he understood something simple and ugly: it didn't matter what you called yourself. The house would still make you play.

Doug staggered to his feet a few yards away, pistol in hand. He fired into the trees.

The gunshots sounded wrong in the wet night—too sharp, too bright.

The wolves did not run.

One moved closer, slow and sure.

Doug fired again. The wolf flinched and then kept coming.

John watched in horror as Doug's confidence drained out of him. "Back!" Doug shouted. "Back, you—"

The wolf lunged.

It hit Doug low, taking his legs out. Doug went down with a yell. The pistol fired once into the air.

John froze, unable to move.

Doug's screams hit John like a shove. For a heartbeat he took a step forward, reflex and adrenaline, the dumb human instinct to grab and pull and fix.

Then the wolves' eyes swung to him—flat, patient, not hunting Doug now so much as reminding John of his place in the story. John saw, in a flash, Alice on the floor and himself standing there too long with a phone in his hand, waiting for someone else to make a decision. The pattern was the same.

He backed away. He hated himself for it. He ran anyway.

Doug screamed as the wolf's jaws closed on his arm. The sound was human in a way the attic thing's scream had not been—raw, terrified, pleading.

More wolves spilled from the trees, converging.

Doug tried to crawl away, boots kicking in mud, but the pack was on him. Bodies piled. Teeth flashed. Doug's screams turned into wet choking sounds.

John backed away, shaking.

One of the horses had broken free from the overturned carriage. It thrashed in its harness, eyes rolling, trying to drag itself away.

A wolf broke from the pack and went for the horse.

The horse screamed and kicked, hooves striking air and mud. It tried to run.

The wolf leapt and sank its teeth into the horse's throat.

Blood sprayed in a dark arc. Steam rose from it in the cool air.

The horse's scream cut off into a gargle. It collapsed, legs folding.

John stood there, frozen in the strobing light of distant lanterns, watching life leave the animal's eyes.

Then he saw something else—something that made his stomach drop.

At the edge of the road, between two trees, hung another boundary line: vertebrae and twine, swaying gently in the still air.

The wolves were not hunting.

They were guarding.

John turned and ran.

His boots slipped in mud. His ribs protested. He didn't care. He sprinted back toward the faint glow of the party, back toward the house he had wanted to escape, because behind him the pack's attention was shifting.

Doug's screams had stopped.

Now there was only the sound of wolves feeding.

John ran until his lungs burned and his vision tunneled. The lantern glow ahead grew brighter, and with it returned the sounds of the party—music, laughter, clapping—as if nothing had happened in the road's darkness.

He stumbled into the yard, nearly falling.

No one looked at him.

The guests danced. They drank. They laughed.

The house glowed warm and welcoming.

It was obscene.

John ripped the mask off his face and gulped air. He let it drop into the mud at his feet. The night smelled suddenly sweet, almost perfumed.

He expected Doug to appear behind him, pistol raised, shouting. He expected wolves to burst from the tree line and tear into the party.

Nothing happened.

The party continued as if the carriage never left, as if Doug had not died screaming in mud.

John stared at his hands. They were smeared with dirt and blood.

He tried to wipe them on his jeans. The smear only spread, turning his palms into something he didn't recognize.

He looked down again, blinking hard, and the blood was thinner—muddy, unreal. Another blink and it was only dirt. The party lights had a way of laundering the evidence, of making violence something that happened offstage. John held his hands up in front of him like he was praying and felt the nausea of not knowing what was true.

He tried to scrape the blood from beneath his nails. It clung.

At the edge of the driveway stood a hand pump, iron and old. John stumbled to it and worked the handle. Water coughed out in a thin stream and splashed his palms.

For a second the water ran pink.

Then it ran clear, as if the blood had never been there at all.

John stared at his hands, dripping, and the nausea rose again—not from gore, but from uncertainty. He could not tell what belonged to his skin and what belonged to his mind, and that felt like the beginning of madness.

He turned toward the line of workers at the edge of the yard.

Phillip stepped out.

His face was calm, but his eyes held something hard. "You tried," he said quietly.

John swallowed, throat raw. "He's dead," he whispered. "They—wolves—"

Phillip nodded once, as if confirming something he had already known. "Yes," he said.

John stared at him. "You let it happen."

Phillip's voice stayed even. "I did not cause it," he said. "But I will not pretend it surprises me."

John's anger rose fast, a familiar heat. "What the hell is this?" he demanded. "A game? A lesson? I didn't ask for any of it."

Phillip's eyes narrowed. "No," he said. "You did not ask. You arrived."

John's breathing came harsh. "How do I get out?"

Phillip glanced toward the porch where Blithe's laughter rang out again. "Not by following him," Phillip said.

John's eyes flicked toward Blithe. The man stood with a drink in hand, smiling at someone as if nothing in the world could touch him.

John felt a pulse of hatred so strong it made him dizzy.

Phillip looked back at John. "Come," he said. "There are those who can speak to you without lies."

John hesitated. "Who?"

Phillip's expression didn't soften. "Those who keep the door shut," he said again. "Those who keep the hunger from spilling into the world."

John swallowed. "The workers?"

Phillip's gaze held his. "The name you use does not change what they are," he said.

He turned and started walking along the yard's edge, away from the music, toward the shadowed outline of the barn beyond the lantern light. John followed, because he had no other direction left.

As they walked, the party's warmth faded behind them. The air cooled. The lanterns grew fewer. The laughter became distant.

By the time they reached the barn, the yard light did not touch it at all.

The barn stood as John had seen it before—rotted, sagging, a dark mouth against the night.

Phillip stopped at the door and placed his hand on the warped wood.

It opened without a sound.

Inside, the lantern John had left in the pit beneath the barn still burned—impossible, distant light rising through cracks in boards. The smell of damp earth rose up.

Phillip stepped inside first. John followed, heart pounding, ribs aching, hands clenched.

In the barn's shadows, figures waited.

Not a crowd. Not a mob. A small circle of men and women dressed in plain clothes—linen, cotton, work-worn. They stood with straight backs and steady eyes.

They were not servants here.

In the lantern's weak light he could see details he hadn't allowed himself to notice earlier: callused palms, cracked nails, the faint puckered lines of old scars. One of the men wore a strip of cloth around his neck that might once have been a collar. Another woman held her chin high as if she had spent a lifetime practicing dignity under someone else's gaze.

They did not look like ghosts out of a story. They looked like people who had been forced into someone else's story and had refused, at the end, to stay quiet.

They did not bow. They did not avert their gaze.

They looked at John the way a judge looks at a man who has already spoken his alibi.

Phillip stood beside John and lowered his head slightly—respect, not submission. "He is here," he said.

A woman in the circle stepped forward. She was older, hair wrapped, hands scarred. Her eyes held exhaustion and steel.

"You brought a lost man," she said.

Phillip nodded. "He tried to cross the line," Phillip replied. "He failed."

The woman's gaze shifted to John. "Most do," she said.

John's throat worked. "Who are you?" he asked.

The woman's voice stayed calm. "We are the ones who hold," she said. "We hold what this land made, so it does not roam free."

John shook his head, confused and angry. "I don't understand."

"You understand hunger," the woman said, and her eyes sharpened. "You understand taking more than you give. You understand calling it something else so you can sleep at night."

John flinched as if struck.

The woman stepped closer, and the others in the circle tightened around her, not threatening but present. Witnesses.

"This house belonged to a man who made his living on pain," she continued. "He made a door. He made a place where suffering could be traded like coin." Her gaze cut toward the distant sound of music. "He is still here."

John's breath caught. "Blithe," he whispered.

The woman nodded. "He remains," she said. "And he is not the only thing that remains. The land remembers. The walls remember. And when a man comes with the right kind of rot inside him, the door opens."

John's hands trembled. "I'm not him," he said. "I'm not —"

"No," the woman agreed. "You are not him."

Her eyes held John steady.

"But you are not innocent either," she said.

The words landed in John like a weight. He wanted to argue. He wanted to scream. He wanted to say all the things he'd said to Alice—excuses dressed as explanations.

Instead he stood there, breathing shallow, feeling the ache in his ribs and the ache deeper than ribs.

Phillip spoke quietly beside him. "They are Gatekeepers," he said. "They keep the door closed."

John stared at the circle. "From what?" he asked.

The woman's answer came without hesitation.

"From you," she said.

From men like you, John heard. From hunger dressed up as need. From the kind of selfishness that didn't look like malice until you counted the bodies.

His mouth went dry.

Chapter Fifteen: The Offer

The barn felt different with the Gatekeepers inside it.

Not warmer. Not safer. Simply... steadier. As if, for the first time tonight, John had stepped into a space where the air didn't lie.

The circle held. No one reached for him. No one threatened him. They just watched, eyes bright in the dim.

Phillip stood at John's shoulder, quiet as a shadow.

John swallowed and forced himself to speak. "You said you keep the door closed," he said to the older woman. "What door?"

The woman's gaze stayed on him. "The one he opened," she said. "The one built out of pain and want."

"He," John repeated, and he didn't have to ask.

"Blithe," Phillip murmured.

John's ribs hurt when he breathed. He pressed a palm against his side, trying to steady himself. "So shut it," he said. "If you're keeping it closed, then shut it. End it."

A man in the circle stepped forward. He was tall, broad-shouldered, face lined as if carved by years. His voice was low and careful. "You think a door closes because you wish it," he said. "You think evil ends because you are tired of it."

John's temper flared. "I think I'm in a house where a dead woman just called me on the phone," he snapped. "I think I've been chased by—by a thing in an attic. I think a man just got eaten alive on the road. I think I'm allowed to be tired."

The tall man held his gaze. "You are allowed," he said. "And you are also responsible."

The words hit John hard enough that he almost laughed. "Responsible?" he repeated. "For wolves?"

The older woman's voice cut in, steady. "Not for wolves," she said. "For what you brought."

John's mouth went dry. "I didn't bring this," he said. "I came here because Hunter wanted me sober. That's it."

The woman nodded slowly, as if listening. "You came here because you had nowhere else to go," she corrected. "You came here because the drink stopped working. You came here because grief made a hole in you, and you wanted something to fill it that wasn't truth."

John felt heat rise in his face. "You don't know me."

The woman's eyes didn't blink. "We know patterns," she said. "We know men who take and call it need. We know men who hurt and call it accident. We know men who fail and call it fate."

The older woman's gaze stayed on John, unblinking, as if she'd learned long ago that looking away was a kind of surrender.

Phillip shifted beside him and spoke her name, quiet but clear. "Miss Ruth."

The name landed with weight. Not a title. Not a role. A person.

Ruth's mouth tightened slightly at the sound of it - not offended, not softened. Acknowledging. She lifted a hand and John saw the deep scarring across her knuckles, old injuries that had healed into hard lines.

They were warning him what the house would do with the parts of him that wanted to be worse.

And the circle of people in front of him were not begging him to be better.

The house was listening.

But his body kept telling the truth.

Some part of him still wanted to argue. To say this was insane. To say the wolves were a symptom and the masks were a fever dream and he was just a man in withdrawal.

John stared at them, breathing shallow.

Eli nodded once. "If you want to leave," he said, "you will be offered a way. It will look like justice. It will sound like mercy. And it will cost more than you can afford."

Ruth cut him off with a look. "No acting," she said.

"I didn't—" he started.

John's mind flashed to Alice on the bathroom floor, to the white rug, to the neat list of practicalities on his phone. To his own hands shaking like they were trying to confess.

Ruth stepped forward again. "We do not ask you to suffer for us," she said. "We ask you to stop making other people the price."

John flinched.

Eli's mouth twitched, almost a smile. "You're already suffering," he said. "Don't turn it into a weapon."

John heard the trap in that and felt anger flare, hot and familiar. "So you want me to starve him," he snapped. "You want me to suffer so you can keep—what? Your door closed? Your righteous line in the dirt?"

Phillip's voice came from beside John, tight. "Blithe feeds on bargains," he said. "He feeds on men who think the world owes them relief."

"The hunger," Ruth said, and this time the word had weight. Not metaphor. Not poetry. A thing with teeth.

John shook his head, frustration and fear tangling. "Walks out as what?" he demanded.

Eli's gaze didn't soften. "We are the ones who stayed," he said. "Not because this land is ours - it never was - but because if we leave, what was made here walks out with you.”

John swallowed. “Then what are you?” he asked, and he hated how small it sounded.

The words landed like a door slamming.

“My name is Eli,” he said. Not a title. A name given back to himself. “And I am not your penance.”

Ruth’s eyes flicked to the young man. Permission.

John’s hands clenched. The mask of his story - the one he couldn’t take off - felt suddenly very thin.

“You didn’t have to,” the man replied. “Men like you come here and think suffering is a currency. You think if you stand in front of it long enough you’ll be forgiven.”

John’s throat tightened. “I didn’t say—”

“You see us and you think we’re here to teach you,” the young man said. His voice was quiet, but it carried. “Like this is a lesson built for you.”

He met John’s gaze without apology.

A young man stood near the back with a split lip that didn’t look old. His eyes were bright and steady. Not defiant. Awake. The kind of awake that came from surviving things that should have killed you.

Then she lowered it and stepped aside just enough that the rest of the circle could be seen as individuals, not an outline.

Ruth held her scarred hand up a moment longer, not as a plea and not as a threat. A statement.

“They took our names here,” Ruth said. “Gave us theirs. Made us answer to it.”

She glanced toward the distant music, the glow of lanterns beyond the barn boards. “He still likes doing that.”

John's throat tightened. "So why stay?" he asked before he could stop himself. "If you hate him, if you hate this place - why stay?"

Ruth's eyes narrowed, not at the question, but at the assumption under it. "Because leaving is what he wants," she said. "The door opens wider every time the ones who know it walk away."

She stepped closer, and the circle subtly adjusted, giving her room. Not because she commanded them - because they chose to.

"We stay," Ruth continued, "because this land made a kind of hunger that doesn't die when the bodies do. It remembers. It waits. If it gets loose, it doesn't stop at this porch."

Her gaze cut into John. "And because men like you keep showing up," she said, "thinking you can outrun the consequences you carried in with you."

John felt heat rise in his face, anger and shame tangled together. He wanted to argue. He wanted to say he hadn't meant it, that he wasn't like Blithe, that he loved Alice.

Ruth didn't give him the room to turn it into performance. "Say her name," she said suddenly.

John blinked, thrown. "What?"

"Say your wife's name," Ruth repeated, voice even. "Just her name. No apology. No story. Say it."

John's mouth went dry. The barn seemed to tilt, the lantern light swimming.

"Alice," he whispered.

Ruth held his gaze for a beat longer, then nodded once, almost imperceptible. "Good," she said. "Now don't wear her like a mask."

Phillip exhaled, the sound tight in his throat, as if Ruth had said something he'd been holding back.

John's throat tightened. He could hear Alice in those words, and it made him want to tear the world apart.

Phillip spoke softly. "They have held this place a long time," he said. "They have seen many men come through the door."

"How?" John demanded. "How are you doing any of this?"

The tall man answered. "By refusing him," he said simply.

John stared. "Refusing Blithe?"

"Refusing the lie," the man said. "He offers bargains. He offers stories that make your hands clean. We refuse."

John's mind snagged on the word. "Bargains," he repeated.

The older woman's gaze sharpened. "He bargains with hunger," she said. "He trades pain for power. He trades blame for relief." Her eyes held John steady. "He will trade you too, if you let him."

John's pulse pounded. "Then why not kill him?" he demanded. "Why not end it?"

The circle's faces tightened, a shared tension that passed through them like wind through grass.

The older woman looked down for a moment, then back up. When she spoke, her voice carried weight. "Because he is a sickness in the land," she said. "And sickness does not leave just because you cut away a symptom."

John shook his head, frustrated. "That's not an answer."

"It is," Phillip murmured. "Just not the one you want."

John turned on Phillip. "You keep saying that. Like wanting to leave a nightmare is some moral failing."

Phillip met his gaze without flinching. "Wanting to leave is not the failing," he said. "Wanting to leave without looking at what is chasing you—" He shook his head once. "That is."

John's hands balled into fists. "I didn't kill my wife," he said, and the words came out like a plea and a threat at the same time.

The older woman watched him for a long moment. "No," she said.

John blinked, thrown.

She stepped closer, and the lantern light caught the lines on her face. "You did not put hands on her throat," she said. "You did not strike her down." She paused. "But you do not get to hide behind that."

John's mouth opened. Nothing came out.

The woman's voice stayed level. "There are deaths that happen in one moment," she said. "And there are deaths that happen by inches. By a thousand small refusals. By making love into something someone has to earn back every day."

John felt the room sway. The words crawled under his skin. He wanted to deny them, to spit them out, to point at the wolves and the attic thing and say none of this is real.

But his ribs hurt. His hands shook. His body was telling the truth even when his mind refused.

The tall man spoke again. "The door stays closed because we hold it," he said. "But when the right kind of man comes, the door strains. It wants to open. Hunger wants to be fed."

John's eyes flicked toward the barn's darkness. "I'm the right kind of man," he said, voice flat.

The older woman's expression didn't soften. "You are a man who knows how to avoid pain," she said. "That is the kind the house likes."

John's jaw clenched. "So what do you want from me?" he asked. "Confession? An apology? You want me to cry? Fine." He laughed, brittle. "I'm sorry I was a bad husband. I'm sorry I drank. I'm sorry I made jokes that weren't funny. Is that what you want?"

The older woman's eyes narrowed. "No," she said.

The single syllable held more disgust than shouting.

"We want truth," she continued. "Not performance. Not the easy words a man uses so he can say he did something."

John's skin flushed hot. "Then tell me what the truth is," he snapped. "If you know so much, tell me."

The circle went still.

Phillip exhaled slowly, and for the first time since John had met him, Phillip looked tired. "They cannot," he said.

John stared. "Why not?"

Phillip's voice was quiet. "Because you would use it as another story," he said. "If they tell you, you will pick the parts that make you the victim."

John's mouth opened. He wanted to argue. The words stuck.

The older woman stepped back into the circle. "You will be shown," she said. "This house will show you what you do not want to see. When it does, you will have a choice. Take it. Or turn away."

"And if I turn away?" John asked.

The tall man's answer was immediate. "Then you will stay," he said.

John felt his stomach drop. "Stay where?" he whispered.

Phillip's gaze held his. "Here," he said. "In this loop. In this hunger. In your own making."

John's mind raced. He pictured himself trapped, running the same halls forever, hearing Alice's voice until it shredded him.

"No," he whispered.

The older woman's voice softened—not kind, but honest. "There is a way out," she said. "There is always a way out. But it is not the way men like you prefer."

John's throat went tight. "Tell me," he said.

She looked at him for a long moment. "Stop lying," she said. "To yourself. To the dead. To the living."

John opened his mouth.

Nothing came out.

The truth crowded behind his teeth like a swarm, each piece sharp: the smell of chemicals, the box under the sink, the way he'd laughed at something that should have terrified him. The way Alice had looked at him, not angry—not anymore—but finished.

His tongue felt thick. His throat felt sewn shut. He could confess to being a drunk. He could confess to being selfish. Those were safe, familiar sins. They let him keep the real thing unnamed.

He swallowed and tasted metal again.

John's temper flared again, but it was thinner now, edged with fear. "That's not instructions," he said.

The tall man stepped forward and nodded toward the barn wall. "You see that door?" he asked.

John followed the gesture. In the barn's gloom, a smaller door sat half-hidden behind stacked boards—an old access door leading down to the pit beneath, perhaps.

John swallowed. "Yes," he said.

"That is where the land keeps what it cannot swallow," the tall man said. "Go there. Stand at the threshold. Speak what you have not spoken."

John's hands trembled. "And then what?" he asked.

The older woman's answer was quiet. "Then we will know whether you are a man who wants freedom," she said, "or a man who wants escape."

John stared at them. The difference felt like a blade.

He didn't answer.

Phillip touched John's elbow lightly, steering him. "Come," Phillip said. "You have heard enough for tonight."

John jerked away. "No," he snapped. "I haven't heard anything. I've heard riddles."

Phillip's eyes hardened. "Riddles keep you alive," he said.

John laughed, harsh. "Alive?" He gestured at his bruised body. "This place is trying to kill me."

Phillip's voice dropped. "This place is trying to make you tell the truth," he corrected. "Death is just one of its tools."

John stared at him, breath shallow.

Phillip's gaze softened a fraction. "I know you want a simple enemy," he said. "A man you can hit. A thing you can stab. The truth is harder. It doesn't bleed when you strike it."

John swallowed. "Then what is the masked man?" he asked. "Because he's out there. I saw him."

Phillip's eyes flicked away for the first time, and the movement was small but telling. "It wears the face you give it," he said. "The more you run, the faster it comes."

John's blood cooled. "What does that mean?"

Phillip looked back at him. "It means you cannot outrun yourself," he said.

John's chest tightened around a sudden, terrible image: the masked man's build. The way it had moved—quick, urgent, familiar. The way it had raised a hand to the glass and waited.

His own hand had risen in answer, like muscle memory.

John shook his head hard. "No," he whispered.

Phillip's voice softened again. "Come," he said. "Before Blithe notices you are gone."

John let Phillip guide him out of the barn.

They stepped back into the yard's edge, where the party's light and music reached like warm fingers. The lanterns swung gently. Laughter rose. It looked, for a heartbeat, like a normal celebration.

Then John saw Doug's absence.

The carriage was gone. No one asked where Doug went. No one looked for him. The party swallowed the missing man as easily as it swallowed spilled liquor.

John's stomach turned.

Phillip stopped beside the line of workers. Their faces watched John—not with hatred, not with pity.

With expectation.

"Why are they looking at me like that?" John whispered.

Phillip didn't answer at first. Then he said, "Because the door strains," he replied. "Because what happens with you matters. Not just for you."

John's jaw tightened. "I didn't ask to matter," he said.

Phillip's voice was quiet. "None of us did," he said.

John's anger rose again, searching for a target. It landed on Blithe's porch, where the man stood laughing, drink in hand, as if he were made of ease.

John felt something like hate, but underneath it was envy. The effortless confidence. The certainty. The way Blithe seemed untouched by consequence.

John walked toward the porch before he fully decided to.

Phillip's hand caught his arm. "Don't," Phillip warned.

John looked at him. "He has answers," John said.

Phillip's gaze sharpened. "He has bargains," Phillip corrected. "And bargains are always paid."

John yanked his arm free. "I'm tired of being told what not to do," he snapped. "I'm tired of—of games. I want this to end."

Phillip's expression tightened, and for a moment John saw something like sorrow there. "Then choose the hard ending," Phillip said softly.

John didn't answer.

He climbed the porch steps.

Inside the house, the air was warmer, heavy with candle smoke and sweet liquor. People moved past him, masked faces turning, laughing, touching. John felt like he was walking through a dream where everyone else knew the script.

He found the office door and pushed it open.

Blithe sat behind his desk as if he'd been waiting. The fire crackled. The decanter gleamed. The glass of whiskey sat where John had left it.

Blithe smiled. "There you are," he said warmly. "I was beginning to think my party bored you."

John stepped inside and shut the door. "What is this place?" he demanded. "What are you?"

Blithe leaned back in his chair, fingers steepled. "A host," he said. "A memory. A hunger. Take your pick."

John's hands shook. "Those people in the barn," he said. "They told me I can't leave."

Blithe's smile softened into sympathy, so convincing it almost made John dizzy. "Ah," he said. "The Gatekeepers."

John stared at him. "You know them."

Blithe chuckled. "Of course I know them," he said. "They've been in my way a very long time."

John's pulse hammered. "Are they telling the truth?" he asked. "Am I trapped here?"

Blithe's gaze slid over John's face—unmasked now, raw. "You are inconvenienced," he corrected. "You are... delayed."

John's throat tightened. "How do I get out?"

Blithe stood and moved around the desk, unhurried. "You want the truth?" he asked. "Or do you want relief?"

John's voice cracked. "Both," he admitted.

Blithe smiled as if John had said something charming. "The Gatekeepers hold the door," he said. "They stand between this place and the world and pretend they are heroes." He shook his head, almost sad. "They call it duty. I call it vanity."

John remembered the woman's eyes in the barn, steady and tired. Vanity didn't fit her.

Blithe watched John's face closely. "Did they tell you to confess?" he asked.

John stiffened. "They said I have to tell the truth."

Blithe's smile widened. "There it is," he murmured. "The trick."

John's jaw clenched. "What trick?"

Blithe leaned closer. His voice was soft, intimate, as if sharing something secret. "They want you to bleed yourself out in words," he said. "They want you to crawl. They want you to say you are the villain and they are the judges." He tilted his head. "And when you do, they'll keep you anyway. Because a man who confesses is a man who can be controlled."

John's pulse thudded. The idea sank into him with the ease of a lie that matches a fear.

Blithe continued, gentle as a priest. "They have had centuries to practice," he said. "They know how to make a man doubt his own hands."

John's breathing turned shallow. "So you can let me out," he said.

Blithe smiled. "I can," he said simply.

John's stomach dropped. "Why?" he whispered. "Why would you?"

Blithe's eyes gleamed. "Because you are useful," he said. "Because you are hungry. Because you already understand how to take what you want and call it something else."

Blithe's words slid into John like a hand into a pocket. You are useful. The phrase didn't sound like praise. It sounded like ownership.

John wanted to deny it. Wanted to say he wasn't that kind of man. But denial had been his talent for years, and he was tired of how easy it came.

John flinched.

Blithe touched John's shoulder lightly. The contact made John's skin crawl. "You want to leave," Blithe said. "I want the door unguarded. We can help each other."

John's voice came out hoarse. "What do you want me to do?"

Blithe stepped back and nodded toward the fireplace. "Sit," he said. "And listen."

John didn't sit. He stayed standing, like he might bolt.

Blithe's smile didn't falter. He moved to a cabinet near the fireplace and removed things that didn't belong to a party: rope, tools, a leather pouch heavy with cartridges, and an ornate wooden box carved with African animals—lion, elephant, giraffe—its green marble knob catching the firelight.

John's breath hitched. He'd seen that box before, upstairs in the wardrobe, like the house had been rehearsing this moment and waiting for him to play his part.

Blithe lifted the box and set it on the desk. He flipped it open.

Inside, a revolver rested in velvet.

John's mouth went dry. "That's—"

"A tool," Blithe said. "A solution. The simple kind you like."

John stared at the gun. "I don't—" He swallowed. "I'm not—"

Blithe's eyes softened. "You've held knives tonight," he said. "You've run. You've fought. You've watched a man die. Don't pretend you're delicate now."

John's hands shook. "What are you asking me?" he whispered.

Blithe's voice was calm. "Remove the Gatekeepers," he said. "One by one, if necessary." He said it the way a man might talk about clearing brush from a road.

John's stomach turned. "They didn't hurt me," he said.

Blithe's gaze sharpened. "They kept you here," he replied. "They accused you. They spoke to you like you were a child. They made your wife's death into a lecture."

John flinched as if slapped.

Blithe leaned in, voice softer. "They are not innocent," he murmured. "They chose this. They chose to stay and play gods on my land."

John almost believed it for half a second, because believing it would make the next step easier.

Then the image of the line of workers—faces down, hands busy, backs straight with learned caution—came back, and the lie cracked. Choice was a word people with power liked. Blithe watched him, waiting for the crack to widen.

John's mind flashed back to the woman's tired eyes. The tall man's steady voice. Phillip's warning.

Blithe watched him hesitate and smiled. "Here is the truth," he said. "They are the lock. If you break the lock, you leave."

John's throat tightened. "And what happens to you?" he asked.

Blithe spread his hands. "I continue," he said simply.

John stared at him. "So you're asking me to murder people so you can keep—what? A house?"

Blithe's smile turned faint. "Don't be dramatic," he said. "It's not murder when the dead are already dead."

John's skin crawled. "They're not dead," he whispered. "They're right there."

Blithe's voice stayed calm. "And yet they have stood in that barn for generations," he replied. "Holding. Judging. Playing at righteousness." He shrugged. "Perhaps it is time they rested."

John's mind spun.

He wanted out. He wanted morning. He wanted a phone in his hand and Hunter's voice in his ear telling him it was going to be okay.

He also wanted someone to blame. Someone living and tangible.

Blithe offered that like a drink.

John's lips parted. "If I do this..." he whispered. "If I kill them... I can leave?"

Blithe's smile returned, bright. "Yes," he said. "You will walk out as if you were never here. You will go back to your world. You will grieve in peace." He tilted his head, eyes warm. "You will stop hearing her voice."

Alice's voice rose in John's head like a tide.

You promised.

John's hands clenched.

Blithe's voice softened. "She would want you to move on," he said. "She would want you to survive."

John's throat tightened. "You don't get to speak for her," he said, but the protest sounded weak.

Blithe lifted the revolver and placed it in John's hands with care, like handing over a sacred object.

The gun was heavier than John expected. Cold. Real.

John stared at it.

He turned it in his hands, watching the cylinder catch the firelight. The click of metal on metal sounded too much like the phone's rotary wheel—an old, patient mechanism doing what it was made to do. He saw brass in the chambers. Real bullets. Real weight. Then, uninvited, the thought arrived: one loud answer, one clean bang. The craving for silence dressed itself up as courage.

He wondered, with a calm that scared him, how many problems could be solved by a single trigger pull.

The thought arrived like an old friend. He'd had it in bar bathrooms at closing time, in the dark of his apartment when Alice had finally stopped arguing. Not the desire to die, exactly. The desire to stop. To end the noise.

He swallowed and told himself this was different. He wasn't pointing it at himself. Not yet.

Blithe's hand closed over John's, firm. "This is the part where you stop being hunted," he murmured. "This is the part where you become the man who decides."

John's pulse hammered. He could feel sweat sliding down his spine.

In the back of his mind, Jim's voice echoed: Don't drink what it offers. Don't follow the mask.

Pay the price.

John looked up at Blithe. "Where are they?" he asked, voice flat.

Blithe's smile widened, satisfied. "In the barn," he said. "Where they like to stand and pretend they own the night."

John's fingers tightened around the revolver.

Blithe stepped back and opened the office door. "Go," he said gently. "Do what you must."

John walked out of the office with the gun hidden under his coat, heart pounding like it wanted to escape his chest. The party noises washed over him. Laughter. Music. The scrape of shoes on wood.

No one stopped him.

On the porch, John paused and looked out into the yard.

Phillip stood near the tree line, face turned toward him. Their eyes met.

Phillip's expression shifted—recognition, then dread.

He started forward.

John turned away before Phillip could reach him.

He descended the steps and headed toward the barn, the revolver's weight dragging at his side like a promise.

As he crossed the yard's edge, the lantern light faded, and with it the laughter. The air grew cold again. The house behind him seemed to exhale.

At the barn door, John stopped.

He could hear nothing inside. No voices. No footsteps.

He reached for the latch, hand trembling.

For a moment, he saw himself as Alice must have seen him—standing on a threshold, choosing whether to come in or stay out.

He swallowed.

Then he opened the door and stepped into the dark.

The door swung shut behind him without a sound.

And somewhere, deep in the house, the television clicked on again.

ACT III

Chapter Sixteen: The Pit

John stood on the porch with the revolver hanging at his side and tried to remember why he had come out here in the first place. The night kept slipping through his fingers. Not like a normal night you forget because you drank too much and the details dissolve into shame. This was different. This was the house taking pieces. This was his own mind tearing its seams.

The yard was a churned-up smear of mud and dead grass. The storm had bent the trees low, branches whipping and hissing. Somewhere beyond the property line, the world still existed - roads, streetlights, diners open late with bad coffee and worse mercy. Somewhere beyond the property line there were people who didn't wear masks.

John's legs wanted the road.

His hands wanted the bottle.

The house wanted whatever was left.

He walked down the porch steps and into the rain. Cold soaked through his flannel immediately, making it cling to his skin like a second, heavy guilt. Each step sent a tremor up his calves. Not just weakness. Not just exhaustion. The tremor had meaning now. His body's Morse code. Need. Need. Need.

He turned his face toward the darkness where the drive should be. He could not see it clearly through the rain, but he could hear it: the faint suggestion of distance, the way open space sounds different from walls.

If he could reach the road, he could call for help. He could flag someone down. He could get out.

He started walking.

The wind shoved at him. Rain stung his eyes. Mud grabbed his boots like hands.

He kept the revolver low, not because he trusted it, but because he did not trust himself. The weight of it was wrong. Too final. Too clean for what he was.

Ten steps.

Twenty.

Thirty.

He forced himself to count because counting was a kind of anchor. Counting was what you did when the world wanted you to drift.

He reached the old oak at the edge of the yard - or he thought he did. Its trunk was black with rain, its branches a ragged crown. He put a hand on the bark and felt the slick, living texture beneath his palm. Real. This was real.

He stepped past it.

The wind shifted.

For a moment, he smelled something that did not belong in rain: stale whiskey. A phantom scent. Memory, maybe. Or the house reminding him what it offered.

John swallowed and kept walking.

The ground sloped. The grass thinned. He should have seen the road by now - a strip of pale gravel, the faint shine of wet asphalt. Instead, the darkness ahead stayed stubbornly featureless, like a curtain.

He slowed.

The sound of the rain changed, becoming louder, tighter. Like he was walking into a smaller space.

John turned his head.

The porch was behind him again.

Not far behind him. Not at the distance it should have been after thirty counted steps. The farmhouse loomed in the rain as if he had never left it, its windows black and watchful. The barn sat off to the side, hulking and patient, a darker shape against the storm.

John stopped.

His breath came in short, hot pulls. He looked down at his boots, at the churned mud beneath them, and tried to make his brain accept what his eyes were telling it.

He had not walked in a circle.

He had walked in a line.

He had counted.

He had touched the tree.

And somehow, he was back.

A laugh scraped out of him, dry and ugly. "No," he said aloud, because saying it was another kind of anchor. "No. That's - that's not how it works."

The rain answered by hitting his face harder.

John turned away from the porch and started again, this time angling to the right, toward where the fence line should run. The fence was old, the kind of thing meant to keep animals in, not people out. He remembered seeing it earlier, half collapsed, buried in weeds.

He found it in three steps.

The boards were there, wet and warped, nailed to posts that leaned like tired men. John grabbed one and followed it, head down against the rain, boots slipping.

He kept counting.

He kept his hand on the fence.

He kept moving.

After what should have been a minute, after what should have been a hundred steps, the fence ended.

Not at a gate. Not at a corner. It simply stopped, as if someone had cut the world off there and decided the rest wasn't necessary.

John stared at the last post.

Beyond it was open darkness and rain.

He took one step forward.

The air changed.

It didn't feel colder. It felt wrong. Thick, like invisible syrup. His ears popped. The sound of rain seemed to mute, then sharpen, as if a hand had turned the volume down and then up again. His skin prickled.

He froze with his foot half raised and thought of Hunter's rules. Do not cross the bone line. Do not answer after dark. Do not go under the house.

Rules were just fear dressed up as control. Until they weren't.

John lowered his foot back to the mud.

The wrongness eased, not disappearing, just retreating, as if whatever waited beyond that invisible boundary had decided to be patient.

John backed away from the last fence post.

He turned slowly.

The yard behind him was a smear of gray and black, rain making everything shine. The farmhouse sat to his left, porch light burning, patient. The drive disappeared into trees to his right.

John stared at the tree line and felt a sudden, childish certainty that if he just picked a different direction—if he refused the obvious path—the house's trap would fail. A maze only worked if you agreed to follow its walls.

He started walking along the fence line instead.

The fence posts were old, their tops split and softened by weather. Barbed wire sagged between them in loose, rusted loops. Rain beaded on the barbs and dropped like slow tears.

John kept his eyes on the ground to keep from losing his balance. Mud grabbed at his boots. His breath came hard, the exertion punching heat into his chest and then leaving it there to cool into shakier panic.

He counted steps without meaning to. Ten. Twenty. Thirty.

A hundred.

The fence should have curved. The property should have ended. He should have found a corner or a break, a place where the world admitted it had edges.

It didn't.

The posts marched on, identical in the rain, identical in the weak porch glow that seemed to follow him no matter where he went. He passed the same knot in the wire twice—he was sure of it. A twisted loop like a question mark, snagged with a strip of gray cloth.

He stopped and stared.

The strip of cloth fluttered once, as if acknowledging him.

John felt his stomach drop. He lifted his boot and looked at the tread. Mud clung in thick ridges. Somewhere in his mind, a small rational voice offered explanations: You're turned around. You're panicking. Everything looks the same in rain.

But the cloth looked familiar in a way that had nothing to do with weather.

He reached into his pocket and pulled out his phone again, even though he already knew what he would see.

Black screen. Dead.

He shook it once, hard, like that could restart time. Nothing.

He slid it back into his pocket and kept walking.

The rain eased. Not stopped—just thinned, as if the storm were deciding whether to stay interested. The sound of it on leaves softened. The yard quieted, and in the quiet John became aware of something else beneath it.

A hum.

Low. Steady.

Like a television left on in another room.

He froze and listened, trying to locate it.

The hum didn't come from the house. It didn't come from the barn. It seemed to come from the ground itself, from the wet earth under his feet, as if the property had a current running beneath it and his bones were the antenna.

John backed up one step.

The hum faded.

He stepped forward again.

It returned, faint but certain.

His skin prickled. He thought of Hunter's list—line stays unbroken—and felt the shape of the rule settle in his chest. Not as a superstition. As a boundary.

He swallowed. His throat clicked. He looked up and realized the fence posts ahead had begun to change.

Not in a way he could point to easily. The wood was the same. The wire was the same. But the spacing was wrong, the rhythm off, like a song played slightly too slow. The trees beyond seemed to lean closer together, branches knitting into a darker wall.

John's breath snagged.

He took another step and felt it: the same wrongness as before, thick as a membrane. The air resisted him. His ears popped as if he'd changed altitude. Rain struck his hood and then seemed to fall in slow motion.

He raised his hand in front of his face and watched his fingers shake.

In the mud at his feet, his footprints stretched behind him—deep boot marks filling with water.

Ahead of him, impossibly, were more boot marks.

Fresh. Sharp. Leading forward along the fence line as if he had already walked this exact route.

John stared at them until his eyes ached.

A laugh tried to rise in his throat, hysterical and thin. He forced it down.

He stepped closer, crouched, and touched the edge of one print with his fingertip. The mud was cold and slick and real.

He could smell himself on it—wet leather, sweat, the sour edge of fear.

The print was his.

John straightened slowly.

He did not remember walking ahead. He did not remember turning back.

He did not remember any of this.

The hum under the ground thickened, pleased, as if recognition was payment.

John backed away from the boot prints. The wrongness eased immediately, retreating the way it had at the fence post—patient, permissive. As if the property was not forcing him, exactly. As if it was simply making sure he made the choice it wanted him to make.

His chest burned. He turned, not running yet because running felt like agreement with panic, and he clung to pride the way he once clung to a bottle.

The porch light was in the same place—exactly where he'd left it.

So was the farmhouse.

The yard was the same churned mud.

And the barn door—he saw it now, from this angle—gaped open in the rain, a narrow wedge of black that looked too deep to be an ordinary space.

The barn's mouth was open.

He did not remember it being open.

A narrow wedge of black yawned between the boards, and in that wedge the darkness looked deeper than night. Not empty. Occupied.

John's stomach tightened.

He could go back into the farmhouse. He could lock the doors. He could sit on the couch and wait for morning like a man waiting for sentencing.

Or he could go where the house was clearly steering him.

Blithe's words came back to him with an intimacy that felt like hands on his shoulders.

One act. Then the door opens.

John stared at the open barn as rain ran down his face like sweat. He tried to decide whether he wanted the door to open or whether he wanted it to stay shut forever.

A whisper threaded through the storm, so quiet it might have been his own thought.

It wasn't your fault.

John's jaw clenched.

Another whisper, closer, warmer, wearing the shape of comfort.

She chose it.

He flinched as if struck. That wasn't comfort. That was poison offered with a clean label.

John lifted the revolver, not aiming it at anything yet, just reminding himself he still had a choice.

"I don't know," he said into the rain, voice shaking. "I don't know what happened."

The barn waited.

John took one step toward it.

Then another.

The mud tried to keep him. The wind tried to shove him back. His body tried to fold in on itself from fatigue and withdrawal and the simple fact of being a man who had finally run out of lies strong enough to stand on.

He went anyway.

He reached the threshold and paused, breathing hard, listening.

Inside the barn, something shifted.

Not a creak.

Not a rat.

A presence adjusting itself, like someone making room.

John took a breath and stepped forward.

The barn swallowed him.

One second he was in the open, wind needling his wet hair, the farmhouse behind him exhaling candle-warm light. The next he was inside a mouth of black timber and old rot, and the door shut with the soft finality of a coffin lid.

John stood still and listened.

No music.

No laughter.

No soft clink of glasses. Just rain on the roof and the slow, patient drip of water somewhere deeper in the building, counting time in a language he didn't know.

His breath smoked in the cold. The revolver hung at his side, dragging his arm down like a weight tied to a river stone. He could feel the tremor in his hand even through the grip--his body insisting, in its own crude Morse code, that it wanted the bottle more than it wanted air.

Blithe had said the Gatekeepers waited in the barn.

John remembered the way Ruth had looked at him there--steady, tired, unimpressed by his suffering. He remembered the tilt of her head, as if she were listening to something behind him, something he couldn't hear.

He remembered Blithe's voice, softer than kindness.

One act. Then the door opens.

John took a careful step forward. The floorboard groaned under him, a wet, wounded sound.

"Phillip?" he called, and hated how small it sounded in the dark.

Nothing answered.

He moved farther in, using the revolver as a kind of talisman. It was absurd, the way the weight of metal could turn into courage. But courage was just a story you told yourself to keep walking, and John had been living on stories for a long time.

The barn smelled like hay gone sour and mouse droppings and rust. Something sweet hid underneath that-- old spilled liquor that had seeped into the wood and lived there, rancid and stubborn. It was the smell of a bar after last call, the smell of cheap regret.

Lightning flashed through gaps in the boards, sketching the interior in hard white strokes: bales slumped like sleeping animals; a ladder up to a loft that might have held children once; hooks on the rafters, dark with age; a length of chain nailed to a post, swaying slightly as if someone had brushed past it.

John's throat seized.

He told himself it was just old farm junk. Old South rot. Old stories people handed down to keep kids out of places where nails stuck up and boards caved in.

But the hush in here didn't feel like abandonment.

It felt like waiting.

John moved deeper, letting the flashlight sweep in slow arcs.

Dust floated in the beam like ash. The air had that particular barn-stale smell—hay that had sweated and dried and sweated again—layered over with the sour ammonia of old animals and the damp mineral breath rising from the ground beneath the planks.

The building was larger inside than he remembered.

Not physically larger—he could see the walls, could count the stalls—but the space between things felt stretched. His footsteps took too long to land. Sound traveled strangely, as if the barn refused to echo in a predictable way.

He passed a row of empty stalls.

The doors hung open on rusted hinges. Halters dangled from pegs, stiff with age. A cracked leather saddle sat on a stand like a relic. In the corner, a salt block had turned gray and pitted, as if something had licked at it in the dark for years.

John's hand brushed the stall door as he walked and came away damp.

He held his fingers up to the light.

Not water.

A thin film that smelled faintly sweet.

His stomach rolled. His brain tried, automatically, to name the sweetness: whiskey. Syrup. Rotting fruit. Blood.

He wiped his fingers on his jeans and kept moving.

A rope hung from a ceiling beam, the loop tied neatly. Not a noose, not exactly—too big, too practical. But the sight of it tightened something in his chest anyway, the old animal part of him that recognized hangman shapes.

He looked away.

The flashlight beam caught on something pale on the floor near the back wall.

A line.

At first he thought it was chalk. Then he saw it wasn't powdery. It was solid.

Bone.

Not one bone. A series of bones—small, white fragments laid end to end, forming a crooked boundary across the boards as if someone had tried to draw a fence inside the barn itself.

John's mouth went dry.

The bone line.

He remembered it from the woods, from Hunter's warnings, from Eli's steady hands. He remembered the way his skin had prickled at it, the way crossing it had felt like stepping into colder air.

Here, in the barn, it looked fresher.

Some of the bones still had dark stains in the grooves.

John stood on the near side of the line and stared down. He could see his breath in the flashlight beam. His hands shook.

"Do not cross the bone line," Hunter's father's handwriting had warned.

John laughed once, sharp and empty. "Yeah," he whispered. "No kidding."

A soft sound came from the darkness beyond the bone line.

Not a creak. Not a scuttle.

A sigh.

John's grip tightened on the revolver. He aimed the light past the line.

The far side of the barn was crowded with shapes: stacked feed sacks, old farm tools, a workbench. A trunk sat beneath the back window, half hidden under a tarp.

The tarp moved.

Just a ripple, like wind had found a seam.

John's pulse spiked. He took one involuntary step forward, then stopped with his toe inches from the bone.

The air thickened again, that membrane-feel. The hum under his skin rose, pleased.

John backed up. The thick feeling faded.

The barn was teaching him. Or reminding him.

Either way, it wanted him attentive.

His throat clicked as he swallowed. He looked down at the bone line and forced himself to study it like a piece of evidence instead of a superstition. The fragments were different sizes. Chicken bones, maybe. Rabbit. A few thicker pieces he couldn't place.

He saw, near the middle, a tooth. Human, maybe. Or pig.

The barn offered that uncertainty the way it offered everything: just enough to make your mind do the worst work for it.

John crouched on his side of the line and reached out carefully, not touching the bone, but pointing the flashlight at the boards just beyond it.

There were marks there.

Scratches. Gouges. The wood was scored as if someone had dragged something heavy and sharp across it again and again, trying to cross without crossing. Trying to erase the boundary by destroying the floor.

John imagined a man in here with a crowbar and an addiction and a belief that if he broke enough wood, the rules would break too.

He thought of himself.

He stood and stepped away from the bone line, moving toward the workbench on his side of the barn. Tools lay scattered in dusty disarray: a hammer, a pry bar, a rusted handsaw. A coffee can full of nails.

Pinned to the wall above the bench was a Polaroid, its edges curled.

John lifted it carefully.

In the photo, a boy stood beside a man in front of this very barn. The boy had a wide grin and a bowl haircut. The man's face was half-shadowed by the porch light, but John could see the jawline, the posture.

Hunter. And Jim Wallace.

They stood close enough that their shoulders touched, and Jim's hand rested on the boy's head with a possessive tenderness that looked, at first glance, like love.

In the corner of the photo, barely visible, was a thin white line across the ground.

Bone.

John flipped the photo over.

On the back, in thick marker, someone had written: KEEP HIM OUT.

Underneath, in smaller letters that looked shakier: KEEP ME OUT TOO.

John's stomach tightened. He pressed the photo back against the wall as if returning it could undo what it implied.

A noise came from the far side of the barn again—past the bone line, near the tarp and the trunk.

John angled the flashlight.

The tarp twitched.

Under it, something hard shifted shape.

John held his breath.

The hum under the floor rose, and for a second, he thought he heard music again—fiddle and clapping—like the masquerade was just outside the barn door, waiting for him to remember how to dance.

Then a voice spoke in the dark.

Not loud. Not a shout. A conversational tone aimed at the space, as if the speaker assumed John was already listening.

"Name it," the voice said.

John's skin went cold.

The voice did not sound like Phillip. It didn't sound like Blithe, either—not exactly. It sounded like a man who had learned that the quickest way to control someone wasn't force. It was invitation.

"Name what you want," the voice continued, patient. "Say it out loud."

John's jaw set. "I want you to leave me alone."

A soft chuckle from the darkness, like that answer was expected.

"That's not what you want," the voice said gently. "That's what you want to want."

John felt his hand tighten on the revolver. "Who are you?"

"Name it," the voice repeated, ignoring the question the way a teacher ignored a child trying to change the subject. "Then name what you'll pay."

John's throat burned. His eyes stung.

The barn waited, the bone line between them like a fence inside his own skull.

He thought of the revolver in his hand. Of Hunter's whisper: The gun is an offer too.

He thought of Alice on the bathroom tile, lips blue, a thin foam at the corner of her mouth. He thought of the rat poison box, ordinary packaging for something that killed quietly. He thought of his own insistence: I didn't mean to. I didn't know.

He thought of the easier story the barn had already offered him outside: It wasn't your fault. She chose it.

His mouth opened before he could stop it.

"She chose it," he whispered.

The words tasted like relief.

The hum rose, approving, and for a second the air in the barn felt lighter, as if something had been unlatched.

Then the light from his flashlight flickered.

In the strobing beam, John saw the tarp lift higher, the trunk beneath it suddenly uncovered.

The trunk was open.

And inside it were masks.

Not one.

Dozens.

White faces stacked and nested, blank expressions frozen in lacquer. Some were smooth and featureless. Some had carved smiles. Some had painted brows and hollow eyes.

Each mask had a name written inside in black marker.

John saw PHILLIP.

BLITHE.

ELI.

RUTH.

And beneath those, other names he didn't recognize. Names written in different hands, some careful, some frantic, as if the act of naming had been a form of protection.

John's stomach lurched.

He took a step toward the trunk, forgetting the bone line.

The air thickened immediately, pressing against his chest, stealing his breath.

John stopped, startled, and looked down.

His boot hovered inches over the bone.

He backed away, gasping, the pressure easing the moment he retreated.

The barn wasn't just a place.

It was a set of rules with teeth.

John stood there trembling, staring at the masks, and realized what the voice had meant.

Name what you want.

Name what you'll pay.

The masks were the payments.

Roles bought with blood and shame.

A sound came from behind him.

He spun, revolver up.

Nothing.

Just the stalls. The rope. The dust.

Then he saw it: on the near wall, above the workbench, someone had carved words into the wood.

Not painted. Not written in marker.

Carved with a knife so hard the grooves splintered.

DO NOT LET IT MAKE YOU CLEAN.

John's breath caught.

He could see, in the carving, the angle of desperation. The way the hand had slipped in places. The way the blade had bitten too deep.

Jim Wallace, maybe. Or his father. Or Hunter, younger, learning the rules before he understood why.

John stared at the words until his eyes blurred.

The voice in the dark spoke again, still patient, still polite.

"You can be done," it said. "One act. One clean balance."

John's grip tightened on the revolver.

The gun felt heavier than before. Not just metal. Meaning.

He found the trapdoor where he remembered it from the masquerade--right where the lantern light had made it look almost ceremonial, a square of darker wood with iron hinges.

In the party-world, there had been hands on his shoulders, masks turned toward him, eyes glittering like wet stones. Now there was only the storm and his own pulse and the quiet insistence of the house that had herded him here.

John set his flashlight on the floor, aimed at the trapdoor. His fingers fumbled on the latch. Sweat slid down his ribs despite the cold.

He lifted.

A breath of air came up from below, damp and mineral, as if the earth itself had exhaled.

There were steps.

He didn't remember steps here.

He didn't remember much of last night, either. Memory, lately, had become a hallway with missing floorboards. You stepped carefully. You tried not to look down.

He swung his legs over and started down.

Chapter Seventeen: The Drive

Hunter's phone buzzed on the kitchen table like a trapped insect.

Hunter hadn't slept. He sat at the kitchen table with his keys lined up in front of him like a ritual he didn't believe in. If the phone rang, he would go. If it didn't, he would still go. The decision kept slipping through his hands.

The quiet in the room felt engineered. Not supernatural —just the kind of silence you got when your own mind refused to make noise because it was listening for something worse.

Three texts to John. All delivered. None read.

He tried to picture John alive, pacing, sweating, doing what he'd promised. He couldn't make the picture hold.

Every other image his mind offered ended the same way: John alone in that old place, bargaining with the dark.

Hunter rubbed a hand over his face.

At 2:14 a.m., his phone lit up again.

It wasn't a call.

It was voicemail.

ONE NEW VOICEMAIL, from John's number.

Hunter stared at the screen long enough that it dimmed. His thumb hovered over play, and he heard his father's voice in his head with the same clarity you heard the last thing someone shouted before a door slammed.

Don't answer it after dark.

Hunter had laughed at that rule when he was sixteen. He'd been sixteen and smart enough to think cynicism was armor. His father had slapped him hard enough to make his ears ring.

"The house offers you things," his father had said, eyes wide and wet, whiskey on his breath. "It always asks for more back."

Hunter's throat tightened.

John wasn't a superstition. John was a man shaking himself to pieces, and Hunter had promised—out loud, to his face—that he wouldn't leave him alone with his own hunger.

Hunter hit play.

Static, at first. A thin hiss, like a dead station.

Then John's voice came through, broken and warped, as if it had been dragged through water.

"I'm sorry," John whispered.

A pause, and then again: "I'm sorry."

Over and over. Not like a message. Like a reflex.

Underneath the words was something steadier than weather—a low hum that didn't rise or fall with the gusts. Could have been the phone's mic clipping. Could have been a generator somewhere out on Van Drake Road. It still sat there, patient and constant, like a television left on in another room.

Hunter's stomach turned.

He yanked the phone away from his ear as if it had burned him.

He called back immediately.

Straight to voicemail.

He called again. Same.

He tried to text, fingers moving too fast: You okay? Answer me. I'm coming.

Delivered.

No read receipt.

Hunter sat back in his chair and stared at the window over the sink where his own reflection looked like someone else—a man in a quiet rental kitchen, mouth half-open, trying not to panic.

The LOCKS notebook sat on the counter where he had left it months ago, after digging it out of a box he swore he would never open. Cheap spiral. Cover stained. Thick marker on the front: LOCKS, underlined so hard it had torn the paper.

Hunter hadn't meant to keep it. He hadn't meant to admit it mattered. He'd told himself it was evidence of his father's alcoholism and nothing else. A prop in an old family drama.

But some part of him liked having proof that the rules had existed outside his own memory. That the fear had been real enough to write down.

He pulled the notebook closer and flipped it open.

Do not answer after dark.
Do not cross the bone line.
Do not bargain.

Under the first three rules were lists. Doors and windows. Times. Notes written by a hand that got shakier the farther down the page you went.

This place hears you. Not your words—your want.

Hunter's pulse kicked.

His father's handwriting had always looked like it was trying to hold itself together. Even sober, there had been a tremor in it. By the end of the notebook, the lines went crooked like a drunk man walking a tightrope.

Hunter shut the notebook hard enough to make the spiral creak.

He found his keys with hands that didn't shake—yet. His body always saved the shaking for later, when the decision had already been made and there was no turning back.

On his way out, he paused by the counter and looked at the chipped white coffee mug sitting by the sink. Alice's mug, the one John had brought out here in a box of her things and set down without comment the first day. Hunter had never used it. He'd never moved it. It had felt like a boundary marker in a house full of boundaries.

He thought of John in the farmhouse, hearing things.

He thought of the way John had looked at the liquor bottle on the first night—not like a drink, like a door.

Hunter grabbed his jacket, his flashlight, the LOCKS notebook, and left.

The storm hit him the moment he stepped outside. Wind like a shove. Rain cold and hard. The porch light flickered once, steadied, then died entirely.

Of course, Hunter thought. Of course now.

He got into his truck and started it. The engine's rumble filled the cab like reassurance. Headlights cut tunnels into the dark.

He told himself this was going to be simple. A drive. A check. A man brought back into daylight.

The voicemail replayed in his head anyway.

I'm sorry. I'm sorry. I'm sorry.

Underneath: the hum.

As he backed out, his phone buzzed again.

Relief hit him so hard he almost laughed.

Then his phone lit up on the seat beside him—no ringtone, no vibration, just the pale glow fighting the rain.

DAD.

Not an incoming call. Just the contact card—opened somehow, the wet capacitive glass registering a phantom swipe.

His father hadn't called in two years. Not since the last fight, the last drive out to Van Drake Road to "check the locks."

Seeing the name now felt wrong. Like a costume. Like someone wearing his father's face.

The LOCKS notebook slid a little on the passenger seat as the truck turned. Hunter's eyes flicked to it.

Do not answer after dark.

He told himself it was water and cheap capacitive glass. Phones did stupid things when they were wet. He was not going to turn it into a story.

The screen went dark. A heartbeat later it woke again and flashed DAD before collapsing back to black.

The hair on his arms lifted anyway.

He thumbed the power button and set the phone face-down in the cup holder.

No missed call. No voicemail. Nothing he could show another person without sounding insane.

The truck drifted. He corrected hard, breath coming fast.

Hunter swore under his breath and kept driving.

The rain smeared the windshield. The wipers worked too hard. The road out of town was empty in the way empty roads always are after midnight: not peaceful—abandoned.

He made it to the highway and turned north.

At a red light, he dialed Hargrove.

It rang until voicemail picked up.

"Hargrove, it's Wallace," Hunter said, voice low, like the darkness could hear him. "John called. I got a voicemail. Something's wrong out there. I'm heading back to Van Drake. If you get this—" He swallowed. "If you get this, call me."

He ended the call and stared at the green light without moving.

The car behind him honked.

Hunter jerked and drove on.

Van Drake Road came off the highway like an afterthought. Narrow. Unlit. The sign bent and faded.

VAN DRAKE RD.

Hunter's chest tightened as if he'd been punched.

He hadn't been out here in years, but his body remembered the turn. His body remembered how the woods swallowed sound. How the air felt thicker, like the trees were leaning in to listen.

He turned onto the road.

The trees pressed close. Headlights tunneled forward, showing only what was directly ahead. Rain clattered on the roof. The world outside the cab became a black wall.

Hunter drove slower.

His phone buzzed again, a brief vibration against the console.

When he glanced down, the lock screen had woken under a film of water. DAD flashed for a fraction of a second —and then it was gone, too fast to be sure he hadn't imagined it.

He kept his eyes on the road after that and held the wheel like it was the only solid thing left.

The road dipped and rose. Mud pooled in ruts. A branch snapped somewhere in the dark and he flinched hard enough that his shoulder twinged.

He passed the old landmark his father used to point out —the stone with the white X painted on it years ago, the paint long gone now.

"The bone starts here," his father had said once, sober enough to sound almost normal. "You cross it, you're on the hook. You understand?"

Hunter hadn't understood then. He understood now, not as a belief but as a sensation. The air changed. The rain sounded different. The woods tightened around the truck like a fist.

He slowed to a crawl.

A flicker of orange light appeared ahead through the trees—weak, as if from lanterns.

Hunter's heart jumped.

The "masquerade" John had described. The impossible party.

Hunter's mind tried to label it: headlights. Reflection. Lightning.

But the light was steady.

Then it winked out.

Hunter's headlights were suddenly the only illumination again. The road was empty. The curve was empty. The woods were empty.

His grip on the wheel tightened until his fingers hurt.

He drove on anyway.

The driveway to the farmhouse was barely visible, a shadowed cut between trees. Hunter turned in. The truck jolted over a rut and the back end fishtailed. He corrected, too late.

The tires sank.

Mud sucked at the wheels like hands.

Hunter tried to rock it free—reverse, drive, reverse. Tires spun and threw mud. The engine whined.

The truck did not move.

He shut the engine off and sat for a second, listening to the rain and his own breathing.

He could go back. He could sleep. He could tell himself the voicemail was nothing.

He saw John's name glowing on the screen in his mind and heard the voice again.

I'm sorry. I'm sorry. I'm sorry.

Underneath: the hum.

Hunter grabbed the flashlight, shoved the LOCKS notebook into his jacket, and stepped out into the rain.

Cold hit him hard. Mud grabbed his boots immediately. The woods smelled wet and rotten. Somewhere deeper in, something moved—branch or body, he couldn't tell.

He raised the flashlight and aimed it toward the house.

The farmhouse loomed at the end of the drive, half-hidden by trees. Its windows were dark.

No porch light. No lanterns. No music.

Just a shape against the night.

Hunter's mouth went dry.

He started walking.

Every step felt like crossing something.

Do not cross the bone line.

He didn't know where the line was, but he felt the world tighten around him as he moved deeper in, like the property was drawing a circle.

His phone buzzed again.

He looked this time, because some part of him needed to know.

The lock screen lit, bright and wrong. DAD.

The call icon pulsed—normal UI animation, and still it felt like a dare.

Hunter's thumb hovered over it.

Do not answer after dark.

He hit the power button until the screen went dark.

The vibration died.

A heartbeat later it buzzed again—another short, useless vibration—and the lock screen flashed the same name.

DAD. Again.

Hunter swore and shoved the phone into his pocket.

The rain changed direction. Wind shoved at him. The flashlight beam shook.

He thought he saw eyes in the trees—two pale points that vanished when he swung the light.

He kept moving.

When he reached the yard, the house was bigger than it had looked from the road. Old wood. Peeling paint. Sagging porch. The kind of place that made you think of termites and inheritance.

The storm cellar doors were open in the grass, like two dark teeth.

Hunter's stomach dropped.

He moved toward them before he could stop himself.

The boards were wet. The hinges slick. The opening below was black.

A low, steady hum rose up from the earth.

Hunter stopped dead.

It was the same sound under John's voicemail. Too steady to be weather. Too patient to be accident.

"John," he called, and his voice sounded thin in the wind.

No answer.

Hunter crouched and aimed the flashlight down.

The beam caught the top step, stone slick with moisture.

From deeper down, a voice floated up—hoarse, shaking, unmistakable.

"Hunter?"

Relief hit Hunter so hard it almost buckled his knees.

"Thank God," he breathed.

He started down.

One step.

Two.

The hum got louder.

And then, somewhere behind him in the yard, his phone buzzed again in his pocket. He didn't check. He didn't have the spare courage.

Hunter did not stop.

He kept going, because responsibility always sounded like a rule when you were too scared to call it love.

Chapter Eighteen: Dispatch

Hargrove sat at his desk with his jacket still on, listening to the rain hammer the station windows. The fluorescent lights above him flickered with each gust, as if even the building's electricity wanted to quit. Detective Hargrove hated storms for reasons that had nothing to do with weather.

In a county like this, storms didn't just knock out power. They knocked loose people's restraint. They made drunks bolder, made bad drivers faster, made domestic calls uglier because everyone was already trapped in the same rooms with the same resentments. They also made ordinary problems harder to solve, and Hargrove was a man who made his living by solving problems.

Lane hovered in the doorway holding a styrofoam cup of coffee, rainwater darkening his uniform at the shoulders, and trying to pretend he wasn't nervous.

"You hear back?" Lane asked.

Hargrove didn't look up from his phone. He'd called Hunter Wallace twice in the last ten minutes. Both calls had gone straight to voicemail. No ring. No delay. Just the polite recorded message that sounded, tonight, like absence made audible.

"Nothing," Hargrove said.

Lane shifted his weight. "Maybe he's driving. Maybe he's in a dead spot."

"Maybe," Hargrove said, and meant: maybe he's already in over his head.

Lane set the coffee down on the corner of Hargrove's desk like an offering and then immediately regretted the symbolism, glancing toward the dark hall as if expecting someone to comment on it.

Hargrove almost smiled. Almost.

He hadn't slept much since the Glisner case landed on his desk. He hadn't expected it to eat at him the way it had. Most deaths in this job came with a logic you could track: a fight, a weapon, a motive that made sense to someone even if it didn't make sense to you.

Alice Glisner's death had come with a kind of domestic banality that made it worse. A kitchen. A mug. A poison box you could buy at any hardware store. A man who said he hadn't meant it while holding the kind of guilt that didn't care what he'd meant.

And then there was the house.

Van Drake Road had a reputation that predated any incident report. The county treated it the way it treated sinkholes and loose dogs: with stories, with avoidance, with the casual superstition that grew in places where people didn't have better tools.

Hargrove didn't believe in hauntings.

He did believe in isolation. In addiction. In violence that repeated because the landscape made it easy.

He was still not sure which category the farmhouse belonged in, and that uncertainty irritated him more than fear would have.

His phone buzzed.

Lane leaned forward instinctively.

Hargrove checked the screen.

A missed call.

From Wallace's father.

Hargrove's jaw tightened.

Lane's eyebrows rose. "Jim Wallace?"

"Yeah," Hargrove said.

He didn't call back immediately. He stared at the name and let himself remember the last time he'd spoken to Jim Wallace—years ago, during a welfare check when the man had refused to let deputies step past the first fence post.

Jim had looked sober then. Angry. Not the loose anger of a drunk. The tight anger of someone guarding something.

House is bad at night, Jim had said, like he was talking about an aggressive dog.

Hargrove hit call back.

The line rang once. Twice.

Then Jim's voice filled the phone, blunt and unpolished. "Detective."

No greeting. No question. A statement like he'd expected the call.

Hargrove sat back in his chair. "Mr. Wallace."

A pause. Rain hissed on the line. "He there?" Jim asked.

"Who?"

"My boy," Jim said. "Hunter."

Hargrove felt Lane's attention sharpen.

"No," Hargrove said. "He's not here."

Another pause. When Jim spoke again, his voice had a different edge. Not anger. Not fear, exactly. Something like readiness. "He went out there."

"He said he was going to check on John Glisner," Hargrove said, keeping his tone even. "We've tried to reach him."

Jim exhaled hard through his nose. "Storm's bad."

"It is," Hargrove agreed.

Jim didn't respond to that. "You tell him to stay out the cellar?"

Hargrove's eyes flicked to Lane, who mouthed: cellar?

Hargrove kept his voice steady. "We didn't talk about a cellar."

Jim's laugh was humorless. "Then you don't know what you're doing."

Hargrove felt irritation flare. "Mr. Wallace, I'm trying to locate—"

"No," Jim cut in, and the sharpness made Lane flinch. "You're trying to make it paperwork. You're trying to make it a call you can clear. You can't clear it. Not out there."

Hargrove's skin prickled—not belief, but the uncomfortable sense of being spoken to by someone who had lived inside a pattern long enough to recognize it.

"You called me," Hargrove said. "Why?"

Jim was quiet for a long moment. Hargrove could hear rain and, underneath, something else—a faint vibration that might have been a truck engine, might have been interference, might have been nothing.

Finally Jim said, "My phone rang."

Hargrove's grip tightened on his own phone. "When?"

"Ten minutes ago. Maybe fifteen," Jim said. "Landline. House line."

Hargrove stared at the station phone on the wall across the room. The ringer switch was down—silent. Lane had flipped it earlier to keep prank calls from tying up the line while the storm rolled through.

"Who was it?" Hargrove asked.

Jim's breath came out slow. "Hunter."

Hargrove went still.

Jim continued, voice low now, as if saying it louder might make it more real. "I heard... I think I heard him. The line was all static, but it sounded like Hunter. Like he said my name."

Lane's eyes widened.

Hargrove kept his own face blank, his voice professional. "Did he ask for help?"

"No," Jim said. "Or—if he did, I couldn't make it out. I caught one word. Sorry. Maybe. Then it cut out."

A cold line ran down Hargrove's spine.

He had heard that phrasing twice tonight—from Hunter himself, drunk and shaking, and now from Hunter's father, describing a landline call that didn't make sense.

"Mr. Wallace," Hargrove said carefully, "where are you right now?"

"In my truck," Jim said. "Headed out there."

Hargrove's mouth tightened. "Don't."

Jim gave a short laugh. "You gonna tell me not to go to my own property?"

"I'm telling you the roads are washed out," Hargrove said. "I'm telling you deputies can't get through the low water. I'm telling you you're going to end up stuck out there and become another problem."

Jim's voice sharpened. "Better me than him."

Lane shifted in the doorway. His coffee cup creaked in his grip.

Hargrove closed his eyes for half a second, collecting himself. This was the part of the job he hated: talking to a man who was already making a decision out of love and stubbornness and terror, and knowing that logic didn't reach that far.

"Listen," Hargrove said. "If you're already on the road, slow down. If you hit water, you turn around. If you get to that drive, you stay at the end until daylight. You do not—do you hear me?—you do not go inside."

Jim's breathing was loud on the line. "Daylight," he repeated, like he was tasting the word.

"Yes," Hargrove said. "Daylight."

Jim didn't promise. He didn't agree. He just said, quieter, "He always comes when people call."

Hargrove's throat tightened. "What does that mean?"

Jim's answer was too quick. Too practiced. "It means my boy's got a problem."

Hargrove heard the lie, heard it in the way Jim's voice tightened around the word problem, as if reducing it made it manageable.

Hargrove let it pass, because arguing with Jim Wallace about the nature of fear in the middle of a storm was not going to locate Hunter.

He ended the call and stared at his phone.

Lane stepped forward, voice careful. "Detective... you believe him?"

"I believe he believes it," Hargrove said.

Lane looked like he wanted more. A conclusion. A verdict.

Hargrove didn't have one.

He stood. "Get dispatch on the line," he said. "I want units staged as close to Van Drake as they can get without swimming. I want EMS on standby. And I want the county to start logging every call that mentions that road tonight—every complaint, every weird report, everything."

Lane's eyes widened. "You think it's going to be one of those nights."

Hargrove grabbed his coat off the chair back. "It's already one of those nights."

Lane moved fast, relief and adrenaline making him useful. He crossed the station to the radio desk, voice clipped as he called in.

Hargrove paused by the wall phone as he passed.

The ringer was still off.

He stared at the quiet handset and the downturned switch.

He told himself that didn't mean anything. Storms did strange things to lines. Old buildings had crossed wires. Humans heard patterns in static.

Still, for a second, he imagined the phone ringing in the dark station, and no one answering because of a rule written on a yellow legal pad somewhere out on Van Drake Road.

Hargrove walked past without touching it.

Outside, the rain kept falling like the sky had decided the county needed to be washed clean.

* * *

The wood held. It creaked, but it held.

The air grew thicker with each step, pressing on his skin. The flashlight beam seemed to shorten, eaten by the dark ahead.

Halfway down, his foot slipped on something wet. He caught himself on the wall, fingers sliding over stone--no longer barn planks.

His light swung.

The walls weren't barn walls.

They were the stone-lined sides of the storm cellar.

John froze, pulse hammering.

He looked up.

The rectangle of the doorway above him had changed. The barn's slats were gone. In their place, he saw the

256

underside of the farmhouse porch--wooden beams slick with rain, old nails, the shadowed belly of the house.

He didn't remember leaving the barn.

He didn't remember opening the storm cellar.

His mind tried to stitch the moments together and failed, like a drunk trying to thread a needle.

For an instant, the darkness above him seemed to pulse, porch beams rising and falling like ribs. He blinked hard, willing the barn back into place, but the rectangle stayed stubbornly porch-shaped.

Maybe he had never been in the barn at all. Maybe the barn was just another room the house could show him when it wanted him to walk.

John dug his nails into his palm until he felt something sharp and honest. Pain was real. Pain didn't lie.

John's stomach lurched.

"You're awake," he whispered to himself, but it sounded like a question.

The last few days had been like this: spaces he couldn't account for, images that didn't belong, time that folded in on itself like bad paper. The shaking wasn't the worst part. The worst part was the way the world refused to hold still long enough for him to trust it.

He forced himself to keep going.

At the bottom, the cellar opened into a low, cramped room. Shelves sagged under dusty jars. Old tools hung on the walls like relics. A pile of broken chairs sat in one corner, half collapsed, as if someone had thrown them down there in anger.

Or as if someone had tried to build a barricade and given up.

The air tasted of mildew and iron and something faintly chemical. Rat poison, maybe. Or the sour tang of vomit that never quite leaves a place.

John's flashlight beam caught a shape on the far wall: a rusted ring bolted into the stone, the kind you might tie an animal to.

There were more. Three. Four.

For a moment, in the hard white circle of light, John saw wrists there. Saw dark hands pulled tight. Saw rope burn.

Then he blinked and it was only rust and stone.

For a second, John couldn't tell if what he'd seen was memory or the house playing dress-up with his guilt.

The rings in the wall looked old enough to be history.

Old enough to be true.

His flashlight beam shook as his hands trembled. He tried to steady it, angry at himself for needing light to prove reality.

A soft sound came from the edge of the beam.

Not a creak. Not the house settling. Footsteps—bare, careful, unhurried.

John's pulse kicked. The revolver rose without him deciding to lift it.

"Who's there?" he demanded, and his voice came out too loud, too thin.

The footsteps stopped.

In the silence, he could hear the rain above, muffled by wood and earth. He could hear his own breath scraping in and out. He could hear the hum under everything, like the house had a heartbeat it didn't bother hiding down here.

Then someone stepped into the edge of his flashlight's circle.

Not masked.

Not costumed.

A woman stood there, hands folded at her waist the way people did when they were trying not to threaten you. She was older than John had first guessed in the masquerade world. Her hair was wrapped in a scarf that looked like it belonged to no time at all. Her eyes were sharp and tired, the kind of tired that came from staying in a place too long because leaving meant something worse.

John recognized her anyway.

He had seen those eyes watching him from behind fabric.

"Ruth," he whispered, and the name tasted like remembering.

Her mouth did not move in surprise. As if she had been waiting for him to say it.

"You brought that down here," she said, looking at the gun. Her voice was calm. Not soft. Calm in the way a door is calm when it's held shut.

John's grip tightened. "Blithe said you were waiting in the barn."

Ruth's eyes flicked over his face, not judging—measuring.

"Blithe says a lot of things," she replied. "He says what you already want to hear."

A second shape moved in the darkness behind her.

A man stepped into the light. Taller than Ruth. Broad-shouldered. Not young. Not old. His hands were empty. His face was set in the kind of patience that wasn't kindness, exactly, but wasn't cruelty either. It was something firmer.

John's memory supplied him: the tall man from the masquerade, the one who had held the edge of the circle without ever looking away.

"Eli," John said.

The man's gaze stayed on the gun.

"Put it down," Eli said.

John barked a laugh that sounded like it hurt. "I can't."

"That's what the house tells you," Ruth said. "That you can't. That you have to choose one clean act and everything balances."

John's throat clicked as he swallowed. "It has to be something," he said. "It has to be... a way out."

Eli's eyes narrowed slightly. "You didn't come looking for a way out," he said. "You came looking for permission."

John flinched. The words landed too close to the truth.

"Permission for what?" he snapped, trying to sound angry instead of afraid.

Ruth tilted her head, considering him. "To make a story that doesn't hurt," she said. "To make your hunger somebody else's fault."

John's hands shook harder.

He wanted to deny it. He wanted to point at the house and say it did this, it did all of it, it offered, it tempted, it pushed.

He wanted to say: I'm sick. I'm shaking. I'm not myself.

He wanted to say: she left me.

He wanted to say: she chose poison.

Ruth's eyes didn't let him hide behind any of it.

"The house offers," Eli said, voice low. "It always offers. That part is simple."

"And the price?" John asked, before he could stop himself.

Ruth's gaze slid, briefly, to the rusted rings in the wall. "The price is always you," she said. "Piece by piece. Memory by memory. Name by name."

John's stomach rolled.

The hum under the floorboards deepened, as if the house approved of being talked about.

Eli took one slow step closer. Not into the beam—just closer enough that John felt it.

"You don't get to buy your way out," Eli said. "Not with blood. Not with a body. Not with a story you can live with."

John lifted the revolver a fraction. "Then what do you want?" he demanded.

Ruth's mouth tightened. "We don't want anything from you," she said.

That hit harder than anger.

John stared at her. "What do you mean?"

Ruth held his gaze. "We're not here to make you better," she said. "We're not here to punish you. We're not your penance."

Eli's voice came again, steady. "We're the lock."

John's breath hitched.

In his mind, the word snapped to the notebook. LOCKS, underlined. His father's handwriting shaking.

Do not bargain.

The house hears your want.

Ruth's eyes stayed on his, and for the first time John understood what had been wrong about the masquerade world. It wasn't that it felt unreal. It was that it felt like a performance built for him—music and masks and flirtation, a whole theater of temptation.

This—this cellar, this damp air, these people who did not smile for him—this felt like something that existed even when John wasn't watching.

"You can't leave," John said, and it came out small. Like a child saying the rules back to an adult.

Ruth did not deny it. "You can," she said. "But not the way you want."

"Then how?"

Eli's gaze flicked, briefly, to the gun. "Not with that," he said.

Ruth's voice softened by a degree—not kindness, but gravity. "Truth is weight," she said. "That's the only thing that holds."

John had heard that phrase from Phillip in the masquerade. Hearing it now from Ruth made it feel older. Not poetry. Physics.

John's throat tightened. "I told the truth," he said. "I told Hunter I drank. I told him I—"

"You told him a story you could survive," Ruth said.

John flinched.

Eli spoke again. "There's truth you carry," he said, "and truth you hand off. Hunger likes it when you hand it off."

John's mind scrambled. "I didn't—" he started, and stopped, because he didn't know what he didn't do.

Ruth stepped closer, just enough that her face caught more of the beam. The lines at the corners of her eyes looked carved by years.

"Say her name," Ruth said.

John's mouth went dry.

He tried to swallow and found nothing.

"Alice," he managed.

The name hit the cellar like a dropped object. It made the air feel denser. The hum changed, almost imperceptibly, like the house had leaned in.

Ruth's eyes didn't move. "Say what you wanted," she said.

John shook his head fast. "No."

Eli's jaw went rigid. "That's the bargain," he said. "You keep the wanting hidden and let it grow teeth."

John's hands shook so badly the flashlight beam danced over the rings in the wall, over the stone floor, over Ruth's face and Eli's chest.

"I didn't want her to die," John said, and even as he said it, he heard how much he needed it to be true.

Ruth didn't argue. She simply waited.

John's breath came faster. His body wanted to run. His mind wanted a bottle. The house wanted the clean story.

A quiet sound came from above.

A voice, far away, filtered through the crack between the cellar doors.

"John?"

John's blood went cold.

Ruth's gaze lifted slightly, as if she had heard the voice too.

Eli's face tightened.

"Hunter," Ruth said softly.

John stared at her. "No," he whispered. "He's not—he wouldn't—"

"He already did," Eli said. "He answered."

The hum deepened, pleased.

Ruth's eyes came back to John. "Don't do it," she said, and for the first time there was something in her voice that sounded like urgency.

John's mouth moved on instinct. A lie rose up, easy as breath.

"Yeah," he called toward the stairs, voice cracking. "I'm down here."

Ruth's eyes closed for a single beat, as if she were bracing for impact.

Eli stepped back into the darkness, not fleeing—making room.

The house listened.

And somewhere above them, footsteps started down.

His throat clicked as he swallowed.

This is real, he told himself.

Or it isn't. And either way, I'm here.

He moved deeper, toward the base of the stairs, and crouched where the shadows were thickest. The revolver felt slick in his palm. He wiped it on his jeans, angry at himself for needing to.

Blithe's voice played in his head again, gentle as a lullaby.

One act.

He tried not to ask what the act was, because some part of him already knew. He had been working his whole life toward the moment when violence felt like a door.

A sound came from above.

Not a creak. Not the house settling. A voice.

"John?"

It floated down through the crack between the cellar doors, thin with distance.

John's blood went cold.

Phillip.

The lie came easy. Lies always did.

"Yeah," John called back. "I'm down here. Come on."

There was a pause. Then another voice, closer now, edged with relief.

"Thank God. Hold on--I'm coming down."

John pressed his cheek to the gun's cold metal, as if that could steady him. He aimed the barrel at the seam of the doors and tried to convince himself he was pointing it at a monster.

His heart slapped against his ribs.

He told himself Phillip wasn't a person.

He told himself the Gatekeepers weren't people.

He told himself they were traps in suits and skin, built to keep him here, built to make him confess, built to make him hurt.

Blithe had said so. And Blithe had sounded like truth.

The voice above had said his name like it meant something.

John stared at the rectangle of light between the cellar doors and tried to decide what kind of trap it was. His mind offered him options the way it always did when he was afraid: make it simple, make it a fight, make it something you can win with force.

He had been good at force.

Force was what he used on himself every morning - white knuckles, clenched jaw, the constant grinding insistence that if he just held tight enough the shaking would stop and the world would behave.

Force was what had brought him here.

The revolver trembled in his hand. The tremor traveled up his forearm and into his shoulder, a chain reaction of need. The metal was slick with rain and sweat. He wanted to wipe his palm on his jeans, but he didn't dare take a hand off the grip.

"Phillip," he whispered again, not because he believed Phillip would answer, but because the name gave the darkness a shape. A target. A story.

The voice above breathed, "John--"

Not the same tone this time.

Not flat. Not calm. Strained.

John's stomach turned. The sound scraped at something familiar. A cadence he'd heard in brighter rooms, over cheap beer and good intentions.

His brain tried to press Phillip's face over the voice anyway. It tried to make the sound foreign, because foreign was easier.

Then another sound threaded through the crack - a faint, steady hum, like a television left on in a room no one was in.

John's skin prickled.

The hum wasn't just a sound. It was an atmosphere. It filled his sinuses, settled behind his eyes.

You're not alone down here, his mind said.

Good, another part of him answered, vicious with relief. Good. Let them come.

Blithe's lullaby voice returned, as if spoken directly into his ear.

One act.

John swallowed. His throat clicked.

He pictured the Gatekeepers from the masquerade - feet on wooden planks, hands folded, faces hidden behind fabric and shadow. He pictured Ruth's gaze, the way it made him feel like a child caught with his hand in a cookie jar full of rot.

He pictured Hunter, too, because Hunter had been in his head since the first day out here. Hunter with his practical hands and his tired eyes and his rules that sounded like superstition until the house started answering.

Hunter who had told him: if it offers you something, call me first.

John squeezed his eyes shut for a heartbeat.

The cellar smelled of mildew and iron and old wood. The smell in his memory was different: his apartment, Alice's shampoo, the sweet burn of whiskey.

The house wasn't offering him a bottle right now.

It was offering him permission.

Permission to call this self-defense.

Permission to make a clean story out of a messy truth.

If something comes down those stairs, his mind reasoned, you have to protect yourself. You have to stop it before it stops you. That's not relapse. That's survival.

He could hear his own heartbeat. He could hear the rain above, muffled by wood and earth. He could hear the hum under the voice.

He lifted the gun higher.

A shadow crossed the crack of light. A figure blocking the storm.

John's finger tightened against the trigger guard.

The voice came again, closer now, and the sound of it made his eyes burn.

"John... it's me."

It didn't say a name.

It didn't have to.

John's mouth went dry.

Because somewhere in his head, he heard Alice say it too - in that last, exhausted tone when she stopped fighting and started leaving.

It's me.

A whisper rose in him, slick and gentle.

Do it.

It wasn't a command. It was a suggestion dressed like mercy.

Do it and it's over.

Do it and you don't have to keep shaking.

Do it and you can finally pay.

John's hands shook so badly the barrel wavered. He braced his elbows against his ribs, trying to steady himself.

"I'm sorry," he whispered, and didn't know who he was apologizing to.

The cellar doors groaned.

A wedge of gray opened. Wind rushed in, carrying rain and the distant smell of wet earth.

A figure appeared at the top of the stairs, silhouetted against the storm.

The figure said, "John--"

The voice was close enough to make the hair on John's arms lift.

Not a shout from the yard. Not a call from the porch.

A voice aimed down the stairwell, threaded through wood and earth, as if the house itself were shaping the sound.

John's grip tightened on the revolver until the metal bit his palm. The tremor in his hands made the barrel wag, a small, shameful motion that felt like betrayal.

He tried to speak and found his mouth full of cotton.

The voice came again, and this time it carried a second layer under it, a faint distortion like the edge of a recording.

John's brain grabbed for the easiest explanation.

The landline.

The house could play voices. It had already done it. It had already used Alice.

Now it was using Hunter.

A small sound rose behind John—no footsteps, no movement he could locate. Just a breath, close to his ear, intimate as a confession.

Do it.

The thought did not feel like his, and that was the worst part. It felt like mercy offered from outside. A clean solution. A single action that would cut the night in half.

John's eyes burned. He blinked hard, staring into the wedge of stormlight, trying to make the silhouette resolve into anything he could name.

For a heartbeat he saw the shape of a mask.

A pale oval where a face should be.

Then it was gone—only shadow again, only rain.

The figure shifted at the top of the stairs.

John's shoulders tensed, ready to fire, ready to stop thinking.

The voice said his name again, and it sounded like someone who loved him trying not to sound afraid.

Lightning flared, and for a single, brutal heartbeat John saw the face.

Not Phillip.

Hunter Wallace.

John's mind rejected it. It tried to rewrite the image, to press Phillip's features over Hunter's like a mask.

The reflex came anyway.

The gun bucked in his hands. The sound was enormous in the confined space, a clap of thunder trapped underground.

Hunter jerked, staggered, and grabbed at himself with one hand like he was trying to hold his body together.

"John?" he rasped, and the word was full of disbelief.

John's stomach dropped through the floor.

He stumbled forward on his knees, the revolver slipping from his fingers. It hit stone with a sharp metallic clack and skittered away, throwing the room into a spinning, sick light.

"Hunter--no--" John choked out.

Hunter made it two steps down before his legs folded. He hit the floor hard and the sound was wrong, too heavy, too final. Blood spread beneath him, dark as spilled ink.

Chapter Nineteen: The Price

John crawled to him, hands already reaching, already shaking, already useless.

"Honey--" Hunter tried, because he always called him that when he was worried, and the word came out wet.

John pressed his palm to Hunter's chest. Then his throat. He felt a frantic flutter and then, under his hand, warmth that didn't belong on stone.

"Hold on," John whispered. "Please. Please--"

Hunter's hand found John's shirt and gripped it, not strong but desperate.

"I got your call," Hunter managed. Each word cost him. "You-- you sounded--"

John stared at him.

"My call?" he whispered.

The memory surfaced like a drowning man: the kitchen phone in the farmhouse, receiver slick and alive with spiders. Alice's voice coming out of plastic. John yanking the cord until it snapped. The receiver hitting the wall.

John's breath hitched.

Hunter's eyes searched his face, trying to find the version of John he knew. The sober one. The trying one. The one who made coffee and apologized and meant it for a full three hours at a time.

"I came as fast as I could," Hunter said, voice thinning. "Road was... hell."

"I didn't call," John said, and the lie landed in the space between them like a body. "I didn't--I couldn't--"

Hunter coughed. Red sprayed his lips. His grip tightened as if to keep himself from falling through the floor.

"You did," Hunter whispered. "It was you. It was your voice. You kept saying–"

John leaned closer, forehead almost touching Hunter's.

"What did I say?"

Hunter's lashes fluttered.

His mouth worked, searching for air and for words at the same time.

"You kept saying you were sorry," he rasped. "Over and over. Like you couldn't stop."

He swallowed, throat clicking. "And under it... there was this hum. Like a TV left on in another room."

John felt the hairs lift along his arms.

"I thought it was the storm," Hunter whispered. "But it didn't sound like weather."

Hunter's lashes fluttered as if he were trying to keep himself in the room.

John could feel the tremor in Hunter's grip. Not strength. Not anger. Just a reflex refusing to accept what had already happened.

Hunter's mouth worked around a breath that wouldn't come clean. "Hargrove..." he rasped.

John's head snapped up. "What?"

Hunter blinked at him, eyes glassy with shock. "He came by," Hunter whispered. "My place. Before I drove out here. He asked... asked about you. Asked about this house."

John's stomach dropped. The detective's name felt like a hook. Like the outside world reaching in.

"What did you tell him?" John demanded, and the anger in his voice sounded insane down here.

Hunter's gaze tightened with effort. "That you were sick," he breathed. "That you were detoxing. That I had you."

A wet cough shook him. John felt the warmth spread under his palm and wanted to scream.

"I told him you weren't alone," Hunter forced out. "Because you weren't supposed to be."

John's throat closed.

Hunter swallowed, throat clicking. "Then my phone buzzed," he whispered. "Your voicemail."

John flinched.

Hunter's eyes held his for a beat, pleading and accusing all at once. "It sounded like you," he said. "But it sounded like... like you were standing in a room full of static. Like there was something under your voice."

John remembered the hum. The way it filled the air like a mood.

Hunter's breathing hitched. "I tried to call you back," he whispered. "No answer. So I drove."

John's hands shook harder.

"The road was bad," Hunter said. "Trees down. Water across the asphalt. I kept thinking I'd turn around. I kept thinking you'd call and tell me you were fine, and I could go home and pretend I hadn't heard it."

His lips pulled back in something that wasn't quite a smile. "But you didn't."

John stared at him, throat tight.

Hunter's gaze drifted past John for a second, toward the dark corner, then snapped back as if he'd burned himself on whatever he saw there. "When I got to the drive, everything was dead," he whispered. "No lights. No music. Just that damn barn sitting there like a black cut."

John's skin prickled.

"I heard you," Hunter said. "From below. I heard you say my name. I thought you were hurt. I thought you'd fallen. I thought -"

His eyes squeezed shut.

"I thought I could fix it," he breathed.

John's stomach twisted. "I didn't call you," he whispered again, and the words tasted like cowardice.

Hunter opened his eyes. In them was a tired kind of certainty. "I know," he said. "But it used your mouth."

John's pulse kicked.

Hunter's fingers tightened weakly on John's shirt. "Listen to me," he rasped. "Don't let it make you pay the way it wants. Don't let it turn this into... relief."

John shook his head, tears burning. "What are you talking about?"

Hunter's gaze flicked to where the revolver had skittered across the stone. "The gun," he whispered. "That's an offer too."

John went still.

Hunter's voice thinned. "It wants one clean act," he breathed. "One story. One price. It wants you to believe you can balance the books with blood and be done."

John stared at him.

Hunter swallowed hard. "Carry it," he whispered. "Carry the truth. Even if it burns."

His eyes squeezed shut. When they opened again, the apology in them was old and exhausted.

"I'm sorry," he breathed.

John's throat closed.

The house had answered his reaching with his own mouth.

Of course it had.

He fumbled for something--anything--to fix this. His belt. His shirt. A towel. A bandage. A miracle. He stripped off his flannel with clumsy hands and pressed it to Hunter's wound, but his tremors made it impossible to keep pressure where it mattered.

"Stay with me," John said. "Stay with me, okay? I can get you out. I can--"

He looked up at the stairs.

Above them, the kitchen was a smear of darkness.

The phone was upstairs. The phone was broken. The phone had been alive.

But Hunter had come.

Because John had reached for help and the house had answered with Alice's voice, and Hunter had heard something else.

Hunter's grip loosened.

"Don't," he whispered, as if John had moved toward the gun again. As if Hunter knew John too well, even now. "Don't do--"

John shook his head hard, tears burning his eyes. "I'm sorry," he said. "I'm sorry. I didn't mean--"

Hunter's gaze drifted past him, to the darker corner of the cellar.

John followed it, and for a moment the shadows there looked crowded. Not shapes. Not things. People.

Bare feet on stone.

Hands folded.

Faces that would not meet his eyes.

John blinked and the corner was empty.

Hunter's breath rattled.

"John," he whispered, and this time it sounded like a question he was afraid to ask. "Alice..."

The name hit John like a shove.

He flinched. He tried to speak and found only air.

Hunter's hand fell from John's shirt.

His eyes stayed open for a few seconds longer, fixed on nothing, as if he were watching something John couldn't see.

Then the light went out of them.

In the silence that followed, something buzzed.

Hunter's phone vibrated once in his pocket, a small, polite tremor against dead flesh. The sound was obscene down here, a reminder that the world still had clocks and networks and people who expected calls to be returned.

John stared at the pocket like it was a mouth.

He reached, stopped, then reached again. His fingers closed around the device and pulled it free.

The screen lit up through spiderweb cracks, then dimmed. One notification flashed before it died again: 1 NEW VOICEMAIL.

John couldn't bring himself to press play. He slid the phone back into Hunter's pocket with shaking hands, as if hiding it could hide what it meant.

Then - because he could not sit still with the silence - he pulled it out again.

His thumb hovered over the screen.

If he pressed play and heard his own voice, it would be proof.

If he pressed play and heard Alice, it would be something worse.

The screen brightened, hesitated, and the battery icon flashed red like a warning light.

John hit call instead, muscle memory overriding thought. 9. 1. 1.

The digits appeared, then blinked, then smeared as the screen dimmed. He put it to his ear anyway.

Static.

A thin, steady hiss that might have been a dead signal or might have been the house breathing through wires and air.

"Please," John whispered into the phone. "Please. I need help."

The static answered with a click.

Then, very faintly, the voicemail tone - that polite little beep - sounded in his ear as if the device had decided on its own to deliver the message.

A voice came through, broken by interference.

"John...?"

Not Hunter's voice. Not exactly.

Too flat. Too close. Like someone standing beside him speaking into a microphone.

John's skin went cold.

The voice continued, the words warping. "You... asked... for... it..."

"You asked for relief," the voice continued, still calm, still measured, as if reading from a script designed to soothe.

John's fingers tightened around the phone until the plastic creaked.

"You asked for silence," the voice said. "You asked for sleep. You asked for a clean hour where your body didn't feel like it was being peeled open from the inside."

Static breathed behind the words. The battery icon on the screen stuttered, flashed red, then steadied again as if the phone couldn't decide whether to die.

John stared at Hunter's chest rising in shallow, wet jerks and felt his own lungs seize.

"I didn't—" John started, but the voice didn't allow interruptions.

"You asked for forgiveness," it said, and the word landed heavy, not comforting. "You asked for a story where you are not the villain."

The voice was close enough to feel like it was inside the phone and inside his skull at the same time.

John's mouth went dry. His tongue felt thick.

"No," he whispered.

A soft sound came through the line—almost a chuckle, almost pity. "Name it."

John flinched.

"Say what you want," the voice urged, patient as a therapist, patient as a dealer. "Out loud. Don't hide behind your shaking hands. Don't hide behind your friend's blood. Name it."

John's eyes burned. He looked down at his hand pressed to Hunter's wound. Blood seeped between his fingers, warm and relentless.

He could feel Hunter's life moving away with each pulse.

John's mind did what it always did in crisis: it reached for the fastest shape that could hold the panic.

A bottle. A pill. A lie.

A clean act.

"I want him to live," John said, and the truth of it surprised him. It made his throat ache.

The voice didn't answer immediately.

When it did, it sounded almost tender. "You can't."

John's stomach dropped.

"You can't put it back," the voice said. "Not the way you broke it."

John's jaw tightened. "Then why are you calling me?"

A faint ringing answered behind the voice, like another phone in another room.

"You don't recognize your own pattern," it said. "You reach. We answer."

John swallowed hard, trying to keep his hand steady on Hunter's chest. "Stop saying we."

The voice ignored him. "You want him to live because then you don't have to carry another body," it said. "You want him to live because then you can pretend this was an accident. A storm. A misunderstanding. A tragedy you didn't mean."

John's vision blurred with tears he refused to let fall. "It was an accident."

The voice softened, dangerous in its gentleness. "Say the other thing."

John's breath stuck. He knew what it wanted. He had already whispered it in the barn.

She chose it.

He heard the phrase like a hook being offered.

"I didn't," John said. His voice shook.

The voice waited. Patient.

Then it spoke again, and for a moment John thought he heard Alice's cadence in it—her way of speaking when she was trying not to cry, when she was trying to keep her voice calm so John wouldn't turn her sadness into anger.

"John," the voice said, and it was so close to her that his whole body recoiled.

His hand slipped on Hunter's blood.

Hunter made a small sound, a wet gasp, and John's focus snapped back to the present like a rubber band.

The voice continued, relentless. "You want the clean story," it said. "You want to be the man who tried. The man who meant well. The man who was forced."

John shook his head, hard, as if he could dislodge the words from the air. "Stop."

"Name what you'll pay," the voice said.

John's laugh came out broken. "Pay? What do you want me to pay?"

Silence.

Then: "Everything you keep pretending you didn't spend."

John's breath hitched.

The phone in his hand suddenly felt heavier, as if it weren't a device at all but a mouth held to his ear.

"You paid with her," the voice said. "A teaspoon at a time."

John squeezed his eyes shut. In the dark behind his lids he saw the kitchen again: Alice's mug, the thin swirl of liquid, the way he had told himself it was just to scare her. Just to make a point. Just to take control back from a woman who had started calling his drinking what it was.

"You paid with yourself," the voice continued. "Every time you reached for the bottle instead of the truth."

John opened his eyes and looked at the gun lying on the cellar floor beside his knee.

The revolver's cylinder glinted in the weak light, indifferent metal.

"You paid with the people who loved you," the voice said. "And now you want a receipt."

The battery icon flashed again, and the screen dimmed so low John could barely see it.

The voice rushed, suddenly urgent, as if time mattered now. "Listen," it said. "I can make it simple."

John's pulse hammered. His hand shook against Hunter's chest.

"The gun is simple," the voice said, almost kindly. "One act. One clean balance. You already understand that language."

John stared at the revolver.

The thought slithered in, familiar: If I'm gone, it stops. If I'm gone, they can rest. If I'm gone, I don't have to feel this.

That was always the offer at the bottom of every bottle. The quiet fantasy of disappearing.

John's throat cinched. "No."

The voice sighed, disappointed. "Then take the other offer."

John blinked. "What other—"

"Say it," the voice cut in, firm now. The gentleness dropped away, revealing the teacher's impatience beneath. "Say she chose it. Say she did it to herself. Say you didn't poison her. Say she wasn't your responsibility."

John's stomach turned. "That's not true."

"It's clean," the voice said, and the word clean sounded like hunger. "It's a story you can live inside."

John's eyes flicked to Hunter's face.

Hunter's eyes were half-open now, unfocused. His lips moved around silent shapes.

John felt a sob tear at his chest and forced it down.

The voice pressed closer. "If you say it," it said, "you get to leave."

John's breath stuttered.

The cellar seemed to listen with him, the walls close, the stairs above like an exit sealed by air.

"You get to walk out of the house," the voice promised. "You get to go home. You get to tell the detectives what they already want to hear: addiction, accident, storm, tragedy."

John's mind, exhausted, reached toward that exit.

He pictured himself stepping into daylight. Pictured a hospital. Pictured a judge. Pictured a rehab room with a bed and a plastic cup of water that didn't taste like pennies.

He pictured sleeping.

He pictured not hearing Alice's voice ever again.

The fantasy was so bright it hurt.

John squeezed Hunter's hand. Hunter's fingers twitched weakly, reflexive.

John's throat burned. "I can't."

The voice went still.

When it spoke again, it was colder. "You can," it said. "You just don't want to because then you lose your favorite drug."

John frowned, confused through blood and panic. "Alcohol?"

A short, contemptuous sound. "Martyrdom."

John's face went hot.

The voice continued, slicing now. "You like suffering because it lets you feel like you're paying. You like shaking because it proves you're trying. You like guilt because guilt is easy. Guilt is a feeling. Truth is a decision."

John's mouth opened, but no words came.

The voice leaned in for the final push. "Name it," it said. "Name the price."

John looked down at Hunter's bleeding chest and realized the price was already here.

It wasn't a future punishment.

It was the present.

He swallowed hard and found his voice. "I did it," he whispered. "I poisoned her."

The words hit the cellar like a dropped weight.

For a second, everything went quieter—as if even the storm outside paused to listen.

The voice on the phone did not answer.

Static rose, thick and wet, swallowing whatever might have come next.

John yanked the phone away from his ear.

The screen went black.

The device died in his hand with a final, indifferent silence.

John stared at it as if he could force it back to life through sheer will.

Above him, the house settled - a soft groan in the beams - like a laugh swallowed.

John kept pressure on the wound long after there was no point. Long after the warmth left. Long after his own arms ached.

The cellar was very quiet.

In the quiet, he could hear the house breathing.

A soft sound came from the corner again.

John's head snapped up.

For a heartbeat, he expected Phillip. He expected Blithe. He expected the cellar to spit out another mask and ask him to wear it.

Instead, Ruth stepped into the edge of his flashlight beam.

Eli was behind her, half in shadow, as if he didn't want the light to make him part of John's story.

Ruth's gaze went to Hunter's body. Not to the blood first —to the face, to the eyes that were open and already too far away.

Something in Ruth's expression tightened. Not grief, exactly. Something older. Something like recognition.

"He came anyway," she said, and the words were not for John. They were for the room. For the lock. For whatever listened.

John's mouth worked. No sound came out.

Eli's eyes flicked to the revolver on the stone. "The offer worked," he said.

"I didn't—" John rasped. "I didn't mean—"

Ruth held up a hand, stopping him. "Want doesn't care what you mean," she said. "Want is a door. You opened it."

John shook his head hard, as if he could shake the sentence loose from his skull. "Help him," he begged, and it sounded pathetic even to him. "Please. Help him."

Ruth knelt beside Hunter. Not as a nurse. Not as a savior. As someone honoring a body.

She reached out and, with two fingers, closed Hunter's eyes.

The gesture was small. It made John's throat burn.

Eli's voice came low. "You can still choose," he said. "Don't take the next offer."

John stared at him. "What next offer?" he whispered.

Eli's gaze slid, just briefly, toward the stairs. Toward the world above. "Relief," he said. "A second shot. A clean ending. Anything that lets you tell yourself the books are closed."

John's stomach rolled. He wanted to vomit. He wanted to drink. He wanted to rewind time and stop his own finger from moving.

He wanted—so badly—to stop feeling.

Ruth rose. Her eyes met John's again.

"We are not your payment," she said. "We do not take your debt."

John's breath hitched. "Then what do I do?"

Ruth's voice was steady. "Carry it," she said. "Carry the truth. Call for help. Let them see what you did. Let it be ugly. Let it be real."

John stared at her as if she'd spoken in another language.

"Carry it," he echoed, hoarse. "You want me to carry it like—like penance?"

Ruth's expression tightened. "No," she said. "Not like penance. Like truth."

The word truth should have sounded abstract. In Ruth's mouth it sounded physical.

John swallowed and felt it in his throat anyway—thick, heavy, lodged.

"Why do you care?" he asked. The question came out sharper than he meant. Anger was easier than terror. "Why are you even here?"

Eli made a small sound, impatient.

Ruth didn't look at him. Her attention stayed on John, on the way he held himself like a man who expected the floor to collapse. "Because it keeps eating," she said simply.

John blinked.

Ruth's gaze drifted, briefly, to Hunter's body. Not to the face. To the shape beneath the blood. The outline of a life reduced to weight.

"My brother came out here one winter," Ruth said. "Not because he was brave. Because he was desperate. He thought the stories were an exaggeration. He thought it was just a bad house with a bad history. He thought he could take what he wanted and leave."

Her voice didn't wobble. The steadiness made it worse.

"He was sober then," she continued. "Newly. Angry about it. He wanted something to prove he was stronger than the cravings. He wanted a test he could beat so he could point to it later and say: See? I'm fine."

John's hands trembled around the dead phone.

Ruth's mouth tightened. "He came home for a while," she said. "He went to meetings. He made coffee. He apologized. He did all the things people do when they're trying to become a story worth telling."

Eli's eyes flicked to Ruth, quick and unreadable.

Ruth's gaze stayed on John. "And then the phone rang one night," she said. "He answered. Because he thought he could."

John's skin prickled.

"He said it was me," Ruth continued. "He said he heard my voice. He said I sounded scared. He didn't ask questions. He didn't check. He got in his truck and drove back out here in the dark because he wanted to be the kind of man who showed up."

The sentence landed like a blow. John felt it in his ribs, in the bruise that never stopped aching.

"He died in this cellar," Ruth said. "Not because he drank. Because he wanted to believe the house would respect his effort. He wanted to believe suffering was payment."

John's throat tightened. "I'm sorry," he whispered, and hated that the words sounded small.

Ruth nodded once, as if acknowledging the impulse, and then dismissed it. "Sorry doesn't change the appetite," she said. "It just makes you feel like you've done something."

Eli's jaw flexed. His voice came out rougher. "We're not here to forgive you," he said.

John flinched. "I didn't ask for—"

"You asked for a way to make it clean," Eli said, and the word clean held contempt. "That's what you people always ask for. A clean version of yourself you can live with."

Ruth shot him another look, warning.

Eli's anger didn't soften, but he shut his mouth.

Ruth turned back to John. "We're here because if it turns you into a story, it doesn't stop at you," she said. "It spreads. It teaches the county a new rule. It teaches the next desperate man how to make an offer."

John's stomach rolled. "So you're... what?" he asked. "Some kind of—"

"Gatekeepers," Ruth said, and the word sounded like a job title. "People who learned that you don't beat a place like this by fighting it. You beat it by denying it what it wants."

"What does it want?" John asked, though he already knew the answer in his bones.

Ruth's eyes held his. "Consent," she said.

John's breath caught.

"It can't take you," Ruth continued, "not the way it wants to, without you handing yourself over. Not with your whole body. Not with your whole voice. That's why it bargains. That's why it offers. Because if you say yes—if you accept its story—then you're not a victim. You're a participant."

John's mouth went dry. "I didn't—"

Ruth lifted her chin slightly. "You did," she said. Not cruel. Just matter-of-fact. "You said yes to it a hundred times before you ever stepped on this property. Every time you chose the bottle over the conversation. Every time you chose the lie that kept you comfortable.”

John’s eyes burned.

Eli shifted, unable to stand still. “And then you came here and brought your mess to its front door,” he said. “Like it’s a dumpster for your guilt.”

John’s anger flared again. “I didn’t ask to be here.”

Ruth’s voice cut through, steady. “No,” she agreed. “You didn’t ask. But you arrived with open hands.”

John swallowed. He thought of the way he’d reached for the phone. The way the house answered reaching.

Ruth’s expression softened a fraction—not kindness, but recognition. “I’m not telling you this to punish you,” she said. “I’m telling you because you have one chance to be a person instead of a role.”

John stared at her. “How?”

Ruth nodded toward the stairwell. “You carry the truth upstairs,” she said. “You take it with you into daylight. You let it be ugly. You let it follow you. You let other people see it.”

John’s stomach twisted. Daylight meant cops. Reports. Prison. His father’s face. His mother’s silence. The mirror.

It meant being known.

“I can’t,” he whispered.

Ruth’s eyes held his, merciless in their clarity. “Then you can,” she said.

For a moment, neither of them moved. The cellar felt too small for the air between them.

Eli’s voice came quiet, almost reluctant. “When you leave,” he said, “don’t look back.”

John turned his head, instinctively, toward Hunter.

Eli saw it and his expression hardened again. "Not for him," Eli said. "Not for closure. Not for payment. That's how it gets you—by turning grief into a chain."

John's breath hitched. "He came because of me."

Ruth nodded once. "Yes," she said. "He did."

Her gaze dropped to the gun. "And it will try to make you pay with another act," she said. "It will offer you the clean ending. Don't take it."

John's hands shook harder. "What if I already did?" he whispered. "What if it already—"

Ruth's eyes lifted to his face again. "Then you do the only thing you haven't done enough of," she said. "You stop performing and you tell the truth."

The idea of the outside world seeing him like this—on his knees in a cellar, hands soaked, Hunter dead—made something in John's chest seize.

"No," he whispered.

Eli's mouth tightened. "That's the bargain," he said. "You'd rather the house eat you than let people know what you are."

John flinched as if struck.

The hum under the floorboards deepened, pleased.

Ruth's gaze moved past John, toward the darkness where the stairs began. "It's listening," she said.

John heard it then, under the rain and under his own blood-rush: that patient, steady vibration. Like a television left on in another room. Like a mouth held just barely shut.

Ruth stepped back into the shadow, and Eli followed. They didn't vanish like a hallucination. They simply retreated, returning to whatever place they belonged.

The cellar felt colder the moment they left the light.

John was alone again with Hunter's body and the gun and the open door in his own chest.

He swallowed hard.

He reached for the outside world anyway, because there was nothing else left to reach for.

He looked around wildly, waiting for Phillip to step into the light. Waiting for Blithe to appear and clap politely. Waiting for the Gatekeepers to rise out of the stone and tell him he had done the act correctly.

No one came.

John crawled backward until his spine hit the wall.

His hands were soaked. His flannel was soaked. The smell of blood was thick in his nose, metallic and intimate.

He swallowed hard and tasted pennies.

He wanted to scream.

He wanted to drink.

He wanted to rewind time and stop his own finger from closing.

Instead, he forced himself up the stairs.

The storm cellar doors were heavier than they should have been. He shoved and they resisted, as if the house didn't want to let him back into the world.

When they finally gave, rain slapped his face.

The yard was gray.

The storm had moved on. Morning had arrived without asking permission.

John stood in the wet grass and stared at the farmhouse like it had betrayed him personally.

The masquerade world--lanterns and music and masks-- was gone like it had never existed. The property was what it had always been: sagging porch, peeling paint, dead grass flattened by rain.

Behind him, Hunter lay in the dark.

John stepped out into the morning and felt the cold hit his face like a slap.

His hands were smeared with dirt and something darker. His fingers kept twitching, trying to close around something that wasn't there.

He looked toward the barn.

In the masquerade it had been alive with voices, crowded with bodies that moved like shadows.

Now it sat collapsed and hollow, its broken windows staring at him. Hunter's truck was parked crooked beside it, mud caked up to the wheel wells.

John's chest tightened.

Hunter had come all the way out here.

Hunter had come because John had asked.

John turned away.

He stumbled to the porch and into the house.

Inside, the air was stale and cold, as if the warmth had been a lie, too. The candles were gone. The chandeliers were dark. The wallpaper sagged.

The living room looked smaller in daylight. Meaner. Like a mouth that had finished chewing.

The red corded phone lay in pieces on the living room floor, base cracked, receiver off the hook and twisted in the cord's slack, like a mouth forced open and left that way.

John stared at it, and his vision swam.

He reached for the receiver anyway.

Static hissed. A faint ticking sound, like a metronome set to a sick rhythm. He waited for a dial tone.

Instead, he heard a whisper, low and familiar, brushing the inside of his ear.

I'm sorry.

John jerked the receiver away as if it had burned him.

He stared at the receiver, at the dull plastic curve of it, and realized his hand was shaking even when it wasn't holding a bottle.

The whisper had not come through the line like a normal sound.

It had come through him.

John set the receiver down beside the cracked base carefully, the way you set down a glass you've already broken.

The line clicked.

He waited for the dial tone to die.

It didn't.

A faint hiss persisted, as if the phone were still open, still listening, still connected to something that wasn't a network.

John's breath hitched.

He yanked the plug free from the wall. The hiss didn't stop. Unplugged, and still listening, as if the cord ran into him instead of into a jack.

He pressed his palm against his eyes until he saw sparks. "DTs," he whispered, trying to make it clinical. Trying to make it manageable.

A sound came from the living room.

Not footsteps. Not a creak.

A click, like electricity deciding to wake up.

The television clicked on.

The remote sat on the coffee table, face down, dark. He hadn't touched it. He hadn't even been in this room since the night the house had dressed itself up in lantern light and laughter.

There was no reason for the screen to be alive.

John froze.

The screen glowed in the dim living room, bright enough to paint the walls in pale light.

It wasn't static.

It wasn't snow.

It was his apartment.

The angle was wrong, too high, as if whoever held the camera had been pinned in a corner near the ceiling, watching the room like prey watches a trap.

The picture stuttered at the edges with faint static, and for a second John thought the furniture was breathing.

The living room. The white carpet. The staircase.

John's throat tightened. He took a step closer, then another, pulled forward by something he didn't want to name.

On the screen, he saw himself.

Not a memory, exactly. A replay. The kind of evidence you can't argue with once it's in front of you—the kind that turns your own story into a lie you can hear.

Not the John who had been trying to get sober. Not the John who had whispered apologies into Hunter's hair.

The other John.

Drunk-John.

His movements were sloppy and slow, like a puppet with loose strings. His eyes were glassy. His mouth moved around words that didn't matter.

Alice stood across from him, rigid, face pale. Her voice was muted by the television's silence, but John could read her anger in the shape of her mouth, the violence of her gestures.

She pointed at him.

She slapped him.

Drunk-John swayed and grinned, like the slap was a joke.

John's stomach turned.

Alice's hand flew to her face again. Then she took a breath that looked like surrender. Her shoulders dropped.

She spoke a sentence John had heard a thousand times in a thousand arguments.

I'm done.

Alice pulled her ring off and threw it.

The ring bounced once on the carpet and rolled, spinning its small circle of gold like a coin, like a dare.

Drunk-John watched it roll like it was a toy.

John in the farmhouse whispered, "No," but the screen didn't hear him.

Alice stumbled into the bathroom and slammed the door. John could see her in the mirror for a moment--hands braced on the sink, breathing hard, as if trying to breathe her way out of a life.

Drunk-John stared at the television's edge of frame for a long moment.

Then he moved.

He stumbled into the kitchen.

John's mouth went dry.

He knew what came next.

He didn't remember it--he had spent the last year building a wall around the memory--but he knew the shape of it the way you know the shape of a bruise under your skin.

On the screen, Drunk-John opened the cabinet under the sink and pulled out the box.

RAT POISON.

The label flashed bright and ordinary in the harsh kitchen light, as casual as paper towels. Then the picture twitched, static chewing at the corners of the frame, as if the house couldn't decide whether it wanted to show him the whole truth or just enough of it.

John's knees went weak. He grabbed the back of the couch to keep from falling.

Drunk-John's hand shook as he opened the box. He didn't measure. He didn't hesitate. He poured.

A pale cloud of powder fell into a glass on the counter.

For a second it hung in the air like dust in sunlight.

Then it vanished into clear liquid.

John's breath came out as a sob.

He had done it.

Not Alice.

Him.

He had wanted the pain to stop. He had wanted to vanish. He had wanted to punish her for leaving. He had wanted all of it and called it despair.

On the screen, Drunk-John capped the box and shoved it back under the sink. Then he walked into the living room and set the glass down on the coffee table like it was nothing.

Like it was a joke.

Like it was a spell.

Then he climbed the stairs, swaying, and collapsed onto the bed in a heap of clothes and sweat.

Alice came out of the bathroom.

She stood in the living room and stared at the glass on the table.

She didn't know.

Of course she didn't know.

She picked it up.

John's throat closed.

Alice lifted the glass to her mouth and drank.

In the farmhouse, John made a sound that wasn't human.

Alice's face changed. Confusion first. Then fear.

She set the glass down, too carefully, as if carefulness could undo what had already happened.

She took a step and stopped.

She tried to call out. No sound came from the television, but John saw the word on her lips.

John.

She stumbled toward the stairs, then changed direction, like she couldn't remember where help lived in her own house.

She made it to the living room.

She fell.

She lay on the white carpet and stared up at the ceiling with eyes that didn't blink.

She died alone.

The television image froze on her face, then dissolved into gray static.

In the farmhouse, John couldn't breathe.

He pressed his hands to his mouth as if he could keep his own scream from escaping.

The screen hissed.

Behind him, a floorboard creaked.

John turned his head slowly.

Phillip stood in the corner of the living room, half in shadow, suit dark, face solemn.

He looked real in the thin morning light. Too real.

John's voice came out small. "I didn't--"

"You did," Phillip said.

Not cruel. Not triumphant.

Just true.

John shook his head, tears streaking his face. "I didn't mean to," he whispered. "I was drunk. I was--"

Phillip nodded once. "You wanted the pain to stop," he said. "So you reached for poison."

John flinched.

Phillip's eyes didn't leave him. "When you couldn't drink it," he continued, "someone you loved paid the price."

The house kept books, and it never lost a receipt.

John pressed his palms to his eyes. The image of Alice on the carpet burned behind his lids.

"I'm sorry," he whispered.

"Sorry is the beginning," Phillip said. "Not the end."

John's chest heaved. He turned toward the cellar door, toward where Hunter lay in the dark, and tasted bile.

He had chosen another poison last night, too.

A gun.

Control.

Relief.

Blithe's lie.

John's voice shook. "What happens now?"

Phillip's gaze held his. "Now you stop running," he said. "Now you face what you have already done."

John let out a broken laugh. "I can't fix this."

"No," Phillip agreed. "You can't."

John's eyes drifted to the revolver on the floor where it had fallen, the metal dull in the gray light.

He had come here to get sober.

He had come here to be forgiven without having to be known.

Instead he had brought his worst self into the house and watched it sharpen.

"I didn't know," John said, and hated himself for how much he wanted that to matter.

Phillip's face didn't change. "You didn't want to know," he said quietly.

John's jaw clenched.

He stepped toward the wall phone again, because he couldn't stand the stillness. He couldn't stand the idea that he could simply stand here and let the world keep turning with Hunter dead in the cellar and Alice dead in his memory.

His fingers closed around the receiver.

Static.

Then, beneath the static, a sound like laughter--soft, distant, easily mistaken for a shift in the line.

John slammed the receiver down.

The plastic cradle cracked.

He ripped the phone off the wall and threw it across the room.

It hit the far wall and exploded into pieces, the cord whipping like a severed vein.

John stood there panting, shaking, staring at the wreckage like it was proof that he was still capable of doing something.

Phillip watched without comment.

John swallowed. "Am I stuck here?"

Phillip's expression softened, but it wasn't comfort. It was pity.

"That depends," Phillip said.

"On what?" John demanded, anger flaring because anger was easier than guilt.

Phillip gestured toward the front door.

"On whether you can walk out," Phillip said, "and carry the truth with you."

John stared at the door.

Outside, morning sat over the yard like ash. Everything was wet from the storm that had moved on, and the air had that thin, rinsed smell that usually meant a clean start. Out here it only meant the house had more daylight to work with.

He could hear nothing but the faint tick of the house settling and the slow drip of water from the eaves.

John stepped closer to the knob.

Phillip didn't stop him.

That was part of the cruelty. Or part of the test.

John wrapped his fingers around the brass. It was cold enough to bite.

He turned it.

The latch released with a clean, familiar click - the sound of any door in any house.

John pulled the door open.

The porch boards shone damp and gray. The yard beyond was a smear of dead grass and flattened mud. Somewhere out there, past the invisible boundary the house kept drawing and redrawing, the road waited.

For a second, hope hit him so hard he almost laughed.

Then he saw the line.

Not drawn in chalk. Not marked with bones. Not labeled.

He saw it the way you see a crack in ice - not the crack itself, but the slight shift in the surface that tells you where the world will give way. The air beyond the porch steps looked thicker. The space was subtly wrong, like a photograph with the edges blurred.

John's throat tightened.

He could step off this porch and keep walking until his legs failed.

Or he could step off this porch and discover the house's geometry again - the loop, the boundary, the invisible hand that turned you back.

He looked down at his sleeve.

There was blood there. Hunter's blood, already cooling, already drying at the edges, turning sticky.

Hunter was still in the dark below, and John had not even tried to pull him up the stairs.

Because some part of him already knew what it would feel like.

Heavy. Impossible.

Truth.

Phillip's voice drifted behind him, not raised, not pleading.

"Shame is lighter," Phillip said. "Shame fits in a bottle. Truth does not."

John swallowed.

"What do you want?" he asked, and the question came out like a snarl, because anger was what he had left when hope failed.

Phillip was quiet for a moment. When he spoke, his voice carried weight that didn't belong to a man standing in a farmhouse.

"I want the door to stay shut," Phillip said simply.

John turned his head.

Phillip's face was calm, but there was strain in the stillness around him, like a man holding something heavy without letting his muscles show it.

"You're not the first," Phillip continued. "Men come here with hunger and call it grief. Men come here with rot in their mouths and call it love. Men come here wanting to be spared the cost of what they've done."

John's jaw clenched.

Phillip's eyes held his. "We keep it contained," he said. "That is our work."

John thought of the corner of the cellar, the way the shadows had looked crowded. Bare feet on stone. Hands folded.

Gatekeepers.

"You can't tell me you're doing this for me," John said.

Phillip's expression didn't change. "I'm not," he replied.

The honesty of it hit harder than kindness would have.

"What happens if I don't?" John asked, and he hated the tremor in his voice.

Phillip glanced past him, toward the open doorway, toward the damp morning. "Then what is behind you keeps wearing your face," he said. "And it walks out instead."

John's stomach dropped.

He pictured the other John from the television - the grin, the empty eyes, the casual cruelty. He pictured that version of himself moving through the world unchallenged, telling stories, spending blame like currency.

Phillip's voice softened by a fraction. "Truth is not punishment," he said. "It is weight. If you will not carry it, something else will."

John stared at the yard again.

The world beyond the porch waited, indifferent.

He could feel the simplest offer in his bones: end it. End it and call it payment.

John's hands clenched into fists. His nails dug crescents into his palms.

"I can't," he whispered, and meant it in a dozen ways.

Phillip's voice was almost gentle. "Then you're still drinking," he said. "Even without the bottle."

John turned, rage hot and bright. "You don't know what it's like."

Phillip's eyes did not blink. "I know what it costs," he said.

John looked away, because he could not bear the steadiness of that gaze. He could not bear the possibility that the house wasn't punishing him so much as simply refusing to let him pretend.

He bent, picked up the revolver with shaking hands, and checked the cylinder like a man checking a prayer.

One spent round.

Five bullets waiting.

Enough.

He stood, legs unsteady, and stepped around the couch.

As he passed the television, it clicked off.

The living room dimmed.

John reached for the doorknob.

His hand hovered there, trembling.

Behind him, Phillip said quietly, "The hard ending is still an ending."

John swallowed.

He opened the door.

Cold air rushed in. Daylight made his eyes ache.

The yard was empty.

Then John saw movement at the tree line.

A figure stood in the wet grass, just beyond the porch steps.

It wore a black ski mask.

The figure's posture was wrong--too familiar. The way it held its shoulders, the way its weight favored one leg. The stance of a man who had never once believed consequences applied to him.

John's blood chilled.

"The mask," he whispered.

The figure tilted its head, as if listening.

Then it began to walk toward the porch.

John backed up a step, revolver lifting without conscious thought.

His hands shook so badly the barrel wavered.

"Stop," John said.

The figure didn't stop.

The wet grass made no sound beneath its feet.

John's stomach twisted. For a moment, he had the absurd thought that the figure wasn't touching the ground at all.

The figure reached the first porch step.

John's finger tightened.

"Don't," he whispered, and the word sounded like a plea.

The figure lifted a hand and, very slowly, reached up to the edge of the ski mask.

John's whole body braced, as if he were about to take a punch.

The figure pulled the mask up.

Underneath was John Glisner.

Same eyes. Same tired lines. Same mouth that had promised and lied and smiled through apologies.

Only the expression was different.

This John wasn't ashamed.

He wasn't afraid.

He looked at John on the porch like he had been waiting for him to catch up.

John's voice cracked. "What are you?"

The other John smiled.

It wasn't a grin. It wasn't a snarl.

It was the smile of a man who has decided he gets to do whatever he wants and call it survival.

"I'm what you keep," the other John said.

The other John's gaze flicked past him, to the dark windows and the open door behind. "They showed you something," he said. "A little movie. A neat little story."

He shrugged, almost careless. "You believe it because it hurts. Hurting feels like paying."

John's mouth went dry. "I did it," he whispered, and hated how the words wanted to become a confession.

"Did you?" the other John asked, voice almost bored. "Or did she? Or did the house need a villain to keep you here? You'll swallow anything if it lets you keep drinking."

He spread his hands, palms up, in a parody of innocence. "Put the mask back on. Let them call her death what it already was. Let them call the man in the cellar a tragedy. You can still walk out and tell yourself you tried."

John lifted the revolver. The barrel wagged. "Shut up," he said, but his voice sounded like a man arguing with an echo.

The other John's smile deepened, pleased. "There you are," he murmured. "Back where you live."

His voice was John's voice, but steadier. Cleaner. As if the shaking belonged to someone else.

John's hands trembled harder. "You're not real," he said, because if he didn't say it out loud, he might believe the worst thing--that the house was right, that the monster was only ever him.

The other John stepped onto the porch.

John lifted the revolver, sighting down the barrel at his own face.

The world narrowed to a small circle: front sight, rear sight, the bridge of a nose he knew too well.

His finger tried to squeeze.

It didn't.

Somewhere inside him, a part of him that still remembered love--still remembered Hunter's hands on his shoulders in rehab, still remembered Alice laughing at a dumb joke--locked his joints in place.

The other John's smile widened.

"You can't," he said softly. "That's why you're here."

He lunged.

John felt the impact like a tackle. The revolver jerked in his grip.

They hit the porch boards hard. The bunched ski mask slid off the other John's head and disappeared beneath the porch.

John's head struck wood. Stars burst behind his eyes.

The other John's hands were on him--strong, familiar hands, hands that had held a steering wheel and held a bottle and held Hunter's shoulder in a drunken hug.

Hands that had never learned gentleness.

John twisted, trying to throw him off, but the other John moved like he knew every weak point, every slow reflex, every place withdrawal had turned John soft.

The revolver was between them, metal slick, barrel sweeping in frantic arcs.

John smelled whiskey.

Or maybe he only remembered it.

Either way, the scent hit him like a slap - the sweet burn, the false warmth, the instant promise of a world made soft. His mouth flooded with saliva. His hands shook harder, betrayed by his own body's hunger.

The other John smiled.

It was not a friendly smile. It was the grin of a man who knows the trick and loves it anyway.

"You miss it," the other John said, voice low. Not quite slurred. Controlled in a way that made it worse. "Not the drink. The excuse."

John's teeth clenched. "You're not real," he rasped, and he didn't know if he meant the man in front of him or the version of himself that had lived for years behind his eyes.

The other John shoved the barrel up toward John's throat, forcing John's chin back, finding the soft place under the jaw where a man could end a story in a second.

John grabbed the other John's wrist with both hands and fought.

The porch creaked under their weight. Damp boards slicked beneath their boots. John's palms slid.

"One clean shot," the other John murmured, pushing. "And you don't have to carry anything."

John's pulse hammered.

He wanted the shaking to stop. He wanted his muscles to unclench. He wanted the world to stop demanding.

His mind flashed bright images - not memories, not exactly, but promises.

A hospital bed. A doctor saying you're stable now. A phone call where Hargrove's voice is distant and procedural and the words not charged with hatred anymore.

Alice's face, calm, forgiving, as if she could be made to look at him again without flinching.

Hunter's laugh.

It all hovered just out of reach like a drink held up and then snatched away.

"You want relief," the other John whispered. "You want to feel paid."

John shoved harder, trying to force the gun away. The other John barely moved, solid as a post.

"You think if you die, it balances," the other John said. "You think if you put the barrel under your chin, you become the tragic husband instead of the bastard who did it."

John's eyes burned. "I didn't know," he whispered.

The other John's grin widened.

"That's the best part," he said softly. "You didn't have to know. You just had to want the pain to stop."

John's hands trembled.

"You still want a story where you're not the villain," the other John said. "So let's make one. You can die out here on this porch and everyone will say grief broke him. They'll shake their heads. They'll forgive you in the same breath they condemn you. You'll be a headline, a cautionary tale, a sad man."

The barrel lifted, just a fraction, and John's throat clamped in anticipation of pressure, of the final click.

The other John leaned closer, breath hot and sweet.

"Or," he whispered, "you can stop fighting and let me live."

John's stomach turned.

Above them, the farmhouse windows stared.

For a heartbeat, John thought he saw movement behind the glass - faces lined in the dark, watching like an audience.

Then his mind supplied the worst possibility: that the faces were his own, dozens of versions of him, all the Johns he had been and would be, watching to see which one won.

John's arms burned.

He wanted to give up.

He wanted to be forgiven without having to be known.

Phillip's words came back to him in a strange, fierce clarity.

Truth is weight.

John's breath came out ragged. He forced his mouth to shape the sentence he had avoided for years.

"I did it," he said.

The other John paused.

Just a heartbeat. Just a twitch in the wrist.

John felt it like a crack in ice.

"I did it," John repeated, louder, as if volume could make it truer. "I poisoned her. I did."

The other John's smile faltered, not from shock, but from irritation - like a man whose favorite joke has been interrupted.

"That's not the whole truth," the other John hissed.

John's hands slipped on damp skin, but he held on.

"I wanted it," John said, voice shaking. "I wanted the pain to stop so bad I didn't care what it cost."

The other John snarled, the sound animal and human at once.

John shoved.

The barrel wavered away from his throat for an instant.

John lunged into that instant, grabbing the gun with both hands, forcing it down and away.

The other John fought him, teeth bared. Their bodies slammed into the porch rail. Wood groaned.

John tried to speak. Tried to say I'm sorry. Tried to say I didn't mean it. Tried to say anything that wasn't a lie.

The other John shoved harder.

John's finger brushed the trigger.

Somewhere, very far away, Phillip's voice drifted through the open door, soft enough to be almost kind.

"Now you know," he said.

The gun went off.

Chapter Twenty: The Unmasking

The first trooper on scene thought the storm cellar doors were a bear den.

They sat half-open in the wet grass like two rusted teeth, rainwater dripping from their hinges. From the road the farmhouse looked asleep, its windows dull and dark, the porch sagging in the gray light. The trooper parked at the end of the drive and listened before he did anything else. That was what you did out here: you listened. Remote places made even confident men cautious.

No barking dog.

No generator.

No voices.

Just water moving in the ditch and the faint hiss of wind through bare branches.

The dispatcher had called it a welfare check. That was the polite language for the things nobody wanted to name. A hunter had found a truck nose-down near the barn with its hazard lights still blinking in the rain. A neighbor had driven by at dawn and seen the storm cellar doors standing open like a mouth. And somewhere in the middle of it, a voicemail had come in—one man's voice sobbing, repeating the same word until it turned to noise.

The trooper walked up the drive with his hand near his holster.

Mud sucked at his boots.

The storm had left the world rinsed and raw. Everything smelled of wet earth and cold metal. The grass was flattened in strange places, as if a fight had rolled across it.

He stopped at the cellar doors and crouched.

The boards were old, scarred, swollen at the edges. Water beaded on the rusty hinges. The dark gap between them breathed out a damp smell that was part rot, part stone, part something faintly sweet, like old liquor spilled years ago and never fully scrubbed out.

There were boot prints leading down.

One set.

Deep, clean tread.

Another set leading back up, staggered, dragging at the toe like the person had been hurt or exhausted or both.

And then the prints thinned and shallowed in the wet grass until they were nothing but disturbed blades and a smear of water—easy to lose, easy to explain, and still wrong in the way they ended.

The trooper's mouth went dry.

A sheet lay crumpled beside the doors.

He didn't want to move it. He also didn't have to.

The shape beneath it was unmistakable.

He backed away, eyes on the farmhouse.

Maybe it was the storm. Maybe it was the quiet. But he had the sudden, irrational certainty that if he turned his back on that house, it would change shape.

He lifted his radio.

"County, this is Unit Twelve," he said, and his voice came out steadier than he felt. "I've got an apparent deceased male at the storm cellar. Need detectives and EMS. Also request K-9 and additional units for a missing person."

He repeated the address.

Van Drake Road.

The line crackled with confirmation. The dispatcher asked him to hold the scene. The trooper didn't need the reminder. He stood at the edge of the yard with his boots planted in the mud and watched the farmhouse like it might blink.

It didn't.

The property stayed quiet and patient.

As if it had all the time in the world.

* * *

By the time Detective Hargrove arrived, the morning had turned flat and gray. The storm had scrubbed the world clean, leaving everything sharper—every broken branch, every churned patch of earth, every small dark stain in the grass where the rain hadn't reached. The sun never truly rose. It only brightened the clouds enough to make them look like a lid.

Hargrove's unmarked car rolled to a stop behind a line of cruisers.

Scene tape snapped and fluttered from the porch rail, loud in the quiet.

Officer Lane stood near the front steps with a notebook open and a face that looked too young for the work. He tried not to look at the sheet near the cellar doors. He didn't succeed.

Hargrove stepped out, adjusted his glasses, and let his gaze sweep the yard in practiced increments.

A bagged revolver rested on the hood of Lane's cruiser, water beading on the plastic.

Two fired chambers in the cylinder.

Two shells that still smelled sharp and new.

One body covered with a sheet.

One man missing.

On the front lawn, near the porch, there was only a dark patch in the grass—blood soaked into the soil—and an empty space where a person should have been.

Hargrove stood at the porch steps and looked up at the farmhouse.

Old houses always looked guilty to him. Maybe because people liked blaming wood and nails for what they did to each other inside.

Lane approached.

"One male," Lane said quietly. "Hunter Wallace. ID confirmed."

He hesitated, then added, "And the homeowner—John Glisner—is missing."

Hargrove's jaw tightened at the second name anyway.

"Glisner," he repeated.

Lane nodded. "You know him?"

"I know the file," Hargrove said.

He did not say: I know the white carpet.

He did not say: I know the cardboard box under the sink.

He did not say: I know a woman on her back at the foot of a staircase while her husband shook in a patrol car and tried to tell me the world didn't make sense.

Lane swallowed. "Looks like a homicide," he offered, and then, after a beat, "and maybe a suicide... if we find him."

Hargrove didn't answer. He crouched near the porch rail and examined the scuffs in the wet wood. Something had scraped here. Something heavy. Rain had tried to wash it away and failed.

There were prints, too—boot soles stamped deep into the mud. Lane had circled them in chalk. One pattern matched the trooper's. Another matched Wallace's boots, based on a quick comparison.

The third pattern did not match either.

It was deeper in one spot than the other, as if whoever made it had been leaning hard, bracing, fighting.

A black ski mask lay crumpled beneath the porch, wedged between the lattice and an old milk crate. Damp at the edges. Strangely dry inside.

Hargrove stared at it for a moment, then looked away.

A man doesn't put on a mask unless he wants to be someone else.

Or unless he's running from something he can't explain.

"Maybe," he said.

Lane flipped a page. "Glisner was in alcohol withdrawal," he said. "We've got that from Wallace's family. He came out here to detox."

Hargrove stood.

"Yeah," he said.

Lane hesitated. "The storm cellar's—" He glanced toward the yard, toward the open doors. "It's bad."

Hargrove didn't ask for details. He already knew the shape of the story. He had seen enough scenes to recognize when a house wasn't the important part. The important part was always the moment inside a person when the decision got made.

"Walk me through," he said.

Lane took a breath. "Wallace got a voicemail from Glisner late last night," he said. "I've got the time stamp— around eleven. Just... just Glisner saying the same thing over and over. 'I'm sorry.' Then the line goes dead."

Hargrove looked toward the house again.

The wind pushed at the porch tape, making it snap.

"So Wallace drove out," Hargrove said.

Lane nodded. "Roads were bad. But he made it. His truck's out by the barn."

Hargrove's eyes narrowed. "He got here in the middle of a storm?"

"Yeah," Lane said. "He came anyway."

Hargrove didn't comment on loyalty. He had seen what loyalty did to people. Sometimes it saved them. Sometimes it put them in the ground.

"Then what?" he asked.

Lane glanced down at his notes. "We've got a gunshot down in the storm cellar," he said. "Blood. Drag marks. It looks like Wallace was hit first. Ballistics matches the revolver."

Hargrove's mind filled in the rest: a man in the dark, shaking, holding a gun like a lifeline, waiting for monsters he could name.

Lane's voice lowered. "Then the phone in the living room is destroyed," he said. "Ripped apart. Like somebody lost it."

He swallowed, eyes flicking to the stain in the grass.

"Then Glisner walks out here," Lane continued, "and there's another gunshot. But no second body."

Hargrove kept his face neutral.

Inside, something in him tightened anyway.

The revolver sat bagged on the hood of Lane's cruiser, rain beading on the plastic.

Two shots.

One accounted for.

One missing.

Hargrove stared at the dark patch in the grass. The blood there was thinner than Wallace's, watered by rain, as if it had leaked out of someone who didn't have much left to give.

Lane rubbed his hands together for warmth. "Why out here?" he asked. "Why not inside? Why not—"

"Because outside is where you go when you want witnesses," Hargrove said.

Lane blinked. "Witnesses?"

Hargrove's mouth twitched, not quite a smile. "Or when you want to make sure no one stops you," he said.

Lane's eyes flicked to the farmhouse. "You believe in haunted houses, Detective?"

Hargrove adjusted his glasses.

"I believe in grief," he said. "I believe in what men do when grief doesn't have a place to go."

Lane hesitated. "Locals say this place is... bad," he said. "They say nobody can leave it."

Hargrove stared at the windows.

They returned only darkness.

For a moment he thought he saw a curtain shift on the second floor, like someone leaning away from the glass.

Then the wind changed, and it was only a loose strip of fabric settling.

Hargrove listened.

He thought, for a heartbeat, he heard something from inside—soft, almost amused, easy to mistake for a board settling or a shutter tapping. Like a man chuckling in a dark room.

Then the porch tape snapped again, and the sound was gone.

He turned away.

"Bag it up," he said. "And call the medical examiner."

Lane nodded and hurried off.

Hargrove took one last look at the farmhouse before following.

He could not shake the thought that the story wasn't done.

* * *

They worked the scene the way they always did.

Slow.

Methodical.

As if attention could stitch a narrative back together.

EMS confirmed what everyone already knew. The man under the sheet was dead. When the medical examiner arrived and pulled the fabric back, Hunter Wallace's face looked wrong in daylight—too pale, too still, the rain tracking clean lines down his cheek like tears someone else had ordered.

The ME spoke quietly to Hargrove about entry wound and trajectory. About the amount of blood in the cellar. About the way Wallace might have stayed alive long enough to move. Long enough to say a last thing.

Lane kept writing.

Hargrove watched the farmhouse.

Two K-9 handlers arrived mid-morning with dogs that strained at their harnesses, eager and anxious. The first dog hit Wallace's scent and pulled toward the barn, then toward the storm cellar, then slowed—nose working hard—and balked at the open doors, whining low the way working dogs did when a smell turned sharp and confusing.

The handler coaxed, clicked her tongue, offered a treat.

The dog refused to descend.

It backed up until its haunches hit the handler's shin, and it stayed there, eyes fixed on the dark gap like it was looking at a cliff.

"Hate enclosed spaces," the handler said, tight smile that didn't reach her eyes.

Hargrove nodded as if that explained the raised hackles and trembling paws.

The second dog took Glisner's scent from the porch rail, where sweat and rain and skin oil still clung to the wood. It tracked across the yard in a crooked line, nose down, tail stiff.

It led them past the dark patch in the grass.

Past the place where the blood had soaked into the dirt.

Toward the tree line.

Halfway there, the dog slowed.

Its ears lifted.

Its paws began to place themselves with careful delicacy, as if the ground had grown fragile.

Then it stopped.

The handler followed its gaze, frowning.

In the wet grass ahead of them, barely visible beneath the sheen of rain, there was a line of pale fragments arranged in a gentle curve.

At first glance it looked like trash. Bone. The leftovers of something small and butchered.

But the pieces were too clean.

Too deliberate.

As if someone had placed them there one by one.

The dog sniffed once, then pulled back, lifting one paw as if the pale fragments might hurt to step on.

The handler muttered under her breath and looked at Hargrove. "She won't step over it," she admitted.

Hargrove crouched at the edge of the line and studied it.

Chicken bones, he thought.

Or rabbit.

Or—if someone wanted to be dramatic—teeth.

"Can you go around?" Lane asked from behind him.

The handler tugged gently on the leash.

The dog stepped left, then right, then refused to move forward.

"It's like the scent just... drops," she said, irritation trying to cover unease. "Could be the rain washing it clean. Could be the wind."

Hargrove traced the curve with his eyes.

On the far side of it, the grass was undisturbed.

No prints.

No drag marks.

No broken stalks.

If Glisner had walked through, the mud would have kept the record.

Hargrove stood.

"We'll grid the property," he said. "Start at the barn, work outward. Check the creek. Check the woods."

Lane nodded and called it in.

They searched for hours.

They found Wallace's truck by the barn, doors unlocked, the cab smelling of wet denim and stale coffee. A set of keys lay on the floorboard. There was no sign of struggle there, just the aftermath of a hurried arrival—tire tracks gouged into mud, a boot print on the door as if Wallace had shoved it open too hard.

They found fresh tire ruts on the drive.

They found a flashlight in the grass with its beam still on, the batteries nearly dead.

They found a torn piece of paper stuck to a thorn bush: a list written in a shaky hand. Lines underlined. Words repeated.

LOCKS.

DOORS.

PHONE.

The handwriting looked like it belonged to a man whose body couldn't stop vibrating.

They did not find John Glisner.

No body in the woods.

No body in the creek.

No body tucked beneath the porch.

No blood trail leading away, only that one dark patch on the lawn and the strange, clean line of bones that no one wanted to step over.

The troopers said it was an animal boundary. A prank. A leftover from hunters.

Hargrove let them talk.

He had seen too many men insist on a simple answer just to keep the world from widening beneath their feet.

By mid-afternoon, the sky began to spit sleet.

Hargrove looked at Lane. "We go in," he said.

Lane's eyes flicked to the farmhouse. "We already cleared—"

"We go in again," Hargrove repeated.

Lane nodded, and the two of them climbed the porch steps.

The wood creaked beneath their weight.

The front door was ajar.

A cold draft rolled out and hit their faces.

Inside, the air smelled of damp and old smoke and something faintly metallic, like pennies held too long in a warm fist.

The living room sat in heavy disarray.

The red corded phone was in pieces on the floor, as if someone had smashed it against the wall until the plastic cracked and the wire guts spilled out. The receiver lay separated from its base, the coil stretched thin and shining like a vein.

The TV was dark, but the glass was warm when Hargrove touched it—warm enough to make him flinch.

Lane stared at the broken phone. "He lost it," he whispered.

Hargrove walked past the phone without answering.

A chair sat in the center of the room at an odd angle, one leg splintered. Dark stains marked the carpet near it. Blood, diluted by rain that had blown in through the open door.

On the coffee table there was a pill bottle tipped on its side, the label half torn.

Hargrove didn't pick it up. He didn't need to. He had seen detox scenes before. He knew the desperate arithmetic of it: anything to stop the shaking, anything to make the walls hold still.

Lane moved to the staircase and looked up. "No one," he said, voice tight.

Hargrove nodded.

The house didn't feel empty.

It felt... paused.

As if someone had walked out of a room mid-sentence.

They checked the kitchen, the bedrooms, the bathroom where water still dripped from a faucet that hadn't been fully turned off. Hargrove paused at the sink and stared into the stainless steel basin.

For a second he saw, in his mind, another sink. Another house. Another box under the cabinet.

A cardboard poison box.

He shook the image away and kept moving.

In a back hallway, a door stood closed. The knob was scratched, the wood around it gouged as if someone had tried to claw their way through.

Lane reached for it.

Hargrove put a hand on his wrist.

"Hold," he said quietly.

Lane looked at him. "What?"

Hargrove didn't have an answer that sounded sane.

He listened.

Nothing.

No movement.

Only the faint tick of the house settling—wood contracting in the cold, nails shifting—ordinary sounds that still felt like a pulse.

Hargrove let Lane open the door.

It was a storage closet.

Empty except for a broken latch on the inside, twisted metal that looked like it had been forced.

Lane exhaled, embarrassed by his own tension. "Jesus," he muttered.

Hargrove stared into the darkness anyway.

He could not stop thinking about doors.

About what stayed shut.

About what got out when a man's hands failed him.

They moved toward the storm cellar.

The doors were still open.

Cold air rolled up from below.

The trooper who had found the body earlier stood nearby, eyes restless. He nodded at Hargrove like a man grateful to hand off responsibility.

Hargrove descended the steps with a flashlight in his hand.

The beam cut down into stone and damp.

The storm cellar was worse than Lane had said, not because of gore—though there was blood—but because of what the room suggested.

There were scuff marks on the walls, as if someone had slid along the stone in panic.

A streak of blood trailed across the floor and ended in a smear near the steps, as if someone had been pulled or had crawled.

In the corner sat an old chair overturned.

Near it, something gleamed: a small metallic button, torn free from a jacket. Hargrove lifted it with gloved fingers. It looked new, bright against the dirt. Like it hadn't belonged here at all.

Lane's light swung, and for a second it caught something on the far wall.

Writing.

Not graffiti. Not carved initials.

Words scratched into damp stone with something sharp.

Hargrove moved closer.

The scratches were shallow, frantic.

I'M SORRY.

Over and over, like a prayer that had been chewed down to its most basic shape.

Lane swallowed.

Hargrove's throat tightened.

He thought of John Glisner's voicemail. The repeating apology. The static.

He thought of the way grief could make a man want to become nothing just to escape being himself.

Lane's light drifted lower.

At the edge of the room, the same pale fragments from the grass lay scattered across the stone, as if the line outside had started down here and then broken apart.

Hargrove knelt.

Bone.

Clean, white.

The flashlight beam climbed the stone walls and found nothing for it to cling to.

No dried blood. No drag marks. No scuffing where boots would have scraped. No dark damp patches where a body had cooled on earth.

Just limestone sweating in the beam and a thin sheen of water on the floor like the cellar was newly washed.

Hargrove stood on the bottom step and let his eyes adjust, unwilling to move farther in. The air down here was colder than it should have been, not by much—just enough to make the hair on his arms lift. He had been in basements all over this county, in houses that smelled like mildew and mouse droppings and old propane. This one smelled like...

Nothing.

Not bleach. Not rot. Not earth.

Nothing was supposed to smell like nothing—unless your own nose was lying to you. Storms did that sometimes. Fear did it, too.

Lane came down behind him, boot heels careful on the steps. He stopped one step above Hargrove, close enough that Hargrove could feel the heat of his body. Lane's usual chatter had been burned out by the morning's work. The jokes were gone. The swagger too.

Hargrove glanced back at him. Lane's face was tight, jaw went hard, eyes scanning the stone as if expecting it to move.

"Stay on the steps," Hargrove said quietly.

Lane nodded once.

Hargrove swung the flashlight across the floor again and tried to think like a detective instead of a man standing in a room that refused to behave like a room.

If there had been blood—and there had been, out in the yard, under the sheet on the grass—then there should have been more down here. There should have been a trail. There should have been transfer. Blood had rules. Gravity had rules.

This cellar looked like someone had taken a sponge to it with obsessive care.

Hargrove crouched and ran the beam along the threshold, the seam where the bottom step met the floor. Even there, in the cracks, there was no dark residue.

He reached down and touched the stone with a gloved fingertip.

Cold. Wet.

When he lifted his hand, he couldn't pull a scent off it.

He hated that detail more than any other.

Lane shifted above him and muttered, "How the hell..."

Hargrove didn't answer because he didn't have an answer that didn't sound like a story.

He moved the light again, slower, forcing himself to inventory.

There was a rusted shelf bolted to the far wall, empty. A stain on the stone that might have been old water. A drain hole in the floor that looked too small to matter.

And then, near the back corner, a thin line of white.

At first he thought it was chalk.

He stepped down onto the cellar floor and approached it, careful, feeling Lane's attention sharpen behind him.

The line was made of bone.

Not a neat row, not symmetrical. A jagged scattering of fragments laid end to end, as if someone had tried to build a boundary with whatever they could find. It ran from wall to wall, cutting the cellar into two halves like a crude border.

Hargrove stopped short of it.

He didn't believe in folk magic.

He did believe in warning signs. He did believe that men in trouble sometimes did strange things to feel in control.

Still, his stomach tightened as he stared at the bone.

Lane's breath came out in a whisper behind him. "Jesus."

Hargrove glanced back. Lane's face had gone pale under the fluorescent harshness of the flashlight. The kid looked suddenly younger. Not a deputy anymore. Just a local boy who had heard too many stories from too many older men and always told himself he'd never be the one standing in the middle of them.

"You ever seen something like that?" Hargrove asked.

Lane swallowed. "Not... not up close," he said. "I've heard—"

"Don't," Hargrove said quietly.

Lane's mouth shut, but the fear stayed.

Hargrove turned back to the line and tried to treat it like evidence.

Bones could come from anywhere. Animal remains. Old trash. Someone bored and superstitious. Someone grieving.

But the placement was deliberate. The way it hugged the stone, the way it turned slightly at the far wall to meet a hairline crack. Whoever had laid it had cared about continuity.

Line stays unbroken.

Hargrove felt the phrase surface from his earlier read of the legal pad. He hadn't wanted to remember it. Now it sat in his mind like a hand on his shoulder.

He raised the flashlight and swept it over the far side of the bone line.

The stone, the water sheen, the emptiness—all of it looked the same.

And yet the air on that side seemed... heavier. Not supernatural. Just wrong—the kind of pressure change that made your ears notice themselves.

Hargrove stepped closer without crossing.

His skin prickled.

Lane shifted again behind him. "Detective," he whispered.

Hargrove didn't respond. He was listening now, and he realized something he hadn't noticed at first because of the rain and the adrenaline and the station chatter in his own head.

There was a sound down here.

Not a drip. Not wind.

A low, steady vibration, barely audible, like an electrical hum.

It reminded Hargrove of the old televisions his grandmother used to keep on with the volume muted—just that faint presence that told you the machine was awake even when the picture was dark.

He held still and listened harder.

The hum didn't come from a single point. It seemed to come from everywhere at once, the way a buried line or a distant generator could.

Hargrove's jaw clenched.

This was the moment where a deputy would crack a joke to break the tension. This was the moment where a man would say, Probably the generator, probably the lines, probably nothing.

Hargrove could not make himself say it.

Lane's voice came again, thinner. "Tell me you see it," he whispered.

Hargrove turned his head a fraction. "See what?"

Lane's eyes were fixed on the far side of the cellar, on a patch of shadow near the back wall where the flashlight beam thinned. His pupils were wide. His face had that strained look Hargrove had seen on witnesses who were trying to decide whether to trust their own senses.

Hargrove followed Lane's gaze.

At first he saw only stone and shadow.

Then, for a heartbeat, he saw something else.

Something in the corner of his vision tried to arrange itself into a person—a darker patch that his mind insisted was shoulders and a head. It might have been Lane's shadow thrown wrong across the wet stone. It might have been nothing at all.

Hargrove's pulse kicked hard.

He swung the light directly.

The shape vanished.

Stone. Damp. Emptiness.

Lane made a sound like he'd bitten his tongue.

Hargrove forced himself to breathe through his nose, slow and controlled. He refused to give the moment language. He refused to turn it into narrative.

Pareidolia, he told himself. Fatigue. Stress. Flashlight artifacts. The brain trying to complete a picture in the dark.

All of those explanations were available.

None of them eased the prickle on his skin.

He stepped back toward the stairs without crossing the bone line. He didn't trust his own impulse anymore, and he didn't like that.

Lane backed up with him, boots scraping lightly, as if sound might provoke something.

At the bottom step, Hargrove stopped and looked back one more time.

The cellar waited.

Not like a room.

Like a jaw held open.

Hargrove climbed the steps and came up into daylight, blinking at the gray sky like a man surfacing from a bad dream.

For a moment he just stood at the top of the steps, letting the porch air hit his face.

The rain had thinned to a mist. The yard smelled like wet grass and diesel and something faintly sour that might have been old hay or old whiskey or simply the imagination of a man who had spent too long in a room that smelled like nothing.

Lane hovered a few feet away, scanning the tree line as if expecting movement. The kid kept licking his lips, a nervous habit Hargrove had never noticed before today.

Hargrove pulled his gloves off and shoved them into his pocket. He didn't trust his hands not to shake if he looked at them too long.

"Photograph the line," he said, voice clipped, professional. "Every angle. Don't step over it. Don't move it. I want CSU to see it exactly as it is."

Lane blinked, grateful for instruction. "You think it matters?"

Hargrove stared at the farmhouse windows, dark now in daylight. "I think it mattered to somebody," he said. "That's enough."

Lane hesitated. "And... the thing I saw?"

Hargrove's jaw bunched. He could have lied. He could have dismissed it. He could have done what cops did when they needed a witness to feel sane.

Instead he chose precision.

"I saw shadow," Hargrove said. "I saw fatigue. I saw a flashlight doing what flashlights do." He looked at Lane. "And I saw you scared. All of those things can be true at the same time."

Lane swallowed and nodded once.

Hargrove turned away from the cellar door and walked toward the living room window, peering through the glass at the dim interior. The red corded phone lay where they'd left it—cracked base, receiver on its side, cord pulled taut. The plug dangled loose beside it, disconnected from the wall.

Unplugged.

Hargrove stared at it for a long moment, feeling the shape of Jim Wallace's voice on the phone: He said he heard my name.

He forced himself to look away.

"Let's finish the house," Hargrove said.

No meat.

No smell.

He looked at Lane.

Lane's face had gone pale.

"Tell me you see it," Lane whispered.

"I see it," Hargrove said.

He didn't say what else he saw.

He didn't say that for a heartbeat, in the beam's edge, he thought he saw bare feet. A shape tucked into shadow. A person standing very still, hands folded, watching.

When he swung the light directly, there was nothing.

Just stone.

Just damp.

Just emptiness.

Lane cleared his throat hard. "We should close it," he said.

Hargrove didn't answer.

He climbed the steps and came up into daylight, blinking at the gray sky like a man surfacing from a bad dream.

On the lawn, the sheet still covered Hunter Wallace.

Behind him, the farmhouse loomed, its windows dark.

Hargrove turned to Lane. "Get the ME to document everything," he said. "Get photos of the writing. The bones. The phone. Every print."

Lane nodded, relief in motion. "And Glisner?" he asked.

Hargrove stared at the dark patch in the grass—the empty space where a man should have been—then let his light drift to the line of bones that his mind insisted was just an animal boundary even as his gut refused to believe it.

"We keep looking," he said.

Lane hesitated. "If he's alive..."

Hargrove's jaw worked.

He pictured John Glisner shaking on a couch, sweat slick on his skin, eyes wide with terror and guilt.

He pictured him holding a gun.

He pictured him telling himself that death was payment.

"If he's alive," Hargrove said, "he's either lost…"

He paused.

"…or he doesn't want to be found."

Lane looked at him, uncertain.

Hargrove didn't blame him.

Some stories demanded a clean ending.

This one didn't feel interested in being clean.

* * *

Near dusk, Hunter Wallace's father arrived.

He drove up in an old pickup with mud caked on the wheel wells, the kind of truck that had seen more fields than roads. He got out without shutting the door. It swung open behind him and stayed there, gaping.

His face was hard in the way grief made men hard when they didn't know where else to put the soft parts.

"Where is he?" he asked, voice flat.

Lane started to answer. Hargrove held up a hand.

"Mr. Wallace," Hargrove said, stepping forward. "I'm Detective Hargrove."

Wallace's father stared at him as if titles were useless here. His gaze slid past Hargrove to the sheet on the lawn.

He stopped walking.

For a long moment he didn't move at all.

Then he made a sound that wasn't a word.

It came from somewhere deep, a place too old for language.

Hargrove watched him go to his knees beside the sheet.

Watched his hands hover, trembling, then lower to touch the fabric like it might burn.

Wallace's fingers found the edge of the sheet and pinched it between thumb and forefinger.

He lifted it a fraction.

Not enough to look. Not enough to face it.

Just enough to see the shape of a hand beneath the fabric, the outline of knuckles, the curve of a wrist.

Hargrove saw Wallace's throat work as if he were swallowing something sharp.

Wallace let the sheet fall again and pressed his palm flat to the top of it. The gesture was not tender. It was a man trying to hold something in place because he did not trust the world to keep it where it belonged.

Lane shifted behind Hargrove, boots scraping wet grass. He looked like he wanted to offer a blanket, a word, a script. His hands hovered uselessly near his belt.

There was no script for this.

Hargrove found himself watching Wallace's hands. They were broad, cracked, the nails rimmed with grease the way a working man's nails were. The skin at his knuckles was split in places, fresh and raw, as if he'd been wrenching on machinery too hard or punching something that refused to break.

He had driven here in a hurry, Hargrove thought.

He had known before the call came.

Wallace's shoulders shook once. He made that same sound again—half breath, half animal noise—and then forced it down so hard the motion traveled through his whole spine.

When he spoke, his voice was quieter.

Not softer. Just smaller, like something had been taken out of it.

"He always came," Wallace said, eyes fixed on the sheet. "Even when he shouldn't."

Hargrove didn't answer. He didn't offer agreement or comfort. Any response felt like theft.

Wallace's gaze flicked up briefly—past Hargrove, past Lane—to the farmhouse. For a second Hargrove thought he might stand, might storm the steps, might put his fist through the front door the way men did in movies when grief needed a target.

But Wallace didn't move.

He stared at the porch light as if it were an eye.

Then his gaze dropped again, back to the sheet, and his jaw tightened with a kind of contained shame that read like familiarity.

"I told him not to come," he whispered, and the words sounded less like blame than like confession.

Hargrove felt his skin prickle, not with belief, but with the uncomfortable sense of pattern. The way people built rules around places that hurt them. The way those rules became part of the family, passed down like inherited bruises.

"I told him not to come," Wallace's father whispered.

Hargrove didn't answer.

He didn't tell the man that warnings rarely mattered to people who believed they were the last tether.

Wallace's father looked up at the farmhouse with an expression that was part hatred and part fear.

"We don't come here," he said, and the sentence sounded like a rule handed down rather than an opinion.

Lane shifted uncomfortably. "Sir, we have no evidence the house—"

Wallace's father cut him off with a look sharp enough to stop the words in Lane's throat.

"Everyone always wants evidence," Wallace's father said. "My wife died in a car wreck, too. Folks said it was the road. Said it was ice. Said it was bad luck."

His voice cracked on the last phrase.

He swallowed hard and lowered his gaze back to the sheet.

"But I watched this place eat my father," he said quietly. "And I watched it try to eat my son."

Hargrove's skin prickled.

Lane opened his mouth again, then closed it.

Hargrove held Wallace's father's gaze. "We're still searching for John Glisner," he said. "We'll keep you informed."

Wallace's father let out a humorless laugh. "You won't find him," he said.

"Why do you say that?" Hargrove asked.

Wallace's father looked back at the farmhouse.

"Because it doesn't give back what it takes," he said.

Hargrove waited for more.

The man shook his head, as if whatever he knew didn't translate into words without becoming nonsense.

After a moment, he stood.

He didn't say goodbye.

He just walked back to his truck and drove away, tires grinding through mud, the sound ugly and human in the quiet yard.

Hargrove watched him go.

Then he turned back to the property.

The farmhouse sat as it always had.

Quiet.

Patient.

As if it had already forgotten the names of the people it had ruined.

* * *

That night, after the search was called off and the last cruiser lights vanished down Van Drake Road, Hargrove stayed a few minutes longer than procedure required.

He stood alone at the edge of the yard and looked at the line of bones.

The rain had stopped.

The air had gone still.

In the silence, the farmhouse seemed to loom larger.

He could have stepped over the line.

He could have walked to the porch and pushed the door open.

He could have gone inside and looked for what everyone wanted him to find: a body, a note, a bottle, a reason.

Instead he stayed where he was.

Because he knew something no one wrote in reports.

Sometimes the only thing holding a man together was the story he told himself about what had happened.

Sometimes the story was a lie.

Sometimes the lie was mercy.

Hargrove turned back toward his car.

Halfway there, he heard it.

A soft click.

Like a latch catching.

He stopped.

Looked back.

The front door was shut now.

It had been ajar all day.

The wind hadn't moved. The air was still.

Hargrove stared at the door for a long time.

Then he got into his car and drove away without turning on his siren.

* * *

Epilogue

That afternoon, in a small warm office miles away, an evidence technician pulled a sealed bag from the Van Drake Road scene - the Glisner case, in office shorthand - and slid a cell phone onto the table.

The phone belonged to Hunter Wallace.

The screen was cracked. The battery icon flashed red with every breath it managed to take.

Marsh set his coffee aside and opened a case file.

He did not read the narrative first. He preferred to let the objects speak before he let other people's opinions get in his way.

He photographed the device.

He logged the serial number.

He plugged it into a charger and watched the percentage crawl upward like a reluctant confession.

When it hit four percent, he pressed play on the voicemail that had been marked in the report.

Audio evidence: caller unknown.

Victim's phone.

Marsh pressed a button anyway.

John Glisner's voice filled the small office, thin and distorted, the sound of a man talking through water.

"I'm sorry," John said.

There was a sob.

A hitch of breath.

Then, again: "I'm sorry."

Again.

The message was not long. It didn't need to be. It was the simplest thing a man could say when he had no other language left.

Marsh listened all the way through, pen moving across his notepad.

Voice identified as John Glisner. Emotional distress. Background noise consistent with wind/rain. No additional voices.

He stopped writing.

Because the last second of the message did not sound like wind.

It sounded like something shifting.

A faint, soft exhale.

Not quite a word.

Not quite a laugh.

Marsh frowned and turned the volume up.

He hit replay.

This time he heard only the sobbing and the static.

He played it again.

Nothing but John.

He played it a third time, leaning closer, headphones pressed tight over his ears.

Still nothing.

Marsh sat back and stared at the phone.

He knew the tricks audio played on people. He knew pareidolia. The brain's hunger for pattern. The way a tired mind could turn interference into meaning.

He also knew the look on the state trooper's face in the doorway when the phone had been handed over.

He knew the way the report had used the word missing instead of dead.

Marsh wrote the line anyway.

No additional voices detected.

He underlined it once, hard enough to tear the paper.

Then he closed the file and set the phone back in its bag.

Outside his office window, the late-day sky hung gray and empty.

Somewhere, far away, an old farmhouse sat in the weather, and it was hard not to imagine it waiting.